love
AND
impediments

A Novel

STEFKA MARINOVA-TODD

North Carolina

Published in the United States by BQB Publishing
(an imprint of Boutique of Quality Books Publishing, Inc.)
www.bqbpublishing.com

ISBN 978-1-952782-81-7 (p)
ISBN 978-1-952782-82-4 (e)

Library of Congress Control Number: 2022940792

Book design by Robin Krauss, www.bookformatters.com
Cover design by Rebecca Lown, www.rebeccalowndesign.com
First editor: Andrea Vande Vorde
Second editor: Allison Itterly

Let me not to the marriage of true minds
Admit impediments.

—William Shakespeare, "Sonnet 116"

To my aunts:
Verna and Villie,
and all the other women—
the size of a sparrow, with the strength of an eagle.

CHAPTER 1

Gray

At three minutes to one, Marta Aneva walked down to the lectern, and looked up. The auditorium was a vortex with raked rows of curved tables, and Marta stood at the bottom of it. She took a deep breath and forced a smile. Teaching was a performance, and like any good actor, she had to put aside troubling thoughts about her personal life and career setbacks and instead focus all of her energy on being inspiring.

For many years, Marta had been teaching classes on child development and dedicated herself to engaging her students in their learning. But today their cool indifference unsettled her. She opened her laptop and began her lecture with a steady voice.

"Emotions permeate and define human existence. We express them through all forms of art. In literature, for example, they are even directly displayed or implied in the titles of books, such as the Jane Austen's novels *Pride and Prejudice* or *Sense and Sensibility*. Or the titles themselves evoke emotional reactions, such as *One Hundred Years of Solitude*, by Gabriel García Márquez, or Joseph Conrad's *Heart of Darkness*." Marta walked closer to the front row of tables. "And more recently, some of Stephen King's novels sport titles such as *Misery* and *Joyland*. But let's agree that some are more apt to his genre than others."

A few students looked up from their computer screens

and some even chuckled, but then their eyes sank back into the blue glow. Marta's voice wavered, but she continued with her lecture on the early stages of emotional development. When several students drifted out of her class early, she pressed her lips together and mumbled, "Perhaps this was enough 'misery' for the day. Next week you'll learn how to recognize emotions in the sounds a baby makes." She seized her laptop and dashed out of the auditorium with her head down.

Upon feeling the satiny smoothness of the doorknob, Marta let out a deep sigh. She was home. The Toronto house was an old Victorian, which had been maintained with a mere fresh coat of paint and an occasional new appliance. Marta cherished the features that preserved the house's origins: the colorful stained glass windows, the dark wood paneling, and the bronze doorknobs. It had been in contrast to her former husband's preference for everything modern and sleek; tingling hints of a failing marriage that she had been willfully ignoring.

Marta carried a steaming cup of tea into her home office and placed it on her desk. She opened her laptop and her eyes skimmed a message from the funding agency, but before she finished reading it, she reclined in her chair and took a sip of her tea. Her application for a grant to support her next big research project had been unsuccessful, for a second time. If she wanted any chance at a promotion to full professorship, she desperately needed the money to support her research on the emotional attachment of children. The repeated rejections were alarming, but not as much as the abrupt realization that all along her life had consisted of tightly wound circles that came back to close at roughly the same spot.

The pattering sound of raindrops on the delicate leaves of

early spring came through the open window. Marta stood up and tried to pull the wooden window down, but it was stuck. She pulled harder and it closed with a thud, but a sharp pain sliced through her shoulder. She rubbed it until the pain subsided and reclined back in her chair.

A crisp chime from her phone startled her and she whispered a curse. It was a calendar alarm reminding her about her dinner plans with a colleague that evening. Marta's first impulse was to cancel. The prospect of having to be pleasant and upbeat drained her. But it would be rude to change plans on such short notice. She placed the still hot cup of tea on her desk and plodded toward her bedroom closet.

The walk to the Italian restaurant in her neighborhood helped her shed some of the gloomy thoughts that had been gnawing at her for most of the day. Now, they seemed to have settled on her aching shoulder. Marta rubbed it again.

As she approached the restaurant door, she recognized the large frame of a man in a trench coat waiting for her. Bruce Mason's wide grin made it easier for her to smile back. They worked in different departments—she in psychology and he in physiotherapy—but they were members of the same committee at the university.

"Howdy," he greeted her. "Judging from the tasty whiff coming from the restaurant, you made a good choice."

Marta smiled and he opened the door for her.

The restaurant was crowded. At one time, the boisterous sound of people, mellowed to a hum by a glass of wine, uplifted Marta's spirits. But tonight it annoyed her, and she could barely hear Bruce over the sound of it. Oblivious to his surroundings, he reveled in stories about himself. He had youthful clean looks despite the thin spot at the top of his head that was surrounded by well-trimmed ash-blond hair. Aware of his insecurity, Marta leaned toward him. She was not troubled by his impending baldness.

As Bruce changed the topic to work, she bit into the mushroom-stuffed ravioli, savoring the smooth cream sauce contrasted by the firmer texture of the pasta. Throughout dinner, he told her pretty much everything about his uneventful childhood in Manitoba, his boring education on the West Coast, and similarly dull academic pursuits. By the time Marta finished her main course, she concluded that they had very little in common, and *that* troubled her.

She took a sip of her strong, dry cappuccino, the only trace of milk in the froth. Bruce was scarfing down a tiramisu, already slightly drunk from the brandy he ordered after the two glasses of wine he had with dinner. When he swallowed the last spoonful, he changed the topic again.

"And did I tell you I'm divorced? The ex and I officially signed the papers last month. She left me for the weaselly guy in her office. And took the kids too. I only have weekly visitation rights. Mind you, the kids are still young. Hell, that's life, eh?"

As the conversation moved on to increasingly more intimate topics, Marta's body tensed, and she gripped the bottom of her seat. She could not suppress the feeling that the innocuous dinner she thought she was having with a colleague was turning into an alarming date.

"And how about you?" His abrupt question pulled Marta from her thoughts.

She hesitated. "What would you like to know?"

"Well, I've been blabbing on all night, and you've barely

said a word. I see shoptalk's boring you. So, tell me about yourself. Are you married? In a relationship?"

Of course, all he wanted to know was whether Marta was single. She was desperate to go home. Her shoulder was now in constant pain, and she was exhausted.

"I'm divorced, too, and I have a nineteen-year-old son who's away at university." A son in college implied that she was a woman of a certain age, and being in her mid-forties she expected Bruce to find it off-putting.

Instead, he smiled. "You don't look old enough to have a grown-up son."

"Looks can be deceptive," she said and looked toward the door.

Despite Marta's gentle objections, Bruce insisted on paying for the dinner and walking her home. They strolled in silence, which was interrupted by his indignant exclamations about the stench wafting from the urine-soaked alleys, the garbage scattered on the street, or the deafening noise from a passing motorcycle—aspects of urban life Marta had come to accept as par for the course.

When they reached her house, she waved her arm toward the door. "This is it." She looked at the keys as she continued to twirl them with her fingers. "Thanks for dinner and for walking me home." She looked up at him. He was smiling, and his eyes sparkled in the dim light.

"Would ya invite me in for a drink?"

"I don't think that's a good idea. I injured my shoulder this afternoon, and it really hurts now." Marta chose to take the easy way out.

"Hey, I can massage your shoulder real good. And it'll be like new by tomorrow."

Shaking him off was going to be harder than she thought,

and Marta was frustrated with herself for not realizing it sooner.

"I can't," she mumbled, avoiding his eyes.

"You can't or you don't wanna?" Bruce's voice still sounded playful.

Marta knew that she had to tell him the real reason and it was bound to end it all. As it *almost* always did in the six years since her divorce.

"Bruce, I barely know you. And I need time to build trust with a person before I can be more intimate with him. And ... I'm not sure that you and I will ever get there." She looked at him. He was no longer smiling. "I'm sorry."

His narrowed eyes, separated by a deep crease, examined her face. He shook his head and walked away. After a couple of steps, he turned back and said, "We live in the twenty-first century, you know. You can let your hair down. See ya." He waved and disappeared in the darkness.

Marta had heard versions of these words before, but it never got any easier to hear them again. She sensed his thoughts—*What a waste of time*—and clutched the smooth doorknob.

$$\twoheadleftarrow\!\!\!\!\text{<<<<<}$$

Marta woke up with a searing pain in her shoulder. The faint glow of dawn seeped through the cracks in the curtains. She reached for her cell phone and gasped in agony. She fussed with a couple of pillows until she found a position that was more bearable, and relaxed.

She was all alone, and this would have been a good time to have someone nearby. But her son, Ilian, was in Montreal. And while one of her friends would come to help her if she called, Marta was not about to trouble them with her silly aches and pains.

She spent the next two days mainly in bed being as still as possible, which gave her plenty of time to think. Frustrated that her neatly planned career path seemed to have veered off course, and seeing no bright prospects for her lonely existence, Marta decided that it was time to take a break before she allowed the ominous curve to close completely, yet again.

Where could she go? She liked to visit busy destinations filled with history and vibrant culture. But this was not to be a typical vacation. She would be taking an unpaid leave from her university. She was restless and craved a quiet, peaceful place. She considered going back to her native country, Bulgaria, but then she would feel obliged to see her family and friends, and she was not ready to revisit her recent past with them. Besides, there were so many countries waiting to be discovered.

Marta leaned back on her pillows and closed her eyes. She saw a young girl who would sit on the floor and stare longingly at a tattered map. The girl had never traveled outside of her country and dreamed of roaming every continent.

Marta jumped out of bed and winced from the sharp pain that pierced her shoulder. She held her injured upper arm as she trudged to Ilian's old room, where a large map of the world was still hanging on the wall. She had been to every continent but Antarctica and South America. Antarctica was too cold and desolate, and she was not prepared for such an extreme degree of social and geographical isolation. She trailed her finger down the South American continent. She tried to remember bits of information about each place when her finger stopped in its meandering track just below the word "Uruguay."

Marta was amused that she knew absolutely nothing about this one country on the whole continent. No longer bothered by the pain in her shoulder, she sprung onto her tiptoes. She went downstairs to her office and opened the laptop on her desk. Her search revealed that Uruguay was a small and stable country—its total population as large as the city of Toronto's—that was not a typical tourist hub, thus not likely to be crowded, and was generally warm all year round.

Four days later and fully recovered from her injury, Marta met with her friend and colleague, Gabrielle, in the coffee shop in the basement of their office building. In between sips of bitter dark coffee, Marta told Gabrielle about her recent challenges with Bruce and in her work.

"But I've concocted a plan to take a six-month leave and go away," Marta said.

"Where are you gonna go?" Originally from Réunion Island, Gabrielle spoke with a heavy French accent. Her head was covered with tightly wound coils of shiny silver-streaked curls, and she wore one of her classic large and brightly colored necklaces and earrings to match. She was vivacious and frank, and Marta braced herself for Gabrielle's reaction to her news.

"Uruguay," Marta answered.

"*Uruguay*? Why Uruguay of all places? Do you like its name?"

Marta laughed.

"It's in South America, right?" Gabrielle continued. "That

means they speak only Spanish there, and it's a language you don't know."

"I can learn it while I'm there. It'll be a bonus. And now that you mentioned it, Uruguay does have an interesting sound to it, but that's not what draws me there."

"Well, what's it then?" Gabrielle pressed her. "An ill-advised wanderlust?"

Marta wrinkled her brows, ignoring Gabrielle's teasing. "I don't know. Perhaps, my choice is a result of growing up in Communist Bulgaria during a period when the word 'options' was considered extravagant."

In the grocery stores, when they had it, there were two types of bread, white and dark; one type of milk, with fat content unknown; two types of cheese, cow and sheep; and two types of yogurt, cow and sheep. When it came to clothes and shoes, the choices were even more limited. As a child, Marta had been exasperated to see other girls wearing the same frilly skirt her mother had bought for her. As an adult, she continued to strive for originality, either in her colorful or embellished locally made clothes, or in her choice of obscure travel destinations.

In the evening, she called Ilian to tell him about her decision. She was both curious and apprehensive about how he would react.

"Maman," he said, "Uruguay isn't your type of place. It has fewer UNESCO heritage sites than Bulgaria."

He was right. There was no logic in her choice of travel destination, but its sudden pull was strong, as if there was something bright waiting for her there. Something exciting and invigorating.

She had to find out.

CHAPTER 2

Blue

Dazed and disheveled, Marta walked through the airport in Montevideo rolling two large suitcases beside her. The small airport was bright and modern, and the floor tiles were glossy without a single scuff mark or dirty glob of chewing gum in sight. Marta researched her destination before she left Toronto, but she did not think to check the airport. She wondered whether all of Uruguay would be new and shiny, thus shattering her hopes for a quaint and warm retreat.

She walked through the sliding glass doors and a fresh breeze tousled her hair. It was a sunny morning in early September, which in Uruguay was the beginning of spring, her favorite season. She was about to get a second spring in one year. Marta inhaled and smiled. The air was warm with the faint scent of the sea, a smell that reminded her of lazy summer holidays by the Black Sea coast. It was the perfect release from the constraints of a multi-leg flight which had started fifteen hours earlier in Toronto.

Flying was a dreaded means to an end for Marta. Despite the fact that she was small and flexible, the cramped seats stifled her. Now, broomsticks and magic carpets would have been a completely different thing, but alas, she lived in the *real* world.

The taxi driver struggled to place her suitcases into the trunk and slammed the lid shut. He sat in the front seat, and after a brief pause to catch his breath, he turned toward her and smiled. He did not speak a word of English, and all he could say was, "*Americana*," to which Marta nodded. She saw no point in clarifying any more than that. She gave him a piece of paper with the hotel name and address. "*Ciudad Vieja*?" he asked.

She already knew that "Ciudad Vieja" meant "Old Town" and replied, "*Sí.*"

The driver was eager to talk, but Marta knew only a few words in Spanish. Undeterred by her silence, he kept talking and pointed out the window from time to time. She examined the scenery that streaked by them. They were in the middle of a residential neighborhood—a wealthy one, judging by the size of the rooftops that jutted above the tall fences surrounding the immense yards. Every once in a while, Marta caught a glimpse of the ocean in the distance. She could not wait to run on the soft sandy beach and dip her feet into the cool water. As they continued, the scenery changed. They were now surrounded by tall, well-maintained condominiums, many of them newly built, but she frowned at the sight of them. They reminded her of the prefabricated concrete buildings of her childhood, and she wondered whether her claustrophobia had something to do with growing up in those tiny, bleak apartments.

The taxi stopped in front of a French-style building that was painted bright red with rounded dormer windows and a copper roof. Marta was relieved that the hotel looked exactly as it did in the photos online. It was not cheap, but she would only stay there until she found a more permanent home. Gabrielle told her that she was crazy to go to Uruguay without having booked her accommodation for the six months she planned to be there. But Marta was on an adventure. She would seek opportunities to discover places locally rather than online. She was willing to move around until she found the right home. She longed to be surprised.

Marta left the unpacked suitcases in her room and went for a walk. She enjoyed the warm sun on her shoulders, and the smoky whiff of grilled steaks revived her hunger. As she neared Plaza Independencia, the main square in the center of the city, Marta shivered at the sight of the imposing buildings that surrounded it. The area reminded her of the streets in downtown Toronto, which were swarming with office employees clad in navy and gray. Some smiled but all had a purpose. There was never a sense of aimlessness among the glass towers of the Town of York.

Marta swerved into the first side street that led back toward the Old Town. This was exactly the kind of place she had hoped to find. The pedestrian street was quiet except for the muffled footsteps and occasional cough coming from the few people who rambled in the shadier side of the street. The row houses on both sides were plain, with flat water-stained facades, and their paint was peeling off in large slabs. The doors, however! Some had elaborate hand-carved wood designs in the shape of vines or flowers, others had glass windows covered with metal filigree-like trellises, and many were painted in teal green, indigo blue, or corn yellow. And each one was unique, as if the door of each house revealed something special about the inhabitants within. She had found a place that was calm yet interesting, without the need to evade meddlesome albeit well-meaning relatives.

At the corner with a larger street, Marta stopped in front of a window that was covered with posters for houses and apartments. She hesitated, intimidated by the embarrassing prospect of communicating in a language she did not know. But she opened the door and went inside.

The real estate office consisted of a single space, which was a curious mixture of old wooden beams, brick-clad pillars, and a dozen or so modern cubicles. As soon as she walked in, a short man in a wrinkled suit greeted her with a smile. *"Buenas tardes."*

She greeted him in Spanish and added, "Do you speak English? *Inglés?"*

"Ah, Inglés. Un momento, por favor," he said and leaned over a nearby cubicle to speak with a woman while pointing at Marta.

The woman stood up and flicked her wavy black hair with her hand. Her dark eyes sparkled, and she introduced herself as Luisa in a voice that rang louder than necessary. Marta looked around, but no one else in the office seemed to have been disturbed. Despite the formidable clicks of her stilettos, Luisa's warm smile comforted Marta, who uttered the first thought that came to her mind. "Your English is excellent."

"No, no. You're joking!" Luisa's unbridled laughter rippled through the air. They walked toward her desk, and Luisa explained that she had learned English while she lived in Arizona for a couple of years. "And where are you from, Marta?"

"I'm from Canada. But I grew up in Bulgaria, a small country in Eastern Europe."

Luisa did not comment on Marta's unusual background, which surprised Marta. She thought that Bulgaria would seem as exotic to Uruguayans as Uruguay seemed to Bulgarians.

"Oh," Luisa said. "I wished to visit Canada but never found the time or the money, really. So, I spent most of my time in Arizona. But I went on a few trips to California and Las Vegas with, what turned out to be, a worthless boyfriend."

"You can still go to Canada. It's easier to visit a place when you have a friend there rather than—" Marta stopped. She knew nothing about Luisa, and a friendship with her was unlikely. For one, Marta had never desired to go to Las Vegas, and she pulled the high heels from the back of her closet only for a wedding or a visit to the opera. But Luisa's unpretentious and bubbly demeanor reminded her of Albena, a close friend from her childhood, who had since been twice divorced and was struggling to make ends meet as a kindergarten teacher with two teenage children. Whenever Marta thought of her, she always heard her uplifting laughter and tasted the sugary syrup from the decadent baklava Albena's mother made for Christmas. Marta had not seen Albena in a long time, and she longed for her company.

Luisa laughed again. "Be careful because I'll come, you know! And what brings you to Uruguay?"

Marta could have explained all the reasons that led her there but chose to focus on the business at hand. She told Luisa the duration of her stay in Montevideo and the amount of money she hoped to spend on accommodation. Without hesitation, Luisa offered a few suggestions for apartments, which she listed in a rehearsed manner while showing photos of the neighborhoods online.

Marta took a fleeting look at the photos. "I'm sure those are great, but I'm looking for something less fancy." Still feeling the uncanny affinity with Luisa, she decided to tell her the true purpose of her trip. "To be honest, I came to Uruguay in search of a simpler, quieter life. I took a leave from my job to take a break, but also to experience a new way of living. Life's too short to do the same things over and over again. And I prefer to live among local people, maybe a small flat in an old building."

"Got it!" Luisa said. "No McDonald's or Starbucks for you." Her eyes brightened. "I have an idea." She turned toward her desk and added over her shoulder, "I'll tell my boss that I'm taking my break now and we can go to my favorite café. It's right around the corner."

In the small coffee shop, filled with the aroma of freshly roasted coffee, Luisa confessed that she did not share Marta's desire for adventure, especially in impoverished circumstances, and burst into a fit of ringing giggles. This made Marta laugh too. She felt silly, but she found it hard to remain serious in Luisa's presence. And Luisa also understood Marta's need for change.

"My friend Sofía is a widow and owns a house a couple of streets over here in the Old Town," Luisa said. "She has a spare bedroom that I'm sure she'd be happy to offer to you. She doesn't rent it to just anyone. But she'll be willing to help you out because she's a good friend of mine. I think this would be a perfect place for you!"

Marta's initial reaction to Luisa's offer was to refuse it. "I've never shared a living space with anyone who isn't family," she confessed. "And that kind of unfamiliarity would make me very uncomfortable."

"That's fine, I totally understand," Luisa said. "But if it makes any difference to you, Sofía also owns a bakery nearby and she spends most days there. She's an early riser and an early sleeper."

"Oh, that's quite the opposite of my typical schedule." Marta took a sip of her coffee. She was tempted by the modest rent that she would have to pay, and the house was in the neighborhood she had already chosen for herself. And since Sofía would hardly ever be home, Marta would have the privacy she desired. Most significantly, she could not remain indifferent to Luisa's kind gesture to offer her a special arrangement through one of her friends, and Marta did not want to appear ungrateful.

"I'd be interested in seeing the place," she said.

"Great. I'll ask Sofía if we could go this afternoon. By the way, did I mention she doesn't speak English? But you wouldn't need to talk to her much, anyway."

Later that afternoon, Marta met Luisa at the address she had given her. It was a small two-story house with a dark-purple door. When the door opened, a large woman greeted them with a smile. She wore a simple sleeveless cotton dress, and a light-blue handkerchief was tied around her hair.

Sofía led them into a modest living room. At one end was a dining table with six chairs around it. The house smelled inviting, a mix of fresh bread and sugar cookies. A large vase of fresh tulips was placed on an ornamental table close to the door. It was the home of a woman who lived alone but was content with her circumstances, unlike Marta who had been restless. Perhaps she could learn from Sofía how to find peace in her own solitude.

Marta and Louisa sat at the dining table, and Sofía brought a pot of tea and a plate covered with a sumptuous variety of cookies. While Marta took a sip of her tea, which was surprisingly bitter, and a bite of a sweet, buttery cookie, Luisa spoke fast in Spanish.

Luisa turned toward Marta. "Sofía's happy to have you as a tenant. But would you like to see the room first?"

Marta nodded and rushed to wipe the crumbs off her

mouth. They followed Sofía up a curving narrow staircase to the second floor. At the end of the dim hallway, Sofía opened a door and invited them inside. A double bed, covered with a quilt embroidered with flowers and birds, took almost all of the space. But there was still room for a dresser, and a narrow armoire was tucked in a corner. Marta loved the faint smell of old wood, which she associated with her grandmother's traditional house in rural Bulgaria, and memories of the past that often managed to delight her, no matter how grim the reality had been. She walked to the window and was pleased to find a door that led to a narrow balcony. It overlooked a backyard that was partially covered with hanging grapevines and surrounded by lilacs and azaleas ready to bloom.

Marta turned back toward the room. "I love it, Luisa! I absolutely love it! When can I move in?"

Sofía did not need a translation of Marta's words and said, "*Inmediatamente.*"

That evening, Marta sat on her colorful bed and ran her hands over the embroidered quilt. The bumpy surface tickled her palms. She had just returned to her room after sharing a simple dinner under the grapevines with Sofía and Luisa. Their cheerful and unassuming company had been in stark contrast to Marta's friends in Canada, who were mostly academics, often smart, witty, and well-informed, but sometimes humorless and self-absorbed.

Marta became aware that she was twirling and pulling on a lock of her hair. She was uneasy again with the reality of sharing a house with someone she had just met, practically a stranger. She wondered whether the awkward feeling would ever go away, or whether it might even get worse. But it was a new experience for her, which was the main reason she traveled to this remote part of the world after all. And it would not hurt her to try it. After all, her past was clear and permanent, unlike her future, opaque but malleable. Marta exhaled and opened the leather-bound notebook she had purchased before she left Toronto and began writing the first entry in her journal.

CHAPTER 3

Orange

As Luisa had predicted, Sofía was gone most of the day, but Marta was surprised when Sofía began to leave freshly baked goods for breakfast. She often cooked a simple meal for dinner and invited Marta as well. The first morning Marta noticed the pastries, she dropped onto a chair and stared at a dark knot on the wood floor. In her adult life, she had taken care of herself and, eventually, her family. At times, the burden had been too heavy for her, but she was proud of her ability to find the strength and energy to go on. Sofía's kindhearted gesture, however, brought on a longing for a long-forgotten existence, that of a loved and carefree child.

Lately, at every recollection of her parents, Marta would become subdued, something she would not have done before her mother's recent death ten months earlier. Her father had died when she was twelve years old, and while she had gotten used to the idea of not having him around, she did miss his loud and contagious laughter. She had been raised by her mother, who had never remarried, and often told her that the love from her daughter was all she needed.

Only since her own divorce had Marta become aware of the sacrifices her mother must have made, and how much harder it was to raise a child as a single parent. It was not just the financial challenges that were inevitable for a high school French teacher. There were also the days her mother had to miss work when Marta was sick, or to attend her ballet performances. And on top of the cooking and cleaning, her mother also changed the fuses and replaced the burned-out lightbulbs because troubling the friendly neighbor was reserved only for more major jobs that required special tools, such as fixing the dripping kitchen faucet.

Her mother never hesitated to rely on Marta's help whenever possible too. Marta liked washing the windows twice a year and scrubbing the parquet with the noxious polish, which smelled so good. Together they painted the whole apartment, wall by wall, which had taken them a whole summer. The painting part was not so difficult, but removing the hundreds of books from the shelves that covered two walls of their tiny living room and placing them back took the most time and effort. Yet, her mother never complained. One day, after they had sat down, exhausted from removing and dusting the books, Marta's mother announced that she was going to take the opportunity to organize and record them. Later, she would look through her list for hours and talk about where the various books came from, and which ones her daughter had to read next. Marta loved listening to the stories, and she dreamed of a future when she could also catalog her most precious memories.

Feeling better, she devoured two of the pastries left by Sofía, emptied her coffee cup, and went outside. She had signed up for a two-week introductory course in Spanish at Academia Uruguay, and she was on her way to the first class. Her route took her to a quaint pedestrian street in the Old Town. The colorful two-story row houses were stacked like tablet candy in pastel shades of yellow, green, pink, and blue. On both sides of the street, the buildings and their black metal balconies were almost symmetrical, as if they were reflected in an invisible mirror framed by the palm trees that ran in the middle of the street. A few people walked past the busy cafés and small grocery stores, which were recognizable by the overflowing baskets of succulent oranges and fragrant verbenas that were placed right outside their doors.

As Marta walked along the street, enjoying the feeling of serenity, she was pulled away from her reverie by the curious sight of a beggar sitting on the sidewalk and reading a book. He was a lean young man, probably in his early twenties. His light brown hair was unkempt but did not look unclean. He wore a newsboy cap, and his eyes were thoughtful with a tinge of sadness.

She noticed him right away because she thought it unusual for a person begging on the street to be reading. Something about him intrigued Marta, and over the next few days she made it a part of her routine to go by and check on him and his book. Sometimes he was writing in a small notebook. A metal can with a few coins in it sat in front of him. There was a sign in Spanish right next to it, but she could not understand most of it.

Marta began to drop pesos in the metal can. At first, the young man was silent and never looked up from his book. But after the first week, whenever her coins rattled, he would lift his head and mutter, "*Gracias.*"

After a few sessions of her Spanish class, Marta felt confident enough to speak Spanish in the stores and was able to have a simple conversation with Sofía. The more she was able to connect to the local people, the less odd she felt. The next time she walked past the young man, she leaned over his can and said, "*Hola.*"

"*Hola,*" he said in return, looking straight at her.

Marta was ready with the next phrase she had learned

in class. "*¿Cómo estás?*" However, she was not prepared for his reply, which came fast and was long. Embarrassed, Marta confessed, "*Hablo poco español.*"

"Why are you bothering then?" he asked in perfect English.

Marta found his words faintly rude, but his bluntness reminded her of her son. Ever since the divorce, Ilian had avoided her company, treating her with cool indifference. He blamed her for the separation because she had been the one who was more volatile, and it had frightened him. Ilian believed that her tears ultimately drove his father away, and he lamented the loss of what he saw as a happy and supportive family. Marta sometimes wondered whether her relationship with her son would have been different, better even, if she had told him the true reason for the divorce. But her conviction that he was too young to understand and her need to protect him from pain prevailed every time, and she remained silent, even when she wanted to wail because she missed him or was hurt yet again by his coldness.

Marta swallowed. "Because I am curious about the books you read, the notes you write, and . . . and what does it say on your sign?"

"Aren't you a nosey one? What if I told you it's none of your business?"

Marta smiled. "You would be right, but I hope that you don't." She reached out her hand to him. "I'm Marta. Nice to meet you."

He shook her hand and mumbled, "Hugo."

"Well, Hugo, it seems that you're not interested in talking to me, so I'll be on my way. I'll come by again tomorrow." She waved at him and walked away.

When Marta approached him again on the following day,

Hugo was reading in his usual spot, but his sign was now written in English: "For the curious one: I need money to buy a wheelchair." She dropped the coins into his tin can and smiled but kept on walking. On her way back from her Spanish class, she noticed that Hugo was on his feet, sort of. It was obvious that he could not bear any weight on them. He had a crutch under one of his arms and was leaning for support on an older woman who was practically dragging him along the sidewalk. Marta stopped and waited for them to turn the corner. She did not think that Hugo would want her to see him in this condition. She was sorry, however, to have just missed him.

The next day, Marta hoped that she would find Hugo in his usual place. When she turned the corner, she was relieved to see him writing in his notebook. His sign was in Spanish again. She walked straight to him, and instead of putting coins in his can, she sat beside him on the sidewalk and folded her legs.

Hugo looked confounded, but before he could say anything, Marta asked, "Tell me, how did you learn to speak English so well?"

"My father was an American," Hugo replied.

"And what is it that you write? I'm curious if you write stories or simply your shopping lists?"

"I write poetry, mostly."

"Poetry? I like poetry—to read, that is. I can't write it myself. I have no sense of rhythm." Marta twisted the hem of her skirt around her finger and looked sideways at Hugo. "And about that wheelchair, how much money have you collected already?"

"Oh, not much. I'll be sitting here for a long time."

Marta's shoulders slumped under the weight of the

silence that followed, and she decided that it was enough for the day. She lifted herself up from the ground and whispered, *"Hasta mañana."*

During the next three days, Marta walked past Hugo's usual spot, but he was not there. She wondered whether something had happened to him, or whether he had picked a different place because he wanted to avoid her. Both options unsettled her. On the fourth day, he was back in the same spot but appeared messier than usual.

"I was worried that you ran away, and I was gathering a search party to scan the whole city looking for you," Marta shouted as she approached him.

"My mother was sick," Hugo said. He sounded congested.

Marta's smile melted, and Hugo assured her that his mother was better and had returned to work. Marta placed herself next to him and leaned her back against the wall. They sat in silence. A couple of people walked by and dropped coins in Hugo's can, and Marta felt a pleasant tingle go down her spine every time she heard the coins clink.

Hugo's voice broke the silence. "Marta, what are you doing? Because if you're trying to be my friend, there's no point."

Marta recognized the familiar bitterness in her mouth. She was resigned to her fate as far as Ilian was concerned, but she did not have to protect Hugo. A seagull swooped down, and the air from its wings ruffled her hair. It picked up a piece of bread from the ground and flew away.

Marta pulled herself away from the wall. "True friendships are never formed for a purpose. But to be honest, I'm not sure what draws me toward you. Maybe it's because you're almost the same age as my son and I miss him. Or because you're so unusual for someone begging on the streets."

"How so?" Hugo's eyes brightened.

"For one, you constantly read, which is unusual even for university students these days. Your goal is to purchase a wheelchair, which suggests that you have a plan, and it's inspiring. And now that I've gotten to know you a little, you seem to be an intelligent young man, and I see a bright path ahead of you, and I'd like to be a part of your journey."

Hugo looked straight into Marta's eyes. "I was raised by my mother. My father died when I was five, and I don't remember him well." His voice was sad but clear. Marta realized how much she missed her own father, but at least she had the consolation of remembering his face, his voice.

"I'm sorry, Hugo," Marta said.

"It's okay, it was a long time ago now." Hugo's voice was flat. "Anyway, my father was a young American journalist who had just graduated from university. And he had progressive ideas. His father was a staunch republican from Alabama, and he disowned him because of their political disagreements. My father left the US and came to Uruguay in search of a simpler life."

Hugo wiped his nose on his sleeve, and Marta pulled a tissue from her purse and passed it to him. While he blew his nose, a passerby dropped a coin into the can, and Hugo continued with his story.

"My father met and married my mother here in Montevideo. They didn't have much money, but they lived happily. But then my father got very sick and eventually died. My mother had to take care of me alone."

"Oh, that must have been very hard for both of you, but

especially your mom," Marta said.

"I guess, and it still is. With only a high-school diploma, she had no skills or training and took whatever low-paying work she could find to support the two of us. Now she works as a maid for a rich family. I couldn't wait to graduate from school and get a job. I wanted to help her," Hugo finished.

Marta wondered whether her own son would have felt the same way in those circumstances.

"Have you met any of your American relatives?" she asked.

"No. My father didn't keep in touch with them, and my mother never met any of them. I might be able to find them based on my last name, and I know the town where they live. But why should I bother? They don't even know I exist."

Marta could not argue with him.

Hugo sniffed. "In my last year of school, I delivered stuff on my bicycle here in the center of the city, and I got hit by a car. Now I can't move my legs, and I can't work or do anything useful. And instead of helping my mother, I'm an even bigger burden on her than I was before."

Marta looked away to hide her tears. Hugo's accident was almost identical to the accident her son, Ilian, had a few years earlier. Ilian was similarly hit by a car, but he had suffered a head injury, and his mobility was not affected. Fortunately, he eventually made a full recovery, but Hugo had not.

"Money from our public healthcare system and the insurance from the person who hit me covered my costs at the hospital. But there was no money for a wheelchair. And since I can't do anything else, I beg on the streets." Hugo blew his nose into the tissue.

Marta looked up toward the sky and the light breeze cooled her cheeks. All she could see was Hugo soaring in the air like a seagull. With the right support he could do so much more, but Marta was already certain that he would never ask for help, a reluctance with which she was all too familiar.

"Have you thought of publishing your poems? You might be able to make some money from them," she said.

"Marta, get a grip on reality. No one reads poetry these days, let alone pays money for it."

Marta nodded. "And what books do you like to read?"

"All types, but lately I'm reading works by communist philosophers, like Karl Marx. His ideas generally inspire me, and I believe socialism is the only way to true equality and life free of materialistic things like money."

Marta was troubled, but considering Hugo's life so far, she was not too surprised by his political and philosophical aspirations. She realized that it had been a long time since she last needed to discuss communism, and the thought of having to do it now did not raise any sentimental feelings in her. She remembered the smell of her old philosophy textbook with its frayed gray cover and the effort it took to understand its convoluted sentences. She had enough confidence in her own intelligence to be certain that it was not a lack of acumen that had precluded her from embracing Marx's theories.

Marta took a deep breath and looked at Hugo. "Let me tell you about my personal experience with Marx's socialism. I grew up in Bulgaria when it was still a communist country. My father also read Marx and Engels, but unlike me, he actually understood a lot of their ideas." Marta chuckled. "He often told me that communism, as originally envisioned by Marx, is a noble, utopian idea. But he was also frustrated by the suppressed and weirdly unequal life we lived. A cardiologist by profession, he would often lament, 'A plumber with no education to speak of makes more money than I do. And I have more than ten years of university. Where's the fairness in that?'"

"I think plumbers make a lot of money here too," Hugo said.

Marta laughed. "You're right. I've heard they're a precious commodity in many places." Her smile disappeared. "But I still doubt that they make more money than a doctor in a country with a free economy."

"I don't know," Hugo said. "But you should know that you didn't live in a real communist system but in a failed one. It's like seeing a five-year-old's scribbles and deciding that you hate books."

"You make a good point. But that was the reality of living in a communist country. We don't have any better examples. Not yet." Marta pulled herself up. "I *believe* that we're not all equal. I mean, we're not all the same, and that's a good thing. Otherwise, life would be boring. But instead of rewarding people with specific strengths and ignoring those who are weaker, we as a society should aim to support people's strengths and help them compensate for their weaknesses." She stood in front of Hugo with her arms crossed and declared, "And only then would everyone have an equal chance at a fulfilling life."

Hugo was silent. To Marta's surprise, this time he was not inclined to argue. She looked at her phone. It was lunchtime, and the street was already busy with people heading to the cafés. Before she left, she leaned toward him and asked, "How about we put my philosophy to practice?"

Hugo looked at her but remained silent.

"I have money saved, and I could afford the price of a manual wheelchair without much difficulty," Marta said. "Looking at the number of coins in your tin can, I think it might take you a few years before you collect enough. So, would you let me help you buy the wheelchair right now? I'll add whatever amount is still needed on top of your savings, and you could be on it tomorrow." Marta was beaming but Hugo was serious.

"I don't want your charity," he said. "It makes rich people feel good about themselves, but it weakens the people it's supposed to help. I'd rather fool myself believing I'm actually working for my money by begging . . . even if it takes years."

Marta was not about to give up. She had long been aware that she had the tendency to put everybody else's needs ahead of her own. But the independent side of her that came along after the divorce insisted that she needed to focus on herself at this point in her life. However, her instincts prevailed yet again. She wanted to help Hugo. She had a rare chance to make a difference in someone's life, especially someone who was young, yet had so much in common with her.

Struck with a new idea, Marta said, "To be honest, I came to Uruguay planning not to work. But I already find it difficult to fill my days, and I'm afraid that my life's starting to lose purpose. And you know, the life of an idle aristocrat isn't that appealing after all. It's well known to be very boring." Marta was encouraged by Hugo's smile and continued, "I've been thinking that maybe getting a part-time job, one or two days a week, would allow me to immerse myself in the world of ordinary people here in Montevideo, and I won't feel so indolent. But I don't really need the money, and I could put it to good use if I bought you a wheelchair with it. And if we agree right now to be friends, it'll be perfectly normal for friends to give each other presents."

"I don't know," Hugo said, fidgeting with the corner of

his book.

"You don't want to be friends?" Marta teased him.

"No, it's not that. It's just that it makes me uncomfortable that you have to work to help me." Hugo kept his eyes fixed on the book.

"Look, Hugo, I don't expect you to be thrilled with the friendship of someone your mother's age. But I also don't see anyone better hanging around here. Maybe you should give me a chance. And, besides, I'll get to meet new people. I'm very fond of the ones I've met here already."

Hugo was silent, and Marta thought it best to give him some time to think it over.

The next morning when she approached him, Hugo still avoided her eyes. She leaned down toward him, hoping to get his attention. Hugo gave her a fleeting look and told her that he had decided.

Marta widened her eyes. "And?"

Hugo looked away again. "My mother is still not fully recovered. Yesterday, when she came home from work, she was wiped out. She coughed most of the night too. I realized that I have to find a way to be the son she needs, my pride be damned." He looked sideways at Marta and a wry smile fluttered across his lips. "And you're cool. You like poetry."

Marta gave him a firm handshake. "We have a deal! I'll start looking for a job this afternoon."

CHAPTER 4

Brown

With her eyes locked onto her laptop screen, Marta took a sip of water and placed the glass on the metal lattice patio table. She had not decided on a specific type of job, and she searched through the dozens of job postings for any suitable part-time position. There were postings for cleaning staff, caretakers of senior adults, handymen, drivers of delivery vans, and nannies. After about twenty minutes of scrolling, she leaned back in her chair and closed her eyes. Listening to the birds sing in Sofía's backyard, Marta took a deep breath and relaxed.

She did not expect this task to be so difficult and was struck by how unprepared she was for manual labor. She had never driven a truck or taken care of a senior citizen, and other than raising her own son, she had no experience raising other children. She also did not speak Spanish well enough. Abruptly, she sat up in her chair and typed, "English tutor." The search only resulted in a few advertisements. The majority were for high school students aiming to improve their grades for graduation, a handful for adults preparing to work in an English-speaking country, and there was just one for a pair of young children. Whenever Marta was presented with choices, she had the tendency to go for the unusual.

She clicked on the post for the young children. Señora Álvarez was looking for a part-time tutor to teach English to two young children, five and three, in Carrasco, and the pay was more generous than the other job posts she had seen. Marta typed on her phone the name of the neighborhood mentioned in the ad. It was a suburb of Montevideo, about a thirty-minute bus ride from the Old Town. She was unenthusiastic about the amount of time she would have to spend traveling there and back, but she was willing to give it a try.

She began to dial the number but stopped. She did not speak Spanish well enough to conduct a phone conversation. She was about to stand up and head toward Luisa's office when she noticed a man approaching her from inside the house. Her heart was racing, and she gripped her cell phone but realized that she did not know the emergency number in Uruguay. She was about to scream for help when the man came out into the light of the backyard. He was carrying a plastic bucket.

"*Buenas tardes*," the man greeted her with a grin. He did not appear to have the right disposition for someone who was about to rob or injure her. He was a stocky man with a round and weathered face. He wore rubber boots and the bottoms of his pants were tucked inside them. His once-black pants and T-shirt were covered with several white jagged circles, which Marta found off-putting. His hands were red and cracked. There was a definite whiff of the sea about him.

Marta was not ready to let her guard down yet, but she gave up on the idea of screaming. Instead, she asked in Spanish, "Who are you?"

"Pedro, Sofía cousin," he answered in heavily accented English.

"You could have knocked or rung the bell. You really scared me."

"I sorry, ma'am. I no ring bell. Sofía tell me Canada lady live her house. I no think I find you here."

"It's all right. I'll live, I think."

With a raspy laugh, Pedro sat across from her at the patio table and placed the bucket on the ground. He observed Marta, his expression still tickled, but his eyes spoke of kindness.

"I fisherman, I catch fish—in sea."

"Oh, I see. I have a general idea of what a fisherman usually does."

"I bring for Sofía. Make dinner. You like little ones? With shells? What you call in English?"

"Shellfish?" Marta offered.

"Yeah, that's right. I bring black ones tonight."

"Mussels."

"Yes, you like 'em?"

"Yes, I do like shellfish in general. I just don't eat raw oysters."

"Oysters best, but I also no eat them. You see, you—I—we same," Pedro said and winked.

Marta could tell that Pedro was one of those men who thought of themselves as funny, but their sense of humor could sometimes come across as inappropriate and crass. She knew she was attractive and had been used to men making advances at her since she was a teenager. With time, they became less frequent but did not cease completely. At forty-six, Marta looked younger than her age, and her small figure was still graceful and trim, even though she had not danced ballet for years. Other than a few strands of gray, her dark brown hair was lush and her eyes, an unusual amber color, were often described as striking.

Eager to escape, Marta stood up from the table, picked up her laptop, and said, "It was nice to meet you, Pedro. By the way, I don't believe I introduced myself. My name's Marta." And she turned toward the house and disappeared inside.

"I here for dinner tonight. I save best oysters for you!" he shouted after her and laughed at his own joke.

Marta sat at a nearby desk and observed Luisa, who was bustling about, getting ready to leave. The agency had closed for the day, and the office was otherwise empty. Marta found it easy to trust Luisa, who herself was not at all inclined to be reserved, but she never pried in Marta's life. It was only natural for Marta to be equally forthcoming, and talking to Luisa always made her feel more cheerful and less burdened. And she was willing to ask Luisa for help.

As soon as they left the office, Marta said, "Are you free for dinner?"

"Well, I was waiting to hear from a guy I met online. We were supposed to have dinner tonight, but he hasn't contacted me yet. So, yes, I guess I'm free."

"Great. Because I just met Sofía's cousin, Pedro. He threatened to be at the house for dinner, and I'd rather not be there."

"Why? What happened? Pedro's a bit unpolished, but he is a nice guy."

"*Unpolished?* More like uncouth."

Luisa's resonant laughter echoed off the buildings along the narrow street. "I don't know what that means, but I'm sure it's fancy for 'unpolished.' Anyway, I can assure you that you're not used to Pedro's manners. But if you give him some time, you'll find him to be a kind person."

As they walked toward the restaurant, Marta wondered whether she would ever come to appreciate Pedro's style. When Luisa spoke again, she sounded pensive.

"There's a doomed love story in Pedro's past, but I don't know the details. He doesn't like to talk about it, and Sofía respects his wishes."

Still, Luisa was undeterred. In high school, Pedro had fallen in love with a girl whose family was from England. They were living in Montevideo temporarily, something to do with her father's job. And she was the reason why Pedro had learned the limited amount of English he knew. The girl returned his feelings, but her family did not approve. Before she and her family were to return to England, Pedro and the girl promised to wait for each other until they could be together again.

"But she never came back. And almost forty years later, Pedro's still not married."

"Wow, that's an amazing and very sad story. I wouldn't have thought Pedro to be such a romantic."

"Don't feel too sorry for him. He hasn't been shy with the ladies all that time!"

Marta kept walking, engrossed by Pedro's ill-fated love story. Her thoughts were disrupted by Luisa's sharp gasp. "I wonder whether you remind him of her?"

"Oh, I hope not. The very thought of it makes me uncomfortable." Marta did not divulge to Luisa that, judging by his wit earlier in the day, she could not imagine herself being attracted to him. And she hated the thought of breaking someone's heart.

"Be clear with him and he'll leave you alone."

"Are you sure?"

"I promise you. He's harmless."

They reached the restaurant, but before Luisa could open the door, Marta gently pulled her back. "Before we go in, I have a favor to ask of you." And she told Luisa about her decision to find a part-time job and that she needed her help with Spanish to call a potential employer.

"That's an unusual plan. I can't imagine why you'd want to tutor two small kids, but I'm happy to make the call for you." Luisa dialed the number, and from her interrupted conversation, Marta could tell that she was talking to a real person on the other side of the line. After a couple of minutes, Luisa hung up the phone. "The meeting with Señora Álvarez is set for tomorrow morning at ten o'clock. By the way, do you know where these people live?"

"Yes, I looked it up. Carraso, or Currasco, or something like that."

"It's called Carrasco, and it's the most affluent neighborhood in Montevideo. It has big mansions, and only the likes of celebrities and the obscenely rich live there."

"Other than potentially working with spoiled and privileged kids, is that a bad thing?" Marta was unsure whether Luisa was trying to warn her to stay away from it or was giving her a hint of what to expect.

"Not necessarily. I wonder who this Señora Álvarez is. I can try to look her up, but without the first name, it'll be difficult. The last name isn't that uncommon."

"That's all right. I don't have anything against fancy mansions. I might enjoy taking on a small anthropological research project. It'll be like observing a new way of life."

"You're the only person I've met who seems to enjoy doing research all the time. It's all you talk about. 'This researcher says this; this research evidence suggests that.'"

"I can't help it. It's what I do for a living," Marta said

as they entered the restaurant. "I'm naturally curious. And research evidence is the most reliable source of information. Other than the sage advice from my grandmother, of course."

Once seated, they ordered wine, and while they waited for their food, Luisa said, "I'm so happy to have dinner with you tonight instead of with some guy I met online who will only disappoint me again." She took a sip of her wine. "Have you tried online dating?"

"No." Marta wished that the topic had not come up because she knew that it would be fruitless. She had to reveal at least part of herself online, which would make her feel extremely exposed and vulnerable. And Marta had been taught—no, indoctrinated—by her mother to avoid unwrapping her soul, to keep her most intimate thoughts to herself, to never reveal to others her fears and weaknesses lest people take advantage of her.

Marta knew that her mother's advice, although extreme, came from an agonizing experience. When Marta was about fourteen, a spurned neighbor had reported to the communist authorities that Marta's mother came from a bourgeois family. Before the communist revolution at the end of the Second World War, Marta's great-grandfather had been a wealthy merchant, and her grandfather was an officer in the king's army. In those days, such information meant that their offspring for generations could be considered "enemies of the people." As a result, Marta and her mother could have been subjected to mild but persistent harassment, such as being called to the police headquarters without warning, and for no reason. This also could have precluded Marta from going to university or severely limited where she could live. Thankfully, her grandfather's good friend, who served in the upper levels of the Communist Party, made sure that the case was put to rest without any long-term consequences—except for Marta's extreme reluctance to open up to anyone who had not proven themselves to be a trusted friend. As a result, online dating was destined to never become her playground.

Luisa's crisp voice pulled Marta out of her thoughts. "You should. These days you aren't going to meet any eligible men anywhere else."

"That's ironic, considering you just said you expect to be disappointed by such an 'eligible man.'"

"Yes, it's not an easy game to play. But being in my forties, I don't have much choice if I'm hoping for a committed relationship. I've never been married, I don't have kids, and I probably never will."

"If you really want a child, you can still have one. These days, you don't have to be in a committed relationship to do that. Or better yet, you can adopt. There are many orphans in the world who would be thrilled to have you as their mother. Have you looked at options here in Uruguay?" Marta was relieved to have moved away from the topic of online dating and marriage in general. While she had no bitter feelings toward her former husband, she was still unhappy with how their marriage had unraveled, and she was unwilling to discuss the details with anyone, not even her son.

"No. I guess I haven't given up on that true love, happily-ever-after, fairy-shmairy illusion," Luisa replied.

"Well, now that I've been through a marriage and a divorce, I would even call the expectation of a happily-ever-after a delusion. To put it plainly, people change over time." Marta shook her head and took a sip of her wine. "But you should stay positive. And if you have the energy and inclination to search for love online, more power to you." She leaned back in her chair.

The waiter came with their plates, and once he was gone, Luisa said, "I'm naive, especially considering my age. Apparently, women over forty are more likely to be struck by lightning than find love. How depressing is that?"

"I didn't mean to suggest that you're too old, or that finding a good partner is impossible." Marta believed that online dating could be rewarding for some, and that Luisa had a personality that was better suited to navigate it more successfully than she did. Luisa was temperamentally the opposite of her. She was outgoing and was not intimidated to strike up quick friendships, especially with men. She was effervescent and, unlike Marta, untroubled by possible rejections.

Marta took a bite of her food. "I'm really more introverted than I look, and this comes out more online than in person. I'm not on social media, either. I don't understand the appeal of it."

"I think people feel more connected through it. I use it to stay up to date on my friends' lives, and mainly to keep up with parties and what's happening in town. Otherwise, I'd miss a lot."

Marta never worried about missing out on anything she did not know about. If a friend really wanted to connect with her, she would find a way to do it. Marta allowed for the possibility that she missed out on some parties and had fewer friends as a result, but she was convinced that, ultimately, the friends she had were the right ones for her.

"Social media brings out people's narcissism," she said. "And I'm not interested in that. No one's eternally happy, consistently witty, or perfectly groomed."

"But how do we find true love, assuming it exists?" Luisa had stopped eating and placed her cheek on her hand.

"I still prefer the old-fashioned way, meeting the person face-to-face. It's the only chance to experience the sparks flying and the butterflies fluttering. And there's still the pleasant surprise of discovering who we are and melding into each other's personalities. I'd take that any day over the modern version: reading our promotional ads on the billboard at some matchmaking website, and discovering with disappointment how the profile doesn't match the person in front of us." She took another bite of her food. "Mine's definitely the harder route, but hopefully more enjoyable and fulfilling."

"But you may never find true love again, or any love for that matter." Luisa picked up her fork.

"I'll take that chance if it means finding it in the best possible way . . . for *me*. But first, I have this job interview tomorrow, and I have to tell Hugo about it."

"Who's Hugo?"

"He's a young person I befriended. He begs on the street near here."

Luisa looked at Marta and squinted. "I think I know who you're talking about. I've seen a young man begging on the street too. And he's always reading a book."

"That's the one."

"And he's your friend?"

Marta smiled at Luisa's befuddled expression. "Yup! And he's the reason I decided to look for a job in the first place."

The next morning, Marta set out to find Hugo before her interview. She was wearing a dark-purple silk blouse with capped sleeves and a loose burnt-orange lace skirt that twirled around her ankles with each step. As she approached him, she announced that she had found a job advertisement for a tutoring position for two young children, and that she was on her way to a meeting with their mother.

"Good luck," Hugo said.

"Thanks. I might need it if the kids prove to be spoiled little brats." Marta reached inside her purse and handed Hugo a gift-wrapped package.

"What's this?" he asked.

"A birthday present."

"But today isn't my birthday."

"I thought the chance of it was pretty slim. But it's bound to be your birthday sometime in the next twelve months, so take this as an early present."

Hugo took the package and unwrapped it slowly, taking care not to tear the paper. It was a book, and before Hugo had a chance to examine it, Marta said, "It's *Animal Farm* by George Orwell. It's an allegory, but it paints an accurate picture of the fear and repression my parents and I experienced during communism in Bulgaria. And you should know that this is light reading in comparison to Orwell's other book on the same general topic, *Nineteen Eighty-Four*. But look on the bright side. That could be your birthday present next year!"

CHAPTER 5

Purple

The long bus ride to Carrasco was not as tedious as Marta had feared. She observed with curiosity the people on the bus who came from all walks of life: some wore dark business suits, others wore hospital uniforms, and many were dressed casually in jeans and T-shirts or simple cotton dresses. Their voices were loud, as if they were shouting angrily at each other, but their smiling faces suggested otherwise. The bus had been full when Marta boarded in the Old Town, but only a handful of people remained by the time the bus reached her stop.

As soon as Marta got off the bus, she felt as if she had been transported back to North America or, more precisely, to an affluent suburb of San Francisco. The main street was broad, neat, and lined with palm trees. The houses were large, and their vast yards were filled with exotic bushes. Marta remembered Luisa's warning about how fancy Carrasco was. She still had to walk another ten minutes before she would reach the address. She crossed the main street and headed up a side street that snaked along a steep hill.

It was almost ten o'clock and it was already hot. By the time Marta reached the address, she was breathing heavily and her cheeks were burning. She paused to catch her breath. The house was a large colonial painted pale yellow, which gave it a warm and welcoming glow. Thick bushes surrounded the yard as far as Marta could see, and a few children's toys were scattered across the neatly trimmed lawn, one of which was a soccer ball. At least one of the children must be a boy, Marta thought, but quickly recognized how ridiculous it was to make such assumptions about gender roles. Her niece was an avid soccer player. The iron gate was ajar, and she walked to the large front door and rang the doorbell. She waited, but she could not hear any noise coming from the inside. She rang the bell again and was about to leave when the door opened.

Marta was surprised to see a young man standing at the door. She had expected a woman. He was barefoot and was fastening the last buttons on his shirt. He was impatient and barely looked at her. In her mild confusion, Marta could not think of what to say in Spanish. She uttered the words, "Señora Álvarez?" and searched in her purse, mumbling to herself, "Oh, where's my phone?"

After the man had finished tucking his shirt into his pants, he leaned toward her and said, "Señor Rodríguez," emphasizing the word señor. "And you don't need your phone. I'm not in a mood for selfies." He spoke in slightly accented English and had a sardonic inflection in his voice.

At first Marta was puzzled by his arrogant presumption. But she assumed that it was a joke and smiled in mild embarrassment. "Thank goodness, you speak English." She reached out to shake his hand. "Marta Aneva, pleased to meet you."

He shook her hand as he looked down the driveway. "How did you get in here? The gate's supposed to be locked."

"Well, it wasn't." Marta shrugged.

The man frowned. "And why are you here?"

Marta realized that he was unaware of the purpose for

her visit, but his indifferent, even disdainful, manner made her feel self-conscious and unwelcome. For a split second she considered leaving, but instead straightened up and said, "I'm here because Señora Álvarez gave me this address when she invited me to interview for a tutoring position for her children."

The man's eyes narrowed, and he moved to one side and gestured her in. Once inside, he led her to a large living room and pointed toward the couch. "You can sit." He turned around and ran up the stairs, taking two steps at a time. Unsure of what his plan was, Marta was confused by his nonchalant, bordering on impolite, behavior. She was not used to being treated with so little respect, but then again, she had never before worked as the domestic help for the very wealthy.

She chose not to sit and, instead, took the opportunity to examine her surroundings. The room was tastefully decorated. The furniture was defined by smooth straight lines and neutral colors, and the artwork on the walls was abstract but engaged Marta's attention. Across from the couch, a soccer game was broadcasting on the huge wall-mounted TV, but the sound was muted. On one side of the room, large French doors led to a patio and a well-kept flower garden, beyond which the ocean shimmered in the distance. On the other side, another set of French doors opened toward a backyard surrounded by a tall hedge. In the middle of the lawn, there was a pond with a fountain that splashed around a statue of a small boy whose foot was placed on a soccer ball. The statue was peculiar and tacky, and Marta was no longer interested in examining it any closer.

She was distracted by loud steps coming down the stairs. When the man reappeared, he was fully dressed, with a linen jacket and shoes. He picked up a remote control from the coffee table and turned the TV off.

He was tall and athletic, with wavy raven-black hair. His eyes were dark but had a sparkle in them that gave his otherwise stern and chiseled face a softer look. He had the confidence of a mature man, one who is used to taking matters in his own hands, but the lack of gray hair suggested that he was probably still in his thirties. Marta was disturbed by how attractive she found him, considering that she would not describe him as her usual type. For one, her former husband had a fair complexion, was generally thin, and cerebrally nonathletic. She was, therefore, confused by her own reaction, but she brushed it off as ludicrous.

The man stood across from her, observing her with a smirk, as if he was enjoying her discomfort. Marta looked him straight in the eye and said in a pitch higher than usual, "Señor Rodríguez, I do *not* wish to trouble you any longer. Is Señora Álvarez at home? Or should I come later?"

"No, Señora Álvarez isn't home, but she'll be back soon. You can wait here, Miss . . . ?"

"Marta's fine."

"Marta, yes. I can remember that." And he pronounced her name with the rolled *r* typical of both Spanish and Bulgarian, which always made her feel sentimental, and she allowed herself to relax.

He left the living room again. He had an annoying habit of disappearing without a word. After a couple of minutes, he returned with two glasses and placed one of them on the coffee table.

"Orange juice," he announced. Marta sat on the couch next to the glass but did not touch it. The man sat across from her and took a sip from his glass. "Señora Álvarez must've found a way to post the ad for a nanny. I know she's been meaning to—"

"I responded to an ad for an English tutor, not a nanny. I hope there wasn't a mistake."

"Tutor, nanny, what's the difference?"

Considering how arrogant the man was, it was to be expected that he would not care about trivialities, such as the exact job description of his domestic employees.

"I'm willing to consider this position only if it's to teach the children English," Marta replied in a businesslike tone. "It's important to me that I'm not expected to clean, or cook, or provide any other type of childcare. I assume that there's another nanny already, or there'll be one soon."

The man took another sip of his juice. He rested his elbows on his knees and looked at Marta with raised eyebrows.

"Where are you from, Marta?"

"I came from Canada, but originally I'm from Bulgaria, a small country in Eastern Europe." Marta often felt the need to provide the additional clarification. Many of the people she had met over the years had not heard of Bulgaria, or had only a vague idea of where it was. And she was certain that the man staring at her, all the way here in Uruguay, would have absolutely no idea.

"I know of Bulgaria," he scoffed. "I'm familiar with some of their players."

"Players?"

"I'm a professional football player. But you'd probably call it 'soccer.'"

"A football player! How interesting." Marta's thoughts were racing, and she was not sure what else to say.

This new revelation explained the self-aggrandizing fountain in his backyard. But Marta was more unsettled by the sudden memory of Emil, the boy who had tortured her when she was in first grade. He chased her relentlessly in the schoolyard during recess, pulled on her hair, and made fun of her that her skirt was uneven or her socks were scrunched. She thought him stupid and was infuriated when the other boys laughed at his witless taunting. One day, she came home from school crying because she had fallen down while running away from Emil, and Marta finally told her mother about her hateful torturer. Instead of giving her a commiserating hug, her mother laughed. "Marta, can't you see? He's showing his preference toward you. He likes you."

Confused, Marta screamed, "But he hates me!" And there was nothing her mother could say to convince her otherwise. Her mother did speak with the teacher, however, and Emil's attentions diminished over time. Marta dreaded the beginning of second grade, but on the first day of school, to her great relief, she discovered that Emil had moved to a new school. The boys were gossiping with unhidden envy that he had been recruited by the national sports school. He was destined to become a professional soccer player. She thought it perfectly fitting for a dumb bully like him. Years later, she had heard his name shouted by sport commentators on soccer game broadcasts that blasted from open windows as she walked past, never looking in.

The revelation that the man sitting in front of her, possibly her potential employer, was a professional football player did not thrill Marta. Instead, she steeled herself to the prospect of limp and insipid conversations, the type she had with people she tried to avoid. But Señor Rodríguez knew of Bulgaria, and that annoyed her.

"I play for an elite professional team in Spain, and I'm gone most of the time," he said and stopped, as if he expected

Marta to say something, to be curious, perhaps, and wanted to allow her the opportunity to ask questions. It was unlike her, but she was not about to become inquisitive. Even if he told her more, she was unlikely to have been impressed. She knew almost nothing about professional football, and she would have considered it a waste of her time. She tried to remember any European teams she might have heard of. Manchester United came to her mind because a Bulgarian player was a member of the team for a while and it was considered a big deal. So big, in fact, that the news had somehow reached her.

Instead, she said, "Europe is very far away from here."

"You really have no idea who I am, do you?" he said, and the same smirk reappeared on his face.

"No. Should I? Do you know who I am?" Marta shifted in her seat. Realizing that he was not joking about the selfies earlier, she grew more irritated with how self-absorbed he was.

The man laughed, and ignoring her question, he explained, "I have two children, Sebastián and Romina. Their mother and I are divorced. They spend their time with her while I'm away, and they spend the short amount of time that I'm here with me. So, this is a casual and extremely part-time position, you understand? I've had no luck with the agencies because no one likes the infrequent and unpredictable schedule."

"That's fine. It works well for me. I won't be relying on the income to support myself."

He regarded her before he said, "And what do you do for a living when you're not a *tutor* for Uruguayan children?"

"I'm a university professor."

"A university professor? How interesting!" The man gasped at her words and bit his lower lip.

Marta scowled at his mockery.

"And why would a university professor want to take care of my kids?" The taunting on his part was unmistakable, but she sensed faint insecurity as well.

Marta's thoughts swirled in her head: the revelation that he was a professional football player, that he was the father of the children, and that Señora Álvarez must not be the mother. His main question of why she wanted to work as a tutor was a reasonable one, but she had no quick answer to it. And judging by Señor Rodríguez's behavior, he would be neither interested nor patient enough to hear it. Instead, Marta decided to begin with the obvious.

"Señor Rodríguez—"

"Eduardo, please."

Marta pressed her lips together and resumed, "I should point out again that I'll be only teaching the children, not taking care of them. As for why I want to do it, teaching is what I do for a living, and I find it to be a rewarding experience. I came to Uruguay during a six-month leave from my work without any specific purpose. The peace and quiet is exactly what I wanted, but it could get boring at times, and I think that a part-time job, as the one you described, would be just fine."

"Okay. But you can't expect me to be excited about someone who"—Eduardo hesitated—"someone who wants to teach my kids because she's bored."

Marta tucked a stray lock of hair behind her ear and nodded. When she spoke again, her voice was softer. "To be completely honest, I have a friend who is an invalid. He is begging near where I live in Ciudad Vieja, and he hopes that one day he could afford to buy a wheelchair. He wouldn't accept a gift from me—apparently, it has something to do with the decaying capitalism that I come from—but he might accept it if I make the money while working here. So, I decided to find a job, and teaching English to children on a part-time basis suits me well." She straightened up in her seat and smiled. "And did I mention? I love children."

At that point the front door opened and a woman came into the house.

"Ah, Señora Álvarez, you've been missed," Eduardo said and continued in Spanish.

Marta was surprised to find her an older woman, with silver and black streaks of neatly arranged hair in a tight bun at the back of her head. She was dressed all in black, and her face was tanned and creased. She smiled and said, "*Buenos días.*"

Marta greeted her back in Spanish and looked at Eduardo. He explained that Señora Álvarez was his housekeeper. She did not speak English, and she usually managed the housework, did the cooking, and often minded the children when he was in town. He leaned back in his chair and crossed his long, muscular legs, with the now familiar smug smile on his lips. "So, are you willing to be the English tutor to my kids?"

Marta knew that the interview with her potential employer had not gone well and had made her unusually uncomfortable. She was eager to leave his living room the same way she had wanted to escape the audition room at the ballet academy all those years ago.

Marta had been barely nine years old, and as required, completely naked but for her panties, which she had chosen carefully for the occasion. While waiting to be called into the audition room, she had seen the girl on her left lift and pull her leg up all the way to her ear—Marta's leg would only go up to just above her hip—and the girl on her right performed a blasted pirouette. Marta turned toward her mother and said, "I wanna go home."

She was jerked back by a painful clutch on her shoulder. Her mother stooped down, and when she spoke Marta shivered. "Marta! Listen *very* carefully. You've dreamed of this ever since you could barely walk, and you're not about to drop it just because you're intimidated. Strong girls fight all the way to the end. And only then will they succeed, regardless of whether they get what they want . . . or *not*." Marta was confused by the swarm of words, but she knew that she had to go into that room. And she opened the door without looking back.

She was devasted when the rejection from the ballet academy finally arrived. With time she had come to accept it, and many years later, she had realized that her mother was right. Marta never had to wonder what might have been if she had never tried.

As Eduardo's pleased expression came back into focus, Marta's confidence in her ability to handle the situation grew. Moreover, since arriving at his house, she was unable to suppress a simmering curiosity about the enigmatic and ever tempting life of a celebrity. She did not want to miss this tantalizing opportunity. The alternative of never finding out was too dull for her to contemplate. Therefore, instead of being annoyed again, Marta was amused by the prospect of the extraordinary entries that she could write in her journal.

"Yes, I'm willing. But could I give you my final answer after I've had a chance to meet the children?"

Before Eduardo was able to say anything, the sound of a car horn came from outside. He stood up and said, "Can you come tomorrow? The children will be here in the morning. Ten o'clock?" Marta nodded, and he said, "*Hasta luego*," and left the house. Her gaze followed him, and through the window beside the front door, she could see a bright red convertible with a stylish blonde with dark sunglasses sitting behind the steering wheel. Without opening the car door, Eduardo jumped into the passenger seat, gave the woman a kiss, and they drove off.

Marta looked at Señora Álvarez and smiled, but she could not think of anything else to say to her. Insecure about her pronunciation in Spanish, she pulled out her cell phone and typed into the translator app, "I will see you tomorrow morning at ten?"

Señora Álvarez looked at the Spanish translation and replied, "*Sí.*"

"*Adiós*," Marta said and left with a deep sigh of relief. It had not been an easy meeting with her future employer. She hoped that she would have an easier time with the children.

CHAPTER 6

Pink

The gate to Eduardo's house was locked. Marta looked around and pressed the only button she could see. She expected to hear someone's voice through the speaker, but instead she heard a click and the gate retreated slowly. A tall young woman answered the front door. She was wearing jeans and a white T-shirt, and her blonde hair was pulled back in a messy knot. At the sight of Marta, she smiled.

"Hi, I'm Isabella, Eduardo's ex-wife. You must be Marta, the new English tutor?"

Marta nodded and shook her hand.

"I knew it, because you arrived right on time," Isabella quipped. "Please, come in. Eduardo's taking a shower after his morning run. He will join us in a moment."

Upon entering the living room, Marta found two children seated primly on the couch. The older one was a boy with dark blond hair and blue eyes, and he resembled his mother. The younger one was a girl with long raven hair, and her eyes were two shiny black olives.

Marta waved and said, "Hi, I'm Marta."

Isabella came closer and addressed the children in English. "Sebastián, Romina, say hi to Marta, please!"

Romina jumped off the couch and approached Marta. "Can you play?" Romina's English was perfect for a three-year-old.

"I'd love to. But you speak English already?"

"Our nanny speaks English," Sebastián said, and he came closer to her too.

"The children have an American nanny at my house," Isabella explained.

"And I hired a *Canadian* tutor to keep things different," Eduardo said as he came down the stairs, his hair still wet from the shower.

Marta realized that the nature of her job would be different than she had anticipated. It was obvious that the children did not need grammar or vocabulary lessons, and she felt compelled to tell their parents that she could not be of any help to them. But she thought of the books she read to her son when he was younger, and the rich opportunities for learning that they had provided to him, and the satisfaction she felt through the interactions she had with him. Marta and Ilian would talk not only about what was in the books, but also how the stories related to their own experiences, their thoughts, and dreams.

Assured that she would find working with Eduardo's children similarly gratifying, Marta reached into her purse and pulled out two toy horses carved out of plain wood. She had bought them the day before from a wood carver at her favorite farmers' market. The only decoration on the horses was a delicate carving of the saddle and stirrups on one horse, which she offered to Sebastián, and an embellished set of reins with flowers on the other, which she gave to Romina. The children thanked Marta after being nudged by their mother. Sebastián lifted his horse above his head and galloped around the room, making loud clip-clop noises with his mouth.

Romina looked at her horse and said, "Hi, horsey! My

name's Romina. And you're Flor. You have flowers on your string."

Marta leaned toward Romina and whispered, "These are called 'reins' in English."

"Okay, I should get going," Isabella said. "The kids will be staying here until the end of the week when Eduardo goes to Europe. Nice to meet you, Marta."

As soon as she left, Romina pulled Marta by the hand. "Come see my room!"

"And I want to show you mine," Sebastián added.

Marta followed them both upstairs. First, she entered Romina's room and exclaimed, "Wow, what a lovely room you have!"

Romina ran toward the most beautiful antique dollhouse Marta had ever seen. It was large—almost as tall as Romina—and had three levels. The house was intricately ornate on the outside, and each room was well furnished. Marta dreamed of a dollhouse such as this when she was a little girl. She had seen pictures of them in her children's books. The closest she came to an experience of playing with a dollhouse was when she visited her aunt, who did not have the actual house but only a few dolls and tiny furniture pieces, which she kept in an old drawer.

Romina pulled her by the hand and said, "Wanna play with my dolls?"

"Yes! But first, I should visit Sebastián's room too. He's been waiting so patiently for his turn. Is that okay with you?"

"Okay," Romina said and brushed her hair off her face before walking toward the door.

It was Sebastián's turn to take Marta by the hand. His room was the same size as Romina's, and the floor was scattered with toy cars, trains, and various plastic animals. A large box of Lego pieces sat in one corner of the room, and there was a partially finished construction set on which Sebastián had been working.

"I'm building a spaceship. But it's not finished yet." Sebastián said as he lifted the structure.

"That's impressive!"

He sat on the floor and began to put Lego pieces together.

"Okay, Romina," Marta said, "show me everything you have in your dollhouse." After a few minutes, Sebastián joined them in Romina's room, but he continued to play on his own with his wooden horse.

While they played on the floor, they heard a knock. Marta turned and saw Eduardo standing at the door, but he was not alone. His arm was wrapped around the waist of a striking young woman who resembled the one in the red convertible. Marta pulled herself up from the floor.

"Marta, this is my girlfriend, Claudia."

Marta smiled and uttered a polite greeting.

Claudia acknowledged her with a slight nod, but her face remained expressionless. She appeared to be very young, but Marta found it difficult to determine the age of women who wore as much makeup as Claudia did. In addition to her youth, Claudia exuded innocence and confidence all at once. She was tall and slim, almost too thin, and her high heels and short dress were obviously expensive and carefully put together. Marta felt self-conscious about the clothes she was wearing: a pair of navy linen pants and a light forest-green top with ruffled three-quarter sleeves. She also could not help but note an undeniable similarity between Claudia and Isabella. Eduardo's taste in women was easily discernible. While Isabella was warm and friendly, Claudia was haughty and aloof. But Claudia probably did not speak English. Marta always felt like an agitated outsider when she did not speak the language, and the current situation perfectly explained Claudia's reticence.

Claudia did not seem inclined to say anything, and an awkward silence ensued. She observed the children with apathy, which Marta found curious. But the children were similarly unenthusiastic to see Claudia.

Eduardo finally broke the silence. "Claudia and I are leaving shortly. You don't mind being left alone with the kids on your first day, do you?" Marta indicated that she would be fine, and he added, "Señora Álvarez is also in the house if you need anything."

Holding Claudia by the hand, he turned to leave just as Marta said, "I have to leave by five at the latest."

"Oh, I hadn't thought about that. I should be back by four. Will that work?"

Marta agreed and made a mental note to discuss the exact plans for her future schedule, if she were to accept his job offer.

As Eduardo and Claudia left the room and headed down the stairs, Marta overheard some of the words Claudia spoke in Spanish: ". . . relieved . . . she's an older woman . . ."

"Most adults are older than you, my love . . ." Eduardo said, but Marta could not distinguish the rest.

She sighed and looked down at the dollhouse. Her mother's assertive voice echoed in her head: *It doesn't matter how old a woman actually is but how old she feels she is.* Marta exhaled and sat on the floor in Romina's room, folded her legs in front of her, and leaned her head on the side of the bookshelf. She was happy to watch Romina play with her dolls, and Sebastián had joined her too. The two played well together, but every once in a while, Romina would shout at Sebastián for putting a piece in the wrong place.

At a more heated moment, Marta asked, "Tell me, Romina, who lives in this house?"

Romina pulled the various dolls from the house. "This is Mommy, and this is her boyfriend. This is Daddy, and this is his girlfriend. This is Grandma and Grandpa, and these are the kids." Then she pulled out a tiny bundle and declared, "And this is baby!"

Marta wondered how closely this strange configuration of the family resembled Romina's own. She guessed that Isabella had a boyfriend too.

"And all of these people live in the same house?" Marta asked.

"Yeah! And it's the birthday party."

"Whose birthday is it?"

"Mine!" Romina shrieked.

"Romina and Claudia have the same birthday," Sebastián mumbled while playing with his horse without looking at anyone in particular.

"That's an unusual coincidence," Marta said.

"I hate it!" Romina shouted.

Marta pulled back. "Oh, Romina, it's not a big deal. Claudia is old enough that she probably doesn't have parties anymore. And even if she does, I'm certain that she invites different friends than yours."

"She is twenty-two and still has birthday parties," Sebastián said.

"Hmm. You're very observant, Sebastián."

"I know because *Papá* made us go to her party, and I counted the candles on her cake."

"She's a model. And she has pretty clothses," Romina said, as if she had heard those exact words somewhere else. She wrinkled her nose and added, "But she don't play. She say we make her dress dirty."

Marta was intrigued by the children's frank observations but chose to change the subject. "We've been playing here long enough. How about we go out for a while? It's a beautiful day outside."

During their outing, Marta took the children to their local public library branch. She expected all the books there to be in Spanish, but to her delight, she discovered a section in English, which was quite varied. A friendly librarian informed her that many of the tourists and some expatriates would donate their books to the library before they left to go back home. Among the typical vacation fare, such as mystery and romance novels, Marta noticed a few classics and a good selection of children's books.

Back at the house, Marta and the children had a lunch that Señora Álvarez had already prepared for them. After lunch, Marta offered to read some of the books to the children, and they piled around her on the couch. While she read, Marta noticed Romina yawning frequently. She realized that Romina was young enough to still take naps in the afternoon but hadn't remembered to ask her parents about that. She asked the children instead. Sebastián was indignant, and he answered that he had not been napping since he was two, but Romina still napped in the afternoon. Marta took Romina to her bedroom and tucked her in bed. She joined Sebastián back downstairs, and he asked if he could watch a movie.

"Okay," Marta said, "but it has to be in English."

As they watched the movie together, Sebastián kept slumping lower and lower on the couch, and finally he placed his head on Marta's lap. She smiled. It no longer surprised her how quickly children warmed up to her.

After her nap, Romina was hungry. Marta went into the kitchen in search of food. She pulled a container of plain yogurt from the fridge, and both children wrinkled their noses in disgust.

"We only eat fruit yogurt. This one's too sour," Sebastián said. Marta ignored him, spooned some yogurt into two bowls, and sprinkled it with fresh blueberries on top. She placed a bowl in front of each child. Then she served some for herself and ate it without hiding her enjoyment from the children.

After observing her for a while, Romina picked up her spoon and placed a yogurt-covered blueberry in her mouth. Her eyes widened. "It's yummy, Sebastián. Try some!"

Sebastián took a bite but was unwilling to give up so easily. He ate the yogurt but kept his nose wrinkled the whole time.

It was shortly past four o'clock when Eduardo came home, alone. He dropped two large grocery bags on the kitchen table and turned toward the children. "Kids, Claudia's coming for dinner, and you have to help me cook."

"Ugh!" both children exclaimed.

"Not again," Sebastián whined.

That was Marta's cue to go home. She got up, and before she headed out of the room, she said. "The children and I had a good day."

"Does this mean you're are taking the job?"

"Yes," Marta replied.

"Can you come for the next three days before I leave for Spain? The kids already seem easy around you, and they'll get to know you better."

"Sure. Ten to four again?"

"Yes, if that works for you."

Marta was assured by the fact that her day with the children was pleasant, and she was relieved that Eduardo was hardly present. She noted with mild disappointment that other than a few children's books, there were no other books in the house. Tributes to soccer, however, were ubiquitous. Marta and her employer came from different worlds and were utterly incompatible. The less they interacted, the more likely they would avoid any potential conflicts between them. But still, she could not resist the enticing promise of discovery, whether in her research or when faced with the curiosities of human nature, even those of a disconcertingly attractive soccer star. Marta smiled at her own inanity.

CHAPTER 7

Amber

"Turns out I'm not working for Señora Álvarez," Marta said after she took a sip of her coffee. "She's just the housekeeper."

"Well, did you meet the actual owner?" Luisa asked. It was mid-afternoon, and they were sitting in the outdoor patio of their favorite café, which was unusually empty.

Marta smiled mischievously. "Oh yes, I did. And all of his women, past and present."

"And? Who is he?" Luisa squeaked with anticipation.

"Someone named Eduardo Rodríguez," Marta replied.

Luisa bounced in her seat. "Get out! You're not serious!" Her eyes were wide, and she was breathless. "Oh my God! Do you even know who Eduardo Rodríguez is?"

Marta laughed, grateful that there were only a couple of other customers at the neighboring tables who appeared undisturbed by Luisa's exclamation. "He actually asked me the same impertinent question. A professional football player, apparently."

"Not just any football player, Marta. He's the *most* famous footballer in Uruguay right now. And this country takes its football very seriously." Luisa stopped to take a breath and said, "And he's gorgeous, don't you think?"

Marta shrugged and Luisa was indignant. "I can't believe you're working in his house and you don't even know who he is. Women here would kill to have your job."

"In this case, he and everyone else around here is fortunate that I'm already working for him. Lives all over Montevideo are safe as a result," Marta said.

"Be serious. You have no idea how lucky you are."

"I'm not sure I'm following you. What's so lucky about working for him? He may be gorgeous, but he has an even more gorgeous girlfriend, and I don't expect to see him hardly at all anyway. I'm lucky because his kids are sweet and we get along splendidly."

"You're such a stiff for not humoring me. And if you're so indifferent yourself, would you at least find a way to introduce me to him? He's delicious. His strong lean body, his dark hair, his beautiful smile . . . it melts my heart every time."

"Luisa, hold yourself together! I refuse to objectify men and treat them as pretty things. Women were treated like that for centuries. And after decades of fighting for women's rights, we shouldn't behave badly now, even if it's only to even the score. We want and deserve to be treated with respect, right? And we should treat everyone else with respect too."

"Oh, come on! But you must find him attractive? It's either that or there's something really wrong with you."

Judging by Luisa's reaction, Marta finally realized how big a celebrity Eduardo Rodríguez was in Uruguay. And it did explain some of his conceited behavior toward her earlier.

"Eduardo's handsome, but that's not enough for me to find him attractive. When I see a billboard with a dashing male model on it, I have the same reaction to it as I do to the statue of *David* by Michelangelo, or the Sagrada Família in Barcelona, or the sunsets I sometimes see outside of my living room window. Beautiful, no doubt about it, but I don't want to have a *relationship* with any of them." Marta paused and a new idea brightened her face. "Well, if *David* steps off his pedestal, puts on some clothes, smiles at me, and charms me with his conversation, then I might consider him. And as for meeting Eduardo yourself, you may be less excited once you get to know him. I get the impression that he's self-absorbed, arrogant, ignorant, and shallow, just as you'd expect from people like him. Though, he does seem to have one redeeming quality. There's a general lightness about him, hinting toward a possible sense of humor, that makes him tolerable. And . . . he cooks for his snooty girlfriend."

"Gosh, you have a way with words." Luisa sounded resigned. She sat up in her chair and asked with a creased brow, "But what makes you think that he's ignorant and self-absorbed? By your own account, you haven't spent a lot of time with him, so you can't know him that well."

Marta tilted her head and pursed her lips. "I just know. You only have to see the fountain in his backyard and you'll know what I mean. And what else could you expect from someone who can't see past the end of his nose?"

"I don't know. I gather you don't like him at all. But I'm not about to give my hopes up just yet."

"There's no point in pining after someone who is so . . ." Marta paused to find the right word that was sufficiently innocuous. "Different."

Luisa sighed. "You're probably right. Now I'm depressed. I was excited to meet him."

"Don't get too downcast. You might still meet him." Marta wanted to be hopeful for her friend, but then she also knew it to be highly unlikely. And she added, "Although at the end of this week, he's joining his team in Spain, and he won't be back until Christmas. So, how's your online dating going?"

"Not great." Luisa sighed. "Remember that failed date

the other night? I haven't been online since. I think I need a break from it for a while." She perked up. "But just yesterday, during our lunch break, this guy walked into our office. He's a software engineer from Buenos Aires and is looking to buy a house on the coast near Montevideo. Prices are cheaper here than in Argentina. His name's Guillermo, and he's kind of nerdy but in a charming sort of way."

"Ah, you like him then?" Marta asked.

"I don't know yet. I barely know him. But I was inspired by what you said the other day, about meeting guys in person and letting the sparks fly. I can't say I saw sparks when I first met Guillermo, but I'm willing to give this a try. *If* he ever comes back to the office."

"He will," Marta assured her. "If he's remotely attracted to you, he will. You're a beautiful, vibrant, and intelligent woman."

"You're all of those things too. But if you could only hear yourself. The way you talked about Eduardo Rodríguez . . . I still can't forgive you for dashing my hopes about him."

Marta laughed. "Tell me more about Guillermo."

The following evening, Marta was dressing the salad when Sofía pulled the last fish from the frying pan. As they brought the food to the table, Pedro walked into the dining room. This time he was expected, and Marta smiled warmly at him. He was dressed in simple but clean clothes, wore slightly worn-out shoes, and had obviously taken a shower—he smelled like soap rather than the sea.

At first, they ate in silence. Eventually, Pedro cleared his throat and said, "You work for Eduardo Rodríguez?"

Marta nodded but was troubled. She did not enjoy

talking about Eduardo, especially when everyone else was so obsessed with him. To temper their excitement, Marta was compelled to highlight his weaknesses and how strongly she disliked him as a result. But she liked people in general and did not feel good being so negative about someone. She barely knew him, after all.

She heard Sofía exclaim in Spanish, "I know. I couldn't believe it when Luisa told me. But apparently, you don't like him much?"

Marta shook her head while she swallowed her bite. She was about to speak when Pedro interjected, "He no your *liga*."

Marta was startled. "Thank you, Pedro, for pointing this out. And here I thought that *I* was out of *his* league."

"Yes, but he not know."

"And how do you know all that?" From the very beginning, Marta had been inclined to tease Pedro. The playful banter had become a natural part of their friendship, and it amused her.

"Life in sea teach me. Much time think. I know much ladies, and I learn their secrets and wants."

"I'd say," added Sofía as she got up to clear the table.

While Sofía was in the kitchen cleaning up and washing the dishes, Pedro said, "I no want you hurt. These men *muy peligroso*. Use woman like nose paper and throw overboard when new woman come."

"Thank you for the advice, Pedro, but I'm not in danger. As you heard already, I don't like Eduardo Rodríguez."

"We see. Now, you give *me* chance?"

Marta felt awkward, and she smiled to hide her indecision about how to best reply to Pedro's brash advances. "Pedro, you are very kind to offer your friendship to a woman you see as needing it. And I thank you for that. But I'm fine right now, and I'm not looking for a partner. I'm happy being by myself and enjoying life as it is."

"I know you, Marta. You think you too good. Very picky with men. You want fruit high on tree, and not see fruit low. These women *solo*."

Marta stirred in her seat. The wisdom of Pedro's words disturbed her. During the years when she was not married, Marta considered herself too busy, first with her university studies, and later with her career, to devote the time necessary to date suitable partners that she liked. Not suffering from lack of attention from men, she had been selective in the ones she let come closer to her, perhaps overly so, because they were few and far apart.

But instead of letting Pedro know that he was right, Marta said, "I'm not alone. I have my son, and I have friends, including you. I consider myself fortunate."

He waved his hand dismissively. "Okay, I see, you—very difficult. Remember, I here—you want man."

Marta blushed. "Thank you, Pedro, I won't forget."

Pedro turned toward the kitchen and shouted in Spanish, "Hey, Sofía, what's left of your pastry that we can have for dessert?"

CHAPTER 8

Ocher

As the heavy front door opened, with Romina almost dangling from its doorknob, Marta knew that it would be a brilliant day. Romina, still in her pajamas, clutched her teddy bear in her arm with a worried look on her face. Marta leaned down to greet her, but before she could ask what was wrong, loud footsteps pounded down the stairs and Romina disappeared into the house.

Today was to be Marta's last day working for Eduardo for a while, because he was leaving for Europe the next day. She had spent three days with the children, and she still marveled at the contentment she felt when greeted by their wide-eyed faces. Their excitement was in stark contrast to the cool indifference she had received from her university students upon entering a classroom. But she also looked forward to a time when she would not need to be with the children and could focus on herself and take the next level of her Spanish class.

As Marta entered the Rodríguezes' house, she was shocked to see that Sebastián was sitting on the bottom step of the staircase in only his underwear. He was crying, which distressed Marta even more.

Eduardo came down the stairs, followed by Señora Álvarez, who was carrying a pile of sheets in her arms. He passed Sebastián without looking at him and hissed to Marta on his way out, "He's about to go to school and still wets his bed. If there are any Canadian tricks you could teach him, that would be good." The front door slammed behind him.

Marta ran to Sebastián and sat on the step next to him. She hugged him and patted his head. Romina jumped from the couch, sat on the step next to them, and placed her head on one of Marta's folded legs. After a while, Sebastián calmed down, but his body still shook with fitful hiccups. Marta told him that it was not uncommon for boys to wet their beds, and with time, it was most likely that he would stop. With even greater conviction, she assured him it was not his fault.

Sebastián lifted his puffy, tear-streaked face. "But . . . it's my fault . . . I'm scared of the dark at . . . at night . . . and I'm afraid to . . . go to the bathroom."

Marta smiled and smoothed the damp tuft of hair at the edge of his forehead and wiped off a tear with the back of her hand. The terrifying monsters she had imagined as a child loomed in her head. She recalled with some embarrassment all the extreme measures she would take to avoid going to the bathroom. Sometimes she would wait until daybreak with a sharp pain in her lower belly before she was brave enough to venture out from the safety of her warm covers. But she had been proud of never wetting her bed. She didn't complain, she didn't ask for help. Whenever she observed other children do that, her mother would scoff and say, "Spoiled brats! They'll never learn to take care of themselves." And Marta had learned to cherish the pain.

Sebastián seemed confused by Marta's reaction, and his eyes would not let go of her face. She rubbed his back and said, "There is a simple solution to this problem, at least one that we can try. Come with me." Sebastián's lips twitched with a hint of a smile, and Romina bounced up and down, relieved that Sebastián was no longer crying.

Marta gathered the children and took them upstairs to get dressed. After such a stressful start to the day, everyone needed to relax. Once downstairs again, the children sat on the couch in the living room, and Sebastián turned on the TV. Marta went to prepare a special drink for them in the kitchen. Señora Álvarez was already working on lunch. Marta poured milk into two glasses and put them in the microwave for a couple of minutes. She asked Señora Álvarez for cinnamon, who passed her a small jar with a golden-brown powder. Marta sprinkled a dash of cinnamon into the glasses and stirred.

Señora Álvarez cleared her throat and said in Spanish, "Señor Rodríguez is a good father. But sometimes he gets upset, especially with Sebastián. He worries that Sebastián won't grow up to be a strong man."

Marta leaned toward Señora Álvarez in a manner suggesting camaraderie and whispered, "Eduardo is foolish to be worried about it. And we both know that his behavior is bound to cause more damage than good."

Señora Álvarez remained quiet. Marta was unsure whether her words were understood, but her disapproval was unequivocal. She took the glasses of milk into the living room and handed them to the children. They took their first sips and, pleased with the taste, gulped down the rest of the warm liquid. Once their glasses were empty, they looked up at Marta in anticipation of what was to come next.

"Can we play, Marta?" Romina asked.

"We are going to the hardware store."

"The what store?" Sebastián said.

"Come, and you'll see." Marta turned the TV off.

The closest strip of shops was about a fifteen-minute walk from the house. The children had already learned that Marta liked to walk, and they followed her without complaining or questioning her any further. Once they reached the hardware store, Sebastián recognized it and announced that he had been there with his father before. Marta raised her brows. Nothing of what she had seen gave her any indication that Eduardo was a handyman.

Marta had already checked on her phone for the Spanish word for "night-light" and headed straight to the shopkeeper. He understood what she asked for and pointed to the shelf.

"Look! This is a night-light," she said to the children and pulled one of the small lights from the box to show them. "You plug it into the wall and it makes a dim light. So, when you have to get up at night, you'll be able to see and not feel scared of the dark."

Marta picked out three lights, then turned to Romina. "Would you like a night-light in your bedroom too?" Romina nodded, her eyes sparkling like black diamonds. Marta paid for the four lights and they exited the store.

On their way home, they walked by a candy shop, and Marta stopped in front of the door. "Hey, kids!" She was amused by the children's puzzled expressions. "How about I buy you some candy today?" At the mention of candy, the two small faces lit up. "But I want to make it clear to you that we won't do this every time we come by this store, okay? Candy is only for special occasions, and I think today is a good day to have a treat. We'll celebrate the last day that Sebastián wets his bed. One piece of candy each!" She turned toward the door and added with a pretend swagger, "And besides, I want a candy myself."

They piled noisily into the shop, and everyone picked their candy. Romina chose a strawberry lollipop with a soft nougat center, Sebastián a red gummy worm, and Marta a small bag of violet drops. She was about to pay when Romina pulled her by the skirt and asked in a whiney tone, "Can I have two lollipops?"

"Absolutely not. Please put one back."

"I wan' it. I give it to Papá." Romina's face was scrunched in a pout, and her bottom lip quivered as if she were about to cry.

Marta kneeled down and looked Romina in the eyes. "Romina, listen. We agreed that we'll get only one candy each. And it's very important that we stick to our deal. We must always keep our promises. You wouldn't want me to change my mind and decide that no one should have any candy."

A couple of tears rolled down Romina's cheek, and she shook her head.

Marta brushed a tear off Romina's face and continued more softly, "Your papa doesn't need candy, but it's awfully kind of you to think of him. If you want to bring him a present, maybe you can pick a flower on the way home."

Romina's eyes brightened again, and she placed one of the lollipops back in the jar.

Finally, Marta paid for the candy and they left the shop. The children ran part of the way up the hill toward their house. Marta could barely keep up with them until Romina stopped and leaned down to pick a few flowers that grew on the side of the road. Sebastián picked a couple of flowers too, but he threw them on the ground.

After Romina had gathered a bunch, she turned toward Marta, lifted her arms up, and whimpered, "I'm tired." Marta picked her up and carried her the rest of the way. When they arrived at the house, everyone was flushed and thirsty, and Marta was panting.

Once inside, Romina handed the flowers to Marta who put them in a glass of water. Instead of following her into the kitchen, the children ran straight upstairs. Marta placed the glass on the kitchen table where their lunch was already waiting for them, and plodded up the stairs. At the top landing, she was greeted by a loud rumpus. The night-lights were scattered on the floor, and the children were skipping around them as if they were performing a wild dance by a ceremonial fire. Marta felt a strong urge to join them, but instead she managed to collect the lights before the children stepped on them.

They plugged one light in each of the children's bedrooms and put one in the hallway separating the bedrooms from the main bathroom. Upon entering the bathroom, Marta exhaled in disappointment. The socket next to the sink had only one place for a plug. An electric toothbrush was already plugged into it. To Marta's questioning look, Sebastián replied that it was his. Marta did not want to make life more complicated for him. With a single plug he would have to switch between the night-light and the toothbrush regularly, which he was sure to forget to do. Moreover, it would not be safe for him to be tinkering with a power plug. And being used to taking matters in her own hands—Marta's former husband had not been a handyman and had been happy to let Marta hire tradespeople as needed—she devised a plan.

She picked up her phone and was about to dial, but stopped. Electrical work carried a degree of risk, even when the repair was as minor as changing a socket. The courteous thing to do would be to check with Eduardo if it was all right with him. But considering his behavior this morning, he was likely to think it an unnecessary hassle aimed at further mollycoddling Sebastián. At the thought of Sebastián suffering even more, Marta made up her mind. Eduardo could fire her, if he pleased, but it was the lesser of the two evils.

She dialed Pedro's phone number. He had been eager to impress her ever since they met, and she felt bad for not being able to oblige him. When he answered, she asked him whether he knew of an electrician who might be available today.

"Why?" Pedro asked.

Marta explained her predicament, and he offered to fix it himself. "But aren't you out at sea today?"

"No, sea bad, no safe. You lucky today! Bring everything. What address?"

The children had just finished their lunch when Pedro arrived, and as soon as he entered the house, he bellowed, "You work for king?"

Marta laughed. "No, just one of his jousting knights."

The children examined Pedro with unabashed curiosity, and Sebastián asked, "Who is this funny man?"

"Sebastián, Romina, this is my friend Pedro. He's a fisherman who has his own boat—"

"Like a sea captain?" Sebastián shouted.

Marta widened her eyes. "Yes! Pedro is a fearless captain who sails the seas in search of fish." She placed her hand on Sebastián's shoulder. "But now he's going to help us with the night-light in the bathroom."

Pedro greeted them with a salute and a wink. He turned toward Sebastián and said in Spanish, "Lead me to that bathroom, young man!" Pedro was about to step onto the thick carpet in the living room but realized that he still had his rubber boots on, and they were covered in sand. He asked, "I take off, ah?"

Marta raised her eyebrows and nodded.

As they reached the bottom of the stairs, Pedro paused and said, "Must no power. Where box?"

"I have no idea," Marta replied.

"¿El sótano?"

"I don't know, Pedro. But come to think of it, I know Señora Álvarez does the laundry in the basement. Sebastián, do you know where the basement door is?"

Before Sebastián could reply, Romina shouted, "I know." She ran into the kitchen and smacked her small hand on a door at the back. Pedro descended into the dim basement. After a minute or so, the low rumble from the fridge stopped. As soon as Pedro emerged again, Sebastián grabbed him by the shirt and led him all the way to the bathroom upstairs. Romina followed them, and Marta went into the living room.

Not long after, Romina came back downstairs, picked a book from the pile that was spread over the coffee table, and sat next to Marta on the couch. Marta began reading, but Romina was restless and kept looking toward the stairs. Pedro's loud talking and Sebastián's giggles rolled down the stairs, and there was a fair bit of commotion. Finally, Sebastián peered from the stairs and announced that the socket was fixed. Romina jumped and ran toward him but stopped.

Pedro's heavy footsteps preceded his booming voice. "Not so fast, boy. First, we need to turn the electricity on," he said in Spanish.

After a few more minutes of going up and down the stairs, Pedro declared the job finished. Unable to resist her curiosity any longer, Romina dashed up the stairs and Marta followed her. The socket looked the same, except that now it had two slots: one for Sebastián's toothbrush, which was already plugged in, and the other had the night-light, which glowed faintly.

"I go. Sofía need help and I say I help," Pedro said while drying his hands on a towel. Turning toward the children, he saluted them again and gently pinched Romina's cheek. Once outside, he waved toward Marta and climbed into his rusty corn-blue truck.

"*¡Muchas gracias, Pedro!*" Marta shouted after him.

Romina yawned. It was past her usual nap time, and Marta took her to her room.

Back in the living room, Sebastián was playing with his toy trains. Marta made herself a cup of tea and sat in one of the armchairs. She observed Sebastián for a while, then sat on the floor across from him. He glanced at her but continued pushing the train up a bridge while making loud puffing noises.

"Can I join in?" Marta asked, tempted by the desire to also push the train around the elaborate train track.

"Hmm . . ." Sebastián stopped the train and looked at the whole setup. "You can be the train master at the next stop." And he pointed to the spot where Marta was supposed to be. She was mildly disappointed but smiled at his reluctance to let go of the train itself.

Marta was not sure how long she and Sebastián had played with the trains when the front door clicked. Eduardo was home with Claudia by his side. Sebastián ran to him while yelling, "Marta made it so I won't pee in my bed," and he pulled Eduardo by the hand. Eduardo looked puzzled, but he followed Sebastián up the stairs. Claudia disappeared after them.

Marta's indignation at Eduardo's earlier treatment of his son returned. She lifted herself up from the floor and went into the kitchen. She took the glass with the flowers Romina had picked earlier in the day and headed toward the vestibule. She heard more footsteps running upstairs. Romina was up, and Marta could hear the children's excited voices.

Eduardo came down the stairs, and as soon as he spotted Marta, he walked straight into the vestibule. The space shrunk around her and she felt slightly dizzy. He stopped in front of her and crossed his arms. "I can't see how the silly lights will help." He was almost a foot taller than her, but he lifted his chin and continued, "Anyway, you should have checked with me first before doing a dangerous repair that involved the electrical installation in my home. Did you change the socket yourself?"

"I could have," Marta replied. "But to assure everyone's complete safety, I asked a friend with more experience." She was about to leave, but then she thought of Sebastián. Eduardo had not considered the effect of his unfeeling behavior on his son or the possible reasons for Sebastián's accidents, and naturally, Marta's solution would seem ridiculous to him. "And you're right. I should've checked with you first. But I didn't because I was worried that you would say no even though the imposition on you and the change to your home were infinitesimal." Her breathing was fast, and Marta stopped to catch her breath before adding, "And I know that what I did was crucial for the well-being of your child and for the success of your relationship with him."

Startled by her eloquent bluntness, Eduardo dropped his arms. "You may be a bloody professor of who-knows-what, but what makes you so confident to tell me how to raise my child?"

Marta was about to retort, infuriated by his response. She contemplated explaining to Eduardo that a bit of empathy would go a long way with his son, but it would have been futile. Her competence was questioned by none other than an uninformed and insolent soccer star. She managed to restrain herself enough to quell her anger, and she remembered the glass with the flowers she was still clutching in her hand. She handed it to him and muttered, "These are a treat from Romina." She picked up her purse and opened the front door, but spun around instead and said with grim urgency, "And don't be such a jock, Eduardo. Talk to your son!"

Eduardo took a sharp breath and blinked. Marta shut the door.

CHAPTER 9

Beige

Marta did not hear from Eduardo, and the unease she felt since their last encounter diminished with time. However, she did hear from Isabella, who invited her for tea about a week after Eduardo left for Europe. Isabella got straight to the point and asked Marta whether she was willing to continue working as a tutor to the children at her house while Eduardo was away. He was not likely to be back for more than a week at a time before Christmas, and it would be such a long time before the children could see Marta again. After considering Isabella's offer, and finding that the demands of her job would be the same at either house, Marta agreed to one day per week. The arrangement also allowed her to stay in touch with the children, who always managed to amuse her, even when they were supremely naughty.

In the evening, Marta went to Luisa's home for dinner. The small but airy one-bedroom apartment was on the twelfth floor of a tall building, and as soon as Marta entered the lobby she smelled wet concrete, an odor that lingered long after people had moved in. Luisa's furnishings were modest and contemporary, and their muted beige tones surprised Marta. She had expected Luisa's home to be as colorful as her personality. But the view of the emerald ocean in the distance was dazzling, and Marta was no longer mystified about Luisa's choice.

She sat on the couch, and Luisa passed her a sweaty glass of lemonade.

"Any news of Guillermo?" Marta asked as she took a sip of her lemonade.

"Yes. He came by the office a couple of days ago, and he wanted me to show him around three different properties. All of them were out of town and it took most of the day. He took me out to lunch *and* dinner."

"Luisa, that's wonderful!"

"I think I like him, Marta. He's the type of guy that I didn't think I'd fall for, but I like him. He's kind and modest, knows a lot about technology, and if I'm patient enough, he could talk about it almost all the time."

Marta was amused by this real example of how opposites attract.

"But he also travels a lot," Luisa continued. "And he's interested in opera, something I'd never thought much about before. But I might give it a try. He invited me to see *La Traviata* on Saturday."

Luisa went into the kitchen, filled a large pot with water, and placed it on the stove. Marta sat on one of the bar stools at the counter. Luisa replaced Marta's empty lemonade glass with a cold glass of white wine and poured one for herself.

As usual, Marta could not resist tempering Luisa's excitement with her more rational thoughts. "This is a promising beginning to your relationship with Guillermo, but I think you should take it slow. We need time to build solid relationships." Marta knew this from her own experience with her former husband, although in their case, as time went by, it became clear that their relationship was doomed. It had started with fireworks, but they had burned out just as fast, and the remainder of their marriage was listless, something they both had come to endure rather than cherish.

Luisa was vigorously stirring the tomato sauce over the stove, and without looking at Marta, she said, "Yeah, yeah, sure. But tell me, what are you up to now that Eduardo is gone?"

"My life doesn't exactly revolve around Eduardo, you know." Marta wrinkled her brows, disturbed by the memory of their last encounter and the way she had admonished him. She brushed the thought away and added, "But I agreed to work for Isabella, his ex-wife, while he's away."

"That's a good idea," Luisa said as she took a sip of her wine. She plunged the wooden spoon back into the sauce. "I know how much you care about those children, even though you don't like their father."

"I do like their mother. But I'm afraid I just may have fired myself from his job."

Luisa spun toward Marta, the dripping spoon still in her hand. "What do you mean? Don't tell me you told Eduardo Rodríguez how much you don't like him?"

"Hmm. I told him a couple of the reasons for my dislike." Marta forced herself to sound upbeat in an attempt to hide the sudden guilt. She had been too harsh toward him.

"I can actually believe this! Marta, don't toy with me. What happened?" The ignored tomato sauce bubbled and spluttered behind Luisa's back.

"I'll tell you, but can I help you with something? I can make the salad."

Luisa placed a cutting board and a knife in front of Marta, then pulled out a head of lettuce and a couple of tomatoes from the fridge. Marta separated the lettuce leaves and brought them to the sink. As she washed each leaf, she told

Luisa about the incident with Sebastián and how upset she had been with Eduardo because of his inappropriate reaction. Marta returned back to her stool and sliced the tomatoes on the cutting board. Through the quick, sharp sounds of the knife chopping against the board, she admitted that she had not handled the situation well. Her pride had been injured and she had allowed her resentment to overwhelm her.

"To be honest, I'm surprised Eduardo hasn't fired me already." Marta scraped the tomato slices into the salad bowl. "But maybe he was too busy getting ready to leave for Spain." As she remembered his angry face and stern reproof, she chopped the lettuce even more vigorously. "Yes, I'm pretty sure that he was offended. At least, I know I wasn't trying to spare his feelings." She transferred the lettuce to the salad bowl. "But I did it because I thought it was for the best for him and his son." She dropped the knife on the cutting board and took a sip of her wine.

"Maybe you're right. Eduardo's more ignorant and less sensitive than his darn smile seems to suggest." Luisa placed a large dollop of fragrant tomato basil sauce in two bowls already filled with steaming pasta. "And by telling him off, you did the right thing." She brought the bowls to the dining table.

Marta followed her with the salad. "Thanks," she said and squeezed Luisa's hand.

The next morning, Marta made a point to visit with Hugo. She had not seen him for a few days, having been too preoccupied with her new job. She realized that she never told him whether she got the job and who her new employer was. She anticipated with some trepidation that he might disapprove of her working for a rich celebrity, whom Hugo was certain to consider a vain ultra-capitalist. Marta also wished that she could tell her son about her new life, but they rarely communicated, and when they did, it was mainly through text, his preferred form of interaction with her.

As Marta approached, Hugo smiled and she sprinted toward him.

"*Hola*, Hugo!" She sat next to him on the sidewalk. "How have you been?"

"Fine." He shrugged. "But I haven't seen you in a while. I thought you went back to Canada or something?"

"Oh no! Do I get the sense that you may have missed me?" Marta bumped her shoulder to his. Hugo blushed and shook his head. "No, of course not," she continued. "Why would you ever miss such a know-it-all who isn't even enchanted with communism?"

Hugo's laugh sounded more like a grunt, but having raised a boy, Marta knew better.

"But to answer your question: no, I'm still here," she said. "I've been preoccupied with my new job, remember?"

"Oh yeah, how's that? Are you tutoring the spoiled brats?"

"Yes, I'm tutoring, but I wouldn't call the kids spoiled brats. They're nice. But their father is something else."

"What do you mean?" Hugo looked at her with mild concern.

"Perhaps if I tell you his name, you'd know exactly what I mean. Does Eduardo Rodríguez ring a bell?" Marta leaned away from Hugo in anticipation of his fiery reprimand.

Hugo remained motionless, and his expression was neutral.

Marta was not sure whether he had heard her. She repeated the name slightly louder. "Eduardo Rodríguez, the football player?"

"I know who you're talking about. Everybody in Uruguay knows his name," Hugo said but remained expressionless.

In complete contrast to how everyone else had been in raptures at her news, Marta expected Hugo to be similarly passionate but critical. She was puzzled by Hugo's tepid reaction.

"I guess you're not a fan?"

"No, not really," Hugo replied. "I've never been into football, even before my accident. And Eduardo Rodríguez is one of those rich guys who makes too much money with his legs and not with his brains."

Now that was more like the reaction Marta had been expecting from him, and she smiled. "I can't say I wholly disagree. But why does it matter how he makes his money? I'm sure he's working very hard for it."

"Come on, Marta, you know what I mean. What he does for a living doesn't help anyone else."

Marta considered his words for a while. "Judging by everyone's obsession with football," she finally said, "Eduardo's sport offers enjoyment and provides an opportunity for people to feel successful by association. And not only for the people in Uruguay but, possibly, all over the world. And even though he isn't producing anything tangible, his work makes other people's lives happier and more productive. Think about it. Writers, or poets for that matter, make money with their brains and not with their legs, but what they produce is similarly intangible."

"Okay, you have a point. But even someone who uses his *brains* shouldn't be making that much money." Marta was about to protest when Hugo continued, "But to be totally fair, I should say that Eduardo Rodríguez isn't as bad as some of the other rich guys."

"How do you know?"

"A couple of years ago, while I was still in school, he came to visit our class. Some famous people like to do that. They promote their sport or cause, and it's good for their image. Most of them come for a few minutes, shake a few hands, and only care to have their photos taken with the students. Then they post them on the internet or have them published in the papers. But Eduardo Rodríguez spent more than an hour with us, and he made a point to talk to us. He also donated money to the school's sports program and the library."

"So, you've actually met him?" Marta was amused by the unexpected twist of fate.

"Yeah, and he asked me if I played football. And when I told him that I didn't, he was surprised but wanted to know what I liked to do instead. And when I said that I wrote poetry, he didn't laugh at me. Instead, he encouraged me to follow my dreams. Even said that sometimes he wished he had more time to read."

Marta was struggling to reconcile Hugo's story with the person she had come to know as her employer. She was both amused and befuddled, in an incongruent state of mind that was brought on when her firm first impressions were subsequently challenged.

"I'm flabbergasted by your story, Hugo," she said. "It even makes me wonder whether we're talking about the same person. So far, all I've seen of Eduardo is that he plays football, he watches football on TV, he jogs and stretches, and he hangs out with his girlfriend, who has the charisma of a life-size doll. He can definitely do with more reading."

Hugo smiled, but Marta was still perplexed. She felt strangely validated, as if her illogical decision to work as a glorified nanny for the ignorant and self-absorbed Eduardo was not completely in vain. Perhaps there was more behind the handsome facade, an inner worth she was able to sense but not yet able to describe.

Marta changed her position to let the blood flow back into her numbed legs. "But enough about Eduardo," she said. "Did you read *Animal Farm*?"

"Yes, I did."

"And? What did you think?"

"It was interesting, but it's an allegory." Hugo cleared his throat. "I'm not sure how much of it is true."

Marta rested her head on her folded knees while looking sideways at him. "It's more true than we might like to believe. It describes a time before I was born, when my parents were young. But I could relate to the fear and deprivation it shows. We were supposed to think that we all had the same chances in life, and that we could all have the same kinds of things. But anyone could see that it wasn't true."

"How so?" Hugo asked.

"Like, take for example, jeans and running shoes. These were things all the kids wanted. But you could only get them in the West. The West was what we called the capitalist countries in Western Europe and North America. And ironically, only people who were well-connected in the Communist Party could go there. And their kids were the ones wearing the jeans and running shoes."

"It's strange that people seem to have been so focused on material things like clothes," Hugo said.

"Yeah, it's natural for people to want the things they can't have. For me and my friends, chewing gum was a precious treat because we rarely had it. And when we did, as most other things in a planned economy, it came in one flavor: peppermint. And if you happened to not like peppermint, or even worse, if you were allergic to it, then you were out of luck. No chewing gum for you!"

"So, how do you think we could achieve true equality? Somehow, dozens of different flavors of chewing gum doesn't seem to be the right answer either," Hugo said and a deep crease appeared between his eyebrows.

Marta sighed. "I don't know. History has shown that it's tricky to find the right balance between people's freedoms and the fair distribution of food and goods. So far, either one has been sacrificed in favor of the other. My father believed that communism can't be imposed on people, but we should be allowed to grow into it naturally. And right after the Second World War, people in Eastern Europe weren't ready, which ultimately resulted in atrocities committed by some of our authoritarian leaders, and numbing apathy and loss of drive for everyone else."

"I wouldn't wish this on anyone." Hugo lifted his cap and scratched his head. "You know, we would probably agree on everything about communism other than our conclusions."

"Fair enough. You're the optimist and I'm the pessimist in this case. I can live with that."

"But your father sounds like an interesting person."

"Yeah, he was. You would've liked him, Hugo. And not only because he was a Marxist. He also loved poetry. He didn't write it, but he liked to read it and recite it by heart. My mother often joked that it was with poetry that he captured her heart."

Hugo smiled, and Marta was uncertain whether he thought her parents silly and old-fashioned, or whether he liked the idea of the romantic appeal of poetry. But she decided that it was not yet a good time to ask him a question that could lead to more personal topics. Instead, she said, "I know the ideas are appealing, especially to those who have a difficult life. But they aren't the panacea for all of our social and political problems. Communist regimes have proven that they could create worse ones." And with that, Marta stood up. "Consider how fortunate you are. You can choose to have a cherry-flavored chewing gum, as well as peppermint, and you can even *choose* not to have any!"

She left invigorated by the conversation with Hugo, but it would have been even more satisfying if she could have had it with Ilian instead.

CHAPTER 10

Cerulean

By mid-October, Marta had been making the most of her free time in Uruguay, and she was impressed by her own commitment to her journal writing. In her past attempts, she had become tired of it by the second or third entry. But now she found something inspiring to write about almost daily even though she did not feel she was accomplishing anything of great significance such as an impactful publication, or a blazing conference presentation, or even a boast-worthy romantic conquest. Her life was ordinary, but she kept cataloging it with relish.

She only wished she could add more entries about Ilian, but his curt replies to her occasional texts were the same: his school was going well and he was fine. No matter how hard Marta tried to get him to say something more about his daily life, he kept shutting her out. Regardless, she remained hopeful about the future and kept texting him every once in a while, just the same.

She was not eager to see Eduardo again and thought it possible that she may never yet. She still expected that he planned to fire her but had not had the time to do it. She had never been fired before, and the prospect of it at this point in her life made her feel self-conscious and unsettled. Several times, she felt the urge to text him and inform him of her desire to quit, but she stopped herself every time. Quitting was also not in the repertoire of strong women, and she continued to wait grudgingly for his return.

One Sunday morning, Marta's phone beeped. It was a text from Eduardo asking whether she could come and meet with him on the next day.

"In Montevideo?" she texted.

"Yes," was his reply.

Marta asked whether he could meet her in Ciudad Vieja instead. It was only fair that, since he requested the meeting, he had to do the trip this time. But his curt answer was that he could not. Marta had the nagging feeling that it was going to be another unpleasant meeting, but considering it was likely to be their last one, she looked forward to the closure it promised.

She arrived at Eduardo's house a few minutes past the arranged hour, and on her way to the front door, she noticed the silver sportscar that he usually drove parked right outside the garage. Señora Álvarez greeted her at the door and explained that Eduardo had not yet returned from his morning run and retreated into the kitchen.

Marta was annoyed. He was very aware of the amount of time it took her to come all the way to his house, and after summoning her there, he did not have the courtesy to be at home when she arrived. She had observed on many occasions that the expectation of being on time in Uruguay was looser than she was used to. However, remembering her last meeting with Eduardo, she was not mollified and her resentment of having to wait for him increased.

After spending several more minutes pacing about the living room, Marta decided it was best to leave. As she reached for the doorknob, the door swung open and Eduardo entered, dripping with sweat and still panting. He smiled and said, "*Hola*, you're not leaving just yet?"

"Yes, I am," Marta replied.

His smile disappeared. "Oh, I see. I'm late. It's been only ten minutes, for Christ's sake!"

Marta felt provoked. She shook her head and stepped around him on her way to the door.

He moved to block her way. "Marta, chill! And come and sit down, will you?" He wiped a drip of sweat from his temple. "I keep forgetting that you are new to Uruguay, and that . . . you're unusual for a . . ." His voice trailed off and he pressed his lips together.

Marta was certain that he was about to say "nanny" and was relieved that he was thoughtful enough to stop himself. Yet, she was unwilling to appear weak by changing her mind. But he still blocked her way out, and it was impossible for her to do anything but to stand awkwardly in the vestibule.

Eduardo moved to the side, clearing her path to the door. "You're free to go, if you'd like. But can we talk?"

Marta hesitated, but now that her way out was unobstructed, she no longer felt the same indignant urgency to fight back. "Okay," she said.

She turned around, walked back to the living room, and sat in one of the armchairs. Eduardo had picked up a towel from a basket in the vestibule and was drying off his face and arms as he sat across from her. He placed the towel on the floor and said, "To be totally honest, I considered firing you after our last meeting."

Marta's whole body tensed but she remained seated. Eduardo rubbed his forehead and continued, "I've been thinking a lot about what you said the last time I saw you"—

he cleared his throat—"and I realized you're right. I've never thought much about my relationship with my kids. I guess I'm too busy." He shifted in his seat. "I also thought children were simple. You know, everyone can have kids. And you don't have to go to school to learn how to raise them. So, it must be easy. And I believed that as long as I provided for them, they'd be fine."

Marta remained silent.

"But you forced me to see that I was wrong. And I want to spend more time to get to know my kids better." He looked straight at her. "I want you to keep working for me. Both Sebastián and Romina seem to like you a lot. And you might be helpful to them in more ways than just teaching them English."

Marta could not help but be affected by his humble confession. She pitied him for thinking that children were simple, but she realized that he was away a lot of the time and did not have many opportunities to spend time with his children. And he was right. There was no school to teach parents how to raise their children, and men, in general, were still at a marked disadvantage when it came to parenting. They were less likely to have been explicitly encouraged as boys to be good caregivers, and instead were trained to be assertive breadwinners.

Finally, Marta broke the silence. "I assume we're talking about a week or so?"

"Yeah, I'm in town for a few matches with the Uruguayan national team, and I'll be here until next Tuesday."

"Okay, I can come any day." Marta was about to stand up but was stopped by Eduardo's sharp intake of breath.

"And feel free to tell me when I'm doing something wrong,

especially with my children. I want to improve myself," he said, his voice barely above a whisper.

Marta was unsure how she felt about his request. She was about to protest, but he continued, "You seem wise and experienced, and I can't say I've known a university professor before. Maybe if I went to university I would meet some." He smiled.

Marta did not expect an insightful self-assessment from Eduardo, but he was in a contemplative mood and her interest was piqued.

"My whole life has been devoted to football. I love the sport and can't complain about my success," he began. "I've been running after a ball ever since I can remember. My father was a youth football coach, and he started my brother and me when we were very young. My mother stayed at home and took care of us. She made sure that we were always comfortable, you know, and well-fed, which isn't a small thing when you are feeding two growing athletes."

Marta remembered how much her son ate at one sitting and smiled.

"My father's only focus was on our training, and like most coaches, he was demanding, sometimes to a fault. I can't blame him. He knew that we have talents for the sport. And he did what he thought was best for our careers. Talent alone was not enough to make us great players, and he didn't hesitate to push us to work as hard as we can. But he never openly expressed his love for us, quite the opposite. I wonder whether he thought it would make him look weaker or something." Eduardo smiled. "So, you see, it's not very surprising that I don't know any better."

Marta sensed his humility and was moved by the sober

and frank account of his upbringing. It must not have been easy for him to come to these realizations, and even more so to share them with her. She compared his conduct with her own, and her cool reserve alarmed rather than assured her. Nevertheless, she was not thrilled by the prospect of "tutoring" Eduardo, as well as his children, which made her feel old and weary. But she realized that if she were to continue working with the children, she would not be able to resist her urge to keep Eduardo in check, as she had done already.

"It's gratifying that you so graciously attribute your inspiration to be a better parent to me," Marta said. "But I can't promise that I can help you in your quest for self-improvement. It would be a tall order for anyone, and I barely know you." She stood up and added, "But you can count on my sincerity. Would that do?"

"I would welcome your sincere opinions as long as you can convey them less . . . forcefully," Eduardo replied. "It's well known in soccer that not all successful penalty shots need to be delivered with a lot of power."

Marta was humbled by his gentle reproof but felt rejuvenated. She examined Eduardo's face, as if she were seeing him for the first time, and said, "I'll do my best."

CHAPTER 11

Pearl

There were only a few people out on the streets on a particularly hot and humid Friday morning. Marta was on her way to Eduardo's house when she saw a man stumbling along the sidewalk and clutching his chest. As she approached him, she recognized Pedro. His face was flushed, and he was perspiring profusely and gasping for breath.

"Pedro, are you okay? Where are you going?" His knees buckled, and Marta grabbed him by the arm.

Pedro mumbled, "I fine."

"No, you're not fine. I'll call for an ambulance."

She heaved him to the nearest building. Pedro tried to protest when Marta pulled out her phone, but she ignored him. After she hung up, she helped him move into the shade. She stayed with him in the ambulance too.

He was admitted to the hospital, and a nurse directed her to sit in the waiting room until someone would come out to give her a diagnosis and an update on his condition. While she waited, she called Sofía and Luisa. She also called Eduardo, who insisted that she let him know once she knew of Pedro's status.

Marta had been at the hospital for half an hour when Sofía arrived, breathless. Marta told her how she had found Pedro on the street, but before she was able to finish, a doctor approached them. He addressed Sofía as Pedro's closest of kin, but he also conveyed the most important parts of his message in English so that Marta could understand. He informed them that Pedro had suffered a mild heart attack and was being prepared for surgery. It was fortunate that the damage to his heart was not extensive, and he was in a stable condition. Before he left, he thanked Marta for bringing Pedro to the hospital when she did because a few more minutes' delay could have been fatal.

At the news, Sofía collapsed in sobs on one of the seats. Her husband had died of a heart attack a few years earlier. Marta sat next to her, gave her a hug, and gently rocked her back and forth. After they had been at the hospital for over an hour, Luisa arrived. Marta was relieved to see her—she was badly in need of her spirit.

Luisa replaced Marta at Sofía's side, and Marta went to get a drink of water when her phone rang.

"How's Pedro?" Eduardo asked.

"He had a mild heart attack. He's in surgery now."

"Are you still at the hospital? Are you alone?"

"No, I'm with my friends. Both Sofía and Luisa are here."

"Good, good." After a brief pause, Eduardo asked, "Which hospital are you at?"

"The British Hospital. When the ambulance driver noticed that I was a foreigner, he took us here because the staff speak English."

"That's a private hospital," Eduardo observed with growing concern in his voice. "Does Pedro have additional health insurance for it?"

"I have no idea." Marta realized that she had not thought about this obvious issue. "But I'll check."

When she returned to the waiting room, Luisa bolted from her seat. "You just missed the doctor. He told us Pedro's surgery was successful!" She explained that the prognosis was good, but he would need to stay in the hospital for a couple of days, and he would not be able to work full-time for at least a few weeks. A smile had softened Sofía's lips, but once she had a chance to process the news fully, her face darkened. "I don't think Pedro has any insurance for this hospital."

Marta tried to comfort Sofía that she would do whatever she could to help Pedro, but she was unsure of the extent to which she could help. She had no idea what amount of money they were talking about, and before she committed to it, she wanted to at least have a clear sense of the costs.

A nurse came to tell them that Pedro would soon be able to receive visitors for a brief time. While they waited, Marta went to the reception desk to inquire about the insurance.

The receptionist typed something into her computer. "All of his hospital expenses are covered," she said.

Pleased, Marta returned to the others and shared the good news. Sofía was relieved and was in tears again, but Luisa was puzzled. She pulled Marta to the side.

"This is extremely unusual, you know," Luisa whispered. "I'm pretty sure that Pedro has only the public insurance. As a fisherman, I don't think he could afford a private hospital, let alone stay for days. It's very expensive."

Marta suspected that she knew the source of the money but decided not to reveal it, at least not until she was certain.

The next day, Marta arrived at Eduardo's house and found the front door ajar. She walked into the quiet house and looked around. Eduardo was sitting on the patio with Claudia on his lap. The children were nowhere to be seen. Marta hesitated but walked toward the open patio door and cleared her throat. As soon as they became aware of her presence, Claudia stood up and Eduardo turned to face Marta.

"Ah, here you are. Claudia and I were waiting for you because Señora Álvarez has stepped out of the house to get groceries. But we really need to go now."

"Where are the children?" Marta asked.

"They are coming from Isabella's but are running late. Remember, you're still in Uruguay," he said with a smile and took Claudia by the hand. They walked to the front door of the house as Eduardo continued, "But you're welcome to stay here and wait for them."

He opened the door for Claudia, but before he left, he called to Marta, "Oh, and if I'm not back by four o'clock, you can leave the children with Señora Álvarez and go home."

Marta could not shake the feeling that he had made these plans intentionally so that she would not have a chance to speak with him. There was nothing she could do but be patient. He could not hide from her forever.

The children did eventually arrive, and the three of them had a calm day. Marta was low on energy. The hospital visit with Pedro had been emotionally draining, and she was not able to sleep well during the night. Four o'clock came and Eduardo was not home. Marta decided to wait for him.

She regretted telling him about the details of Pedro's hospitalization, which she assumed prompted him to act more charitably than it made any sense. No one in her experience had ever been this generous. Even if they wanted to, most of her family and friends did not have the same resources. It was not just the amount of money that made Marta uncomfortable, but also his benevolent gesture, which she was unable to explain. After all, he did not even know Pedro. And deep down, she was also embarrassed by her lack of discretion because she feared that Eduardo may have interpreted her news about Pedro as an implicit call for his help. And Marta was *not* a "spoiled brat," and she could not rest easy until she'd had a chance to clear it with Eduardo. It would be a problem if he came back with Claudia, but she made up her mind to ask him directly for a brief private meeting.

Señora Álvarez served them dinner and left for the day since Marta was going to stay with the children. After she put the children to bed, Marta went into the kitchen and made herself a cup of tea. By now, she was exhausted, but she had to stay awake until Eduardo came home. She sat at the kitchen table and read the news on her phone. Her eyelids closed intermittently, and eventually, Marta fell asleep on the table.

She was awoken by a gentle nudge on her shoulder. Marta's body twitched, and she pulled herself up. As her eyes adjusted to the bright light, she saw Eduardo's amused expression.

"I'm sorry to wake you up. You seemed so cozy," he said.

Marta blushed with embarrassment.

His face became serious. "What are you doing here, anyway? I told you to leave the children with Señora Álvarez."

"I have to speak with you, and I decided not to leave until I've had a chance to do it. What time is it?"

"Just after ten."

"Is now a good time?" Marta said and looked around for a sign of Claudia. But she had either gone upstairs already, or she was not in the house.

"I'd rather go to bed, but if you insist, I'm here"—
Eduardo leaned toward her, and raised his eyebrows—"and
alone."

Marta was not in a playful mood. She was too tired and
preoccupied with the question she wanted to ask him. She
walked past him and sat on the couch in the living room.
Eduardo followed her, and once he was seated in one of the
armchairs, he crossed his legs and looked at her with calm
anticipation.

Marta took a deep breath and said, "Eduardo, did you
pay for Pedro's private hospital expenses?"

Eduardo's expression did not change. After a while, he
said, "What if I did?"

Marta felt trapped by his words but decided to be direct.
"For one, my friends and I want to know to whom we are all
indebted." And she breathed, "And if it was you, I'd like to
pay you back."

"In this case, no, I didn't. Is this all you wanted to talk to
me about?"

Eduardo was about to stand up when Marta pleaded,
"Please, don't be coy. It must've been you because there's no
one else. And it was thoughtless of me to tell you. I didn't
realize that you would do such a thing. I wasn't thinking
clearly at the time, and I was ignorant of the whole insurance
process in this country."

Eduardo placed his elbows on his knees. His expression
was serious, his voice lower than usual, as he said, "Marta,
your friend needed help, and I know that you would've
helped him. But I'm darn sure that I have more money than
you do, and I was happy to put it to good use for a change."
His face lighted, and his voice resumed its familiar tone. "As
for your friends' gratitude, I'm asking you to make sure they

don't know the real source. And a 'thank you' from you alone would get rid of the debt, as you call it." Eduardo leaned back in his chair.

Marta sat motionless, staring at her trembling hands. She could not remain indifferent to the sincerity in his words, and the even more shocking revelation that his generous gesture appeared to have been done with her in mind. Eventually, she turned her grave face toward him and murmured, "Thank you."

Eduardo smiled. "Now that we've dealt with this concern of yours, I'm going to bed." He stood up and headed toward the stairs. Marta remained in her seat, still stunned by his revelation. After a couple of steps, he stopped and turned back toward her. His eyes sparkled with whimsy again. "You can sleep on the couch or in one of the spare bedrooms upstairs."

Marta jumped to her feet, bid him good night, and left the house.

≪≪≪≪≪

Marta approached Pedro's hospital room for her last daily visit, and hearing a loud bellow from within, she rushed inside. Pedro was sitting on his bed, bouncing in his seat, and gesticulating with his arms. The small TV set on the table across from his bed was blasting a sustained, "*Goooooooooooal!*" Pedro was beaming, and as soon as he noticed her, he shouted, "Marta, Eduardo Rodríguez mark goal!"

"Oh, is that all? I was worried you were in distress." Marta squinted at the TV screen. "What's the score?"

"Two-one Uruguay!" was Pedro's jubilant reply.

"Who are they playing against?"

"Chile." The camera zoomed onto one of the players, and

Pedro pointed to the screen and shouted again, "Eduardo Rodríguez!"

Marta recognized the face. "Yeah, that's him, all right."

But was it? she wondered. The person on the screen felt strangely removed and unfamiliar, like the faces of other people she had seen on TV but never encountered in person. Only then did she realize that she never thought of Eduardo as the celebrity he was to everyone else. He was merely the father of the children she worked with. She was aware that he played professional soccer and was famous, but seeing him on TV was as if she was seeing someone else.

Marta was rattled by an alarming thought. How did Eduardo see her? She had been on TV, but on the news, not on the sports channels. And she had been in the papers, but in the science section, not in the gossip columns. Therefore, Eduardo seeing her in a glamorous guise was out of the question. Did she appear as a pretentious, drab professor who knew a lot of useless information and thought too highly of herself? He had said as much himself after Sebastián's bed-wetting accident. Or did he see a pitiful middle-aged woman who had traveled almost halfway across the globe and taken up a low-status job just so she could escape her stale life? Perhaps it was feeling sorry for her that had compelled him to help Pedro. While Marta could allow both personas to be conceivable, they were still inaccurate, and she found the idea of Eduardo seeing her as either one extremely distasteful. Her niggling suspicion that her own initial opinion of him was just as flawed continued to grow.

She turned toward Pedro, who was still exuberant. He moved restlessly and, every once in a while, made unintelligible noises and slapped his arms on the bed covers.

"Pedro, does your doctor approve of this much excitement so soon after your surgery?"

Pedro did not remove his eyes from the TV screen and waved at her. "No matter."

Marta smiled, realizing that Pedro was not going to give her his attention while the match was on. She leaned back in her chair and patiently watched the rest of the game with him. There were less than ten minutes of regular play left, and she was willing to wait it out. Luckily for her, no one scored any more goals and the game was soon over. Pedro turned off the TV and looked at Marta, still smiling, his usual teasing mood returned.

"I fine. You no worry. Uruguay win—I ready go home!"

"But you'll have to stay with us in Sofía's house for a while," Marta said. "You'll need help, and it would be easier for us to provide it when you're near us."

Earlier, when Sofía had broached the idea to her, Marta had hesitated at first. The thought of sharing her living space with yet another person did not appeal to her. But realizing that she no longer felt threatened by Pedro, and that he really needed their help, at least initially, she had agreed.

Pedro looked at Marta. A lot of emotions were mixed in his gleaming eyes. "Thank you, Marta. To you, my life in debt—always."

"Oh, no! You owe me nothing. I'm only glad I happened to see you when I did, and it was in the nick of time. Now, you need to rest and gather your strength, and nothing would make me happier but to see you back at sea."

Pedro wiped a tear from his face and closed his eyes. They sat in silence for a long time, and eventually Pedro lifted his head and smiled with a mischievous spark in his eyes.

"How you love life?"

"You can't be serious!"

"You no give me chance?"

Marta was troubled by the true answer to his question. She had grown to like Pedro. Luisa was right. He was a warm and guileless person, ill-educated but naturally intelligent, which gave him a rare insight into other people's hearts—Marta did not like that it was only her heart he was able to read so well. And she could tell that he really liked her, and she wished she could reciprocate his feelings. But she couldn't.

Instead of answering him, she said, "You need to get back on your feet and to your usual routines first."

Pedro sighed. "You love life go around and around. And you alone, also when with someone. You—believe me! I know."

Marta was startled by this revelation. "Pedro, we don't need to talk about my love life right now. Your recovery is much more important."

Ignoring her, Pedro asked, "Who hurt you very bad, Marta?"

Marta was about to answer "no one," but memories of her past slithered into her consciousness.

It was in the early 1990s, right after the Berlin Wall had fallen down, that she met Chris. They were both students at the University of New Hampshire, where Marta had come to from Bulgaria after winning a scholarship. Chris was an American who was completing a master's degree in political science. He was witty, his fine features gave him a Noble-Elf-like aura, and Marta was in love. He was similarly charmed by Marta's idiosyncrasies, which he contributed to her upbringing in Eastern Europe, and it intrigued him.

They were married the summer after Marta graduated from college.

They moved to Chicago in order for her to pursue her doctorate at Northwestern University. Chris began working as an assistant on the campaign of a local politician. He also freelanced as a political opinion writer for local newspapers. Marta and Chris were busy but lived in harmony. Halfway through their time in Chicago, Ilian was born, and by the time he was two, Marta graduated from university and was hired as a university professor in Toronto. At first, Chris was unsure about his political career prospects in Canada. But he found a full-time position as the political writer for the *Globe and Mail*, which suited him well. He eventually was put in charge of the section devoted to US politics, and Chris gladly gave up on his political ambitions for good.

Marta was relieved because she did not look forward to being put in the spotlight as the spouse of a politician. Also, Chris's schedule was less stressful, although he spent a significant amount of time traveling for work. He was supportive of her career, even when it appeared to be for the wrong reasons. As time went on, Chris's trips became more frequent, his wittiness acquired acerbic tones, and his elvish qualities fused into a cold detachment. Marta was frustrated with the enormous burden of raising Ilian while also managing a demanding full-time career mostly on her own. She complained to Chris, who usually retorted in a calm and rational manner, which infuriated Marta even more. Her husband grew even colder and his trips increased in frequency and in length.

Marta looked at Pedro, having just realized why she had been distrustful and cautious around men. The end of her fifteen-year marriage had felt like a betrayal. Chris's bouts of impotence, especially toward the end, did not make Marta feel as if she was foremost in his thoughts. As a result, with the exception of a couple of brief attempts, she had not been in a committed relationship ever since the divorce. During bursts of weakness, she yearned for the companionship, but generally she was content with her independence.

Pedro finally muttered, "I knew." He took her hand. "Marta, you like oyster—plain outside, beautiful pearl inside. Chance find it—one in millions. Close shell tight, oyster no let anyone in. And people go by and no see it. But if open it, they find pearl. But much trouble for people—find pearl no much possible."

Marta stood up. "Pedro, even though you dared to call me 'plain,' I know you mean well. You're an extremely kind and intuitive man. Now, get well." She leaned over and placed a soft kiss on his temple.

CHAPTER 12

Ecru

Marta struggled to walk up the hill. Earlier in the day, on their way home from the hospital, Pedro had told her that a big storm was coming, and that it might be a good idea to stay home for the rest of the day. If he were working, he would take the day off. But Eduardo had a business meeting that afternoon, something to do with a commercial he was going to do for a sports equipment company. Señora Álvarez could always mind the children, but Marta knew that they preferred her company. Moreover, she had already promised that she would spend the afternoon with them, and she had to remain true to her word.

The sky was steel gray and the trees swayed violently. Marta was struck by the thought that a big branch could break free, and she hastened her step. But during particularly strong gusts of wind, she barely moved. Finally, she arrived at the house, breathless from the effort, her hair tangled with a few leaves caught in it.

Eduardo opened the front door. "You made it!"

"Of course, I made it. And if I wasn't going to come, I would've called you." Marta stepped past him into the vestibule, straightened her clothes, and ran her fingers through her hair.

Eduardo pulled out the remaining leaves from her hair. Seized by untoward modesty, Marta looked at her feet.

"It's a tempest out there," he said.

"Yes, I believe it was Ariel who sprinkled the leaves on my head, that mischievous being." Marta had already recovered her usual spirit.

Eduardo paused, as if unsure what to say. Then he reached for his leather jacket and told her that he had sent Señora Álvarez home. She had been worried about getting stuck in the house in case the storm worsened. But she had prepared food for dinner. When Eduardo opened the front door, a gust of wind promptly dumped a few leaves and grass clippings onto the vestibule floor.

"Where are the children?" Marta asked.

"They're playing with Lego in Sebastián's room," Eduardo said as his hair became the next tousled victim of the roguish wind.

Upstairs, at the door to Sebastián's room, Marta stopped to observe the children. They were building a structure with Lego blocks, and it was obvious that Sebastián was in charge. From time to time, he would tell Romina that she had put a block in the wrong place and he would remove it. Romina went along with it, but when Sebastián reached to remove the blocks she had carefully assembled, she shrieked in protest and hit him with her fist.

"Hey! Hey, kids, stop that!" Marta shouted as she rushed into the room. As soon as she saw her, Romina ran toward her, grabbed her by the leg, and glared at Sebastián. He continued playing with his blocks while Marta took Romina by the hand, and together, they went downstairs.

Marta prepared two glasses of warm milk with a dash of cinnamon in them, and Romina eagerly drank hers. Marta placed the other glass on the coffee table, picked three picture books from the shelf, and sat on the couch. Romina tucked in next to her. They were about to finish the second book when Sebastián joined them. He gulped his glass of milk, exhaled loudly, and announced that he was bored and wanted to watch a movie. Marta did not mind, and Sebastián picked a movie that was one of Romina's favorites, *My Neighbor Totoro*. There was peace before the movie even began.

Marta watched the movie with the children for a while, but before it was over, she left the couch and went closer to the window. It was still afternoon, but the sky was as dark as dusk. The wind howled louder than before, and the trees in the yard twisted and swung in all directions, their branches bending down to the ground as if in exhausted defeat.

Suddenly, it got quiet in the room, and the children's disappointed whines joined the wind's zealous whistling. The power had gone out. It was quite dark in the house, and without TV or the internet, their usual forms of diversion were no longer available. Marta went on a search to find some candles before the house became completely dark and in case the power was out for a while. She searched in the drawers in the kitchen, where she found matches but no candles. Finally, she gave up and picked up the fancy candle holders from the dining table and brought them into the living room.

It was quite dark by now, and Romina had snuggled closer to Sebastián on the couch. Marta lit the candles, placed them on the coffee table, and sat next to the children.

"I'm scared," Romina whimpered.

"What are we going to do? I'm bored," Sebastián said.

While looking at the candles, Marta said, "Did you know that, not so long ago, no one had electricity and everything was done by candlelight? And computers became common only during my lifetime." She stopped and smiled. To the children, she probably seemed ancient and her point was lost on them. "There must be something we can do. We have to be creative."

Marta's thoughts drifted to a lazy afternoon on a hot summer day in a small Bulgarian town. Sitting under a big walnut tree, little Marta was snuggled in the crook of her grandfather's arm as she listened to the whimsical stories he told her about animals. They were, what he called, fairy tales. Sometimes he entertained her with the usual fairy tales familiar to all children, but often he told her stories that he had invented, and she found those to be the most amusing. Marta still remembered the one about the hedgehog.

"How about I tell you a fairy tale?" she suggested. The children were puzzled, and seeing the ambivalence on their faces, Marta knew that they had never been told stories before. "The story of the hedgehog my grandfather told me many, many years ago."

"What's a hedgehog?" asked Sebastián.

"Of course you don't know what a hedgehog is because they don't live in the Americas, including Uruguay." And Marta described to the children what hedgehogs looked like, what they ate, and where they lived.

"Do you see hedgehog, Marta?" asked Romina.

"Yes, and I've held one in my hand. They're cute but extremely prickly animals." And she told them the story about the hedgehog, who had only three clever tricks, but they were good ones.

It was past six o'clock when the front door swung open and Eduardo stumbled in looking disheveled. There were a few drops of rain on his leather jacket, and he was panting slightly.

"A huge tree has fallen down, and it's blocking the road leading to the house. And it took some of the power lines with it. I had to leave my car on the road and walk up the rest of the way." And turning toward Marta, he added, "The reason for being late."

Eduardo slumped on the couch and exhaled. "Ah, candles. How romantic!"

The children piled around him and recounted all their emotions of the past few hours, and everything they had learned about hedgehogs.

"Hedgehogs! Where on Earth did you hear about hedgehogs? Do you even know what they are?"

"Yes," Sebastián replied, "Marta told us."

"So," Eduardo said, "in addition to English lessons, you're also teaching the children biology. I should remember to give you a pay raise."

"That won't be necessary," Marta mumbled. "And besides, it wasn't a biology lesson, it was just an old fairy tale that my grandfather used to tell me when I was about Sebastián's age."

"Yeah, except that the children seem to know what a hedgehog looks like, where it lives, what it eats, and how many tricks it knows. And all of that revealed in the glow of candlelight. Undoubtedly worth a pay raise!"

"The candlelight only stirred our imaginations," Marta said. She was willing to go along with the teasing, but she was unwilling to give up on her protest over the ridiculous pay raise.

A bright bolt of lightning lit the room and a powerful rumble of thunder followed.

Romina jumped in her seat and hid in the crook of Eduardo's arm. "I'm scared," she whimpered again.

Outside, the rain was a steely curtain, tossed by the wind in all directions.

"Kids, how about you have dinner and go to bed. Once you're safely tucked in, you won't be afraid of the storm," Eduardo said with forced cheerfulness.

By candlelight, they ate in the living room in complete silence, which was intermittently interrupted by loud thunder and Romina's startled sobs. When they finished eating, Marta picked up the dishes and took them to the kitchen. Back in the living room, she found Eduardo observing the storm raging outside.

"It's not safe for you to go home in this weather. You should spend the night here," Eduardo said.

Marta hesitated. She did not have any of her personal belongings and was not mentally prepared to spend the night in someone else's house. She looked out the window. The visibility was low, and the roads were probably flooded too.

"Thank you. I believe I have no choice," she said. At her words, both children ran toward her and chanted her name as they skipped around her. She smiled and picked up one of the candle holders. She took Romina by the hand and led her upstairs. Sebastián and Eduardo followed them.

After Romina was tucked in bed, Marta came downstairs. After a short while, Eduardo joined her in the living room. The thunderstorm continued to rage with the same intensity as before. Unable to suppress the need to find something to do to while away the hours, Marta said, "Since we can't do much in the dark, let's make the best of the situation."

"What do you have in mind?" Eduardo said, but his tone was far more teasing than his plain question implied.

Marta chuckled when she realized that her words could be interpreted in a different way than she had intended. "A cup of tea would be nice. But come to think of it, it would take forever to heat the water on the flame of a candle."

"I have an idea," Eduardo said and went into the kitchen. He returned shortly with two glasses filled with a cold golden liquid, and orange and lime pieces floated on the top. "*Clericó*," he said, handing one of the drinks to Marta, and sat down on the couch across from her. "Or the best I can do under the circumstances."

"What is it?" Marta asked as she inhaled the aroma.

"It's the Uruguayan version of sangria. But this one I made with white wine."

Marta took a sip of the cool and fruity liquid, which was sweeter than typical sangria but with a stronger citrus flavor. She loved the tartness and the novelty delighted her.

Eduardo stared at the candles. "It's scary to realize how dependent we've become on electricity. There seems to be nothing we can do without it."

"We can still think, and dream, and tell stories. Those are worth a lot."

"Then tell me a story, Marta. Do you know any more about hedgehogs?"

Marta laughed. "I do, as a matter of fact." She became thoughtful and stared at the candles for a while. "I love candles, their soft glow and playful flutter that makes shadows dance on the walls. They seem to calm my heartbeat and spur my thoughts all at once. They remind me of a time in my life that was difficult in some ways, but looking back, it seems romantic now."

"Go on," Eduardo said. "I think I might enjoy this story even more than the one about hedgehogs."

"Don't be so sure!"

Marta described to Eduardo the period during the
political changes in Eastern Europe when the Berlin Wall fell.
It had been a difficult period, and especially the winter of
1989 when Marta was still in high school. The sudden loss of
central control and the demise of the planned economy had
led to chaos and food shortages. The stores were virtually
empty. The government had introduced coupons to control
the distribution of basic foods, such as flour and sugar,
similarly to how food distribution was handled right after
the Second World War. Marta's mother and grandmother
hoped it would be the hardest time in their lives, but alas,
they were reliving it again forty years later.

"It sounds like something you see in movies or hear
about in the news," Eduardo said and took a sip of his drink.
"In some parts of Latin America there's a lot of poverty, and
some of the football players I know come from very poor
families. But the situation in Uruguay has been stable most
of my life, and I've been lucky."

"Yes, you're lucky. It's only through the difficult times that
we city folk realize how incapable we've become of taking
care of ourselves. My mother and I lived in a small apartment
in the capital city, and my grandmother would spend the
winters with us. My father passed away when I was twelve.
We had no other source of food other than what was available
in the stores. But when the stores were empty, we were left
to starve. People in the villages had yard animals and grew
and preserved some of their own fruits and vegetables. And
they fared better during these spartan times. To make things
worse, the government decided to ration power consumption
by switching the electricity on and off every two hours. Fun!
Half the city would have electricity for two hours and spend

the other two hours without it. People joked that the city was like a disco club, with the lights flashing on and off."

"Sounds exciting," Eduardo said.

"Yeah, as long as you don't *live* in the club!"

Eduardo lifted his eyebrows and nodded.

"We had to plan according to the government's schedule," Marta continued. "In the evenings, I often did my homework in the candlelight while my mother listened to the news. Back then, there were no computers or the internet. We had a battery-powered radio."

She emptied her glass and placed it on the coffee table. She leaned back and folded her legs to one side. "One day my mother brought home a whole turkey. The grandfather of one of her students, who lived in the countryside, had given her the turkey as a present. 'Take it, *madame*, I know you and your family are starving,' he had said. We hadn't eaten meat for at least a couple of months, and, oh, the joy! My grandmother portioned it carefully. She made at least five different dishes out of it. We ate it for what felt like an entire month. I wonder whether this is the reason why I don't like turkey now."

"I like turkey, but you can have too much of a good thing," Eduardo said. "But I'm guessing, you and your family survived the hard times somehow?"

"Yes, it was hard for sure, but for some reason I remember those times fondly now. We were together a lot more, and we were forced to rely on each other more during those difficult times." Marta was pensive. "And I liked doing homework in the candlelight. When I was done, my mother would talk about the various people throughout history who wrote some of the most important pieces of literature. George

Eliot, Shakespeare, Flaubert, and all of those writers who still influence our lives today. Or those who created beautiful art—you know, Michelangelo is believed to have partially lost his eyesight while working on the Sistine Chapel. It was mostly done in the dim light of candles."

"I don't think I'll look at a lighted candle the same way again," Eduardo said.

Marta smiled and looked languorously at the flickering flames.

"It's getting late. And I have to get up early to go for a run before I face the rest of the day." Eduardo stood up, and with a candleholder in hand, they headed toward the stairs.

Once in her room, Marta took off her pants, blew out the candles, and slid under the cool sheets. The storm had subsided slightly.

Another loud thunder shook the window, and soon after, Marta's door opened, and she could make out a small silhouette barely visible in the dark. "Marta, I'm scared!" Romina said. "Can I stay with you?"

"Of course, Romina. Come into my little hut."

Romina climbed onto the bed and snuggled closely under the covers. Marta turned toward her and held her tight. Romina's body relaxed, and Marta heard another soft voice in the dark. Sebastián placed himself next to Romina, but he wanted to hold Marta's hand.

As the storm continued to rage late into the night, sleep eluded Marta. Sebastián and Romina's unreserved trust made her think of Ilian's current detachment. Marta lamented the time when he had been dependent on her, and she yearned for his willingness to seek comfort in her arms. A lone tear soaked into the pillow, and Marta, lulled by the children's peaceful but noisy breathing, eventually fell asleep.

Marta woke up disoriented. She noticed the two sweaty heads next to her and remembered that the children had come in the middle of the night, afraid of the storm. They were still fast asleep. Marta checked the time on her phone. It was a few minutes before six o'clock. She carefully got out of bed, tiptoed to the window, and peeked behind the blinds. The clouds had cleared and the sky was pale blue. The ocean was a pool of gold that reflected the warm sun. The lively and carefree chirping of birds lifted Marta's spirits too.

As she came down the stairs, Marta could hear clutter from the kitchen and wondered whether it was Señora Álvarez preparing breakfast. She found Eduardo busy over the stove instead. She leaned on the doorframe and observed him for a while. Eventually, he turned around and said, "Good morning. Are you hungry?"

"Not yet," Marta replied and reached for the coffee pot.

Eduardo removed the omelet from the frying pan and divided it onto two plates, which he brought to the kitchen table. Marta sat across from him and held onto her cup. After taking a bite from his omelet, he said, "The kids seem to be attached to you now, and it happened fast."

"Yeah, I'm really lucky," Marta said, observing him while he ate his breakfast.

Eduardo took a bite of his toast. "They've known Claudia for almost a year, and they're still not easy around her. Why do you think that is?"

Marta remained silent while she searched for a delicate reply to his abrupt question.

"I'd say it's as if they've been enchanted by you," Eduardo continued. "I haven't seen them behave this way with people who aren't family members." He took another bite. "Are you sure it's cinnamon and not magic powder that you sprinkle in their milk?"

Marta laughed. "Yes! My real name's Elphaba and my true skin color's green, and I cackle and brew potions in a large cauldron. And sometimes I'm known to fly on a broomstick. I wish!" Her voice grew more somber as she continued, "I do love children. I always have. And they seem to be fond of me." She wanted to add that her magic only worked while they were little, but she took a sip of her coffee instead.

Eduardo leaned back in his chair. Marta finally cut a piece of her omelet with her fork.

"It's not lost on me how special it is to be loved by such pure hearts, and I consider myself fortunate because of it." She cut another piece, more meticulously than the soft egg required. She had come up with what she thought was a discreet answer to his original question. "And as for Claudia, she's still very young and inexperienced. And she doesn't seem to be particularly interested in children right now. Perhaps with time, and especially when she has children of her own, she'd change. All she needs to do, really, is to play again."

Marta finished the rest of her omelet in silence and took her plate to the kitchen. Back at the table, Eduardo had not moved.

"Thanks for breakfast. I should go and check on Pedro while Sofía is at work."

"How is he?" Eduardo asked.

"Much better. Your goal the other day had him almost running."

Eduardo smiled but did not say anything. Marta still could not connect the man in front of her with the one on

TV in Pedro's hospital room. With increasing unease, Marta realized how wrong she had been about him, as she had been wrong about other men before him. Except, with time, the others paled while Eduardo seemed to flourish. And so far, no conversation about the weather was necessary to rescue them from the deluge of chilly silence.

CHAPTER 13

Lavender

Eduardo went back to Spain and Marta went back to work at Isabella's house. She no longer took Spanish classes, and instead put her new language skills to practice in her daily interactions. She ventured on day trips outside of Montevideo, and she often talked to strangers on the bus, or to the waiters when ordering lunch, or to the salespeople in the markets where she bought small souvenirs. On some weekends, she went hiking with Luisa in the hills on the outskirts of Montevideo, or for a walk along the coast. Occasionally during the week, Marta accompanied Luisa on her trips to show homes to prospective buyers. While Luisa talked, Marta listened. She found the home interiors not so different from those in North America, and she spent most of her time waiting for Luisa in the yards, which were usually filled with exotic plants and trees. Sometimes the ocean views were breathtaking too.

One day in early November, as soon as Marta arrived for work, Isabella pulled her aside and spoke with quiet urgency, avoiding the possibility that the children would overhear her. "Marta, have you heard?"

Marta shook her head. "No, what's up?"

"Eduardo has been injured and has a concussion."

Marta was startled by the news and cold sweat pearled down her back. She had learned a thing or two about head injuries after Ilian's bike accident.

"Oh, that sounds serious," Marta said. "Is he going to be okay?"

"I hope so. He's had a couple of concussions before, but they haven't lasted long, and usually he'd be back playing within a week or less. But it's been a few days since his injury, and he's still not feeling well. And I'm a bit concerned."

"How did he get injured?" Marta asked, although she knew that the answer would not make much of a difference on her mounting concern.

"He tried to head the ball but hit his head against the head of another player. Apparently, the other player is fine, but Eduardo has been injured, and the symptoms haven't gone away yet."

For the rest of the week, the reports were that Eduardo's condition was unchanged. When Marta arrived for work the following week, Isabella pulled her into the kitchen, away from the children, who were watching TV in the living room.

"It's been two weeks since Eduardo's injury and he's still not able to play. Claudia has gone to be with him to keep his spirits up. Apparently, he's been frustrated with the lack of improvement. His doctors are concerned about his mental health as well as his physical trauma. Oh, Marta, I'm getting really worried. What are we going to do?" Isabella cried in anguish.

Marta felt the tingling sense of panic in her feet and it crawled up her body. She tried to remain calm. "He'll be fine. You said he's had concussions before."

"Yes, but they haven't lasted this long." Isabella sighed. "But I seem to remember from his past doctors that after repeated concussions, it's not unusual for the symptoms to get worse or to last longer. And no one knows how each person would react to each injury. It's hard for them to say how quickly he'll recover."

The tingling sensation began to subside. "This explains in part some of his current condition, which is comforting," Marta said. "But you should go and visit him. It might be easier when you see him in person rather than relying on the news from a distance."

Throughout the next week, Marta did not hear any news from Isabella. She did not trouble her for updates because Marta was no longer confident in her own ability to remain calm if faced with more distressing news. Instead, she assumed the situation was, at least, stable. It was the only way she could manage her own strangely pressing anxiety.

Marta was sitting in the shade of the grapevines in Sofía's backyard. Soothed by the rustle of their leaves, she slipped into the imaginary world of her book. The jarringly artificial ring of her phone pulled her back into reality. Puzzled, she answered the call.

"*Hola*, Marta. How are you?" Eduardo sounded surprisingly cheerful.

"I'm fine, thanks. But I hear you've been seriously injured. How are you feeling?"

"Oh, it comes and goes. It's part of the trade."

Marta was relieved to hear that he sounded like his usual self.

"Hey, listen, I'm in your neighborhood," Eduardo said. "Can I come by for a short visit?"

What? Marta almost screamed in surprise but was able to contain herself. Instead, she said, "Are you in town? I thought you were in Spain with Claudia."

"Yeah, that was true until two days ago when we came back to Montevideo. Today I came down here to visit a boys' football club that's run by one of my friends. And since I was already nearby, I thought it might be easier to come over and talk than to text you."

Marta knew that it was her turn to say something, but she was distracted while surveying her surroundings for clutter. She still could not resist her training in Bulgarian hospitality, which required that you and your home had to be presentable when a guest arrived, no matter how unexpected.

"Marta, are you still there?" Eduardo said.

"Yes, yes, sorry." She entered the house to examine the living room, but it was tidy as usual.

"I know it's short notice. I don't have to come if it's a bad time."

"No, it's fine." Marta was short of breath as she ran up the stairs to drop off her book in her room.

"What's the address?"

Marta gave him the address and hung up the phone. She considered the clothes she was wearing. Her linen shorts and baggy T-shirt were perfectly presentable, but she changed into a simple sleeveless cotton dress. She brushed her hair and was coming down the stairs when the doorbell rang.

Marta opened the door, but she could hardly recognize Eduardo. "Are you on your way to rob a bank?" she exclaimed.

Even though it was hot, he wore a jean jacket with the collar turned up to cover his neck and the sides of his face. He also wore a baseball cap and a pair of large sunglasses, which he removed as soon as she opened the door.

Eduardo smiled and looked impatiently down the street. "Can we get inside first and I'll explain?" She closed the door behind him and led him through the house all the way to the backyard. They sat around the patio table, and Eduardo took off his jacket and baseball cap, and he looked like himself again.

"When I'm out, I have to cover up. Or I could spend a lot of time talking to fans or being hunted by the paparazzi."

"Sorry, I keep forgetting what a big celebrity you are around here. I see it's a hard life," Marta said.

Eduardo shrugged. "As with everything, it has its pros and cons." He looked around Sofía's backyard and said, "This is a cool place. But to be honest, I'm surprised."

"Why should you be surprised?"

"Because this isn't a very good part of town. You must be able to afford to live somewhere better?"

"I like the area. I get to hang out with interesting people who are kind and unaffected, and it's been a lot of fun. I wouldn't have met the special friends and eaten the good food that I have if I didn't live here. Fancy hotels are the same wherever you go."

Eduardo remained silent, and Marta could not fathom the real reason for his unexpected visit, especially in his condition. It had not been very long ago, just over a month, since they last saw each other. It was strange for him to go to all the trouble to visit her in Ciudad Vieja, which was densely populated and did not provide nearly as much privacy as his sprawling neighborhood. Moreover, its pedestrian streets were busy during the day, and he would have had to walk for a block from the closest street where, Marta assumed, he had parked his car. And he seemed to have anticipated that obstacle, which explained his disguise.

Feeling hotter than usual, Marta went into the kitchen and returned shortly with a pitcher full of lemonade and two glasses. She placed them on the table and disappeared again.

When she emerged from the house, she was carrying a plate piled with cookies. She sat on the patio chair and Eduardo poured the lemonade into the glasses.

"Tell me what's going on with your concussion. You look fine to me," Marta said.

Eduardo picked up his glass and leaned back in his chair. "It's a strange one. I've had concussions before, but the symptoms had gone away pretty quickly. You learn to do the right things that get you better, and it usually works." He took a sip from his glass. "But this time's different. It's lasting way longer than anyone expected, especially me. The doctors don't seem too surprised. They did many scans and tests already, and they all came out fine. I've been told to keep taking care of myself and, with time, I'll be back to normal."

"And how long do you expect the recovery to take?"

"I don't know. The injury happened over three weeks ago. It's been too long, and now no one can tell how soon I'll recover. We'll have to go by the symptoms. I generally feel okay, but once I start more vigorous training—*wham!*— my symptoms come back and I have to stop." He placed his empty glass on the table, picked up a cookie from the plate, and took a bite. "Hmm, these are good. Is it lavender I taste? Did you say your friend owns a bakery? I should go and buy some for the kids. They'll be happier to see me."

"Yes, Sofía owns a small bakery a block away from here. And the kids are happy to see you even when you don't bring cookies."

"I know," Eduardo said. "But speaking of the kids, are you up for resuming your tutoring at my place again? They'll be with me next week."

"Okay," Marta replied. So, that was the real purpose for

his visit, but he could have called her instead. *Why did he come?* She took a sip of her lemonade but was disappointed that it did not have the cooling effect she desired. "I'll be glad to. But how long do you think you'll be in town? A week? Longer?"

"As I said, this has been an unusual one. I should have remained with my club in Barcelona. But having to watch my teammates practice every day while I sit on the sidelines, weak and injured, somehow made me feel low. If I improved faster, it would have been different. But as time drags on, my mood seems to be getting worse. And after some long talks with the coaches, the doctors, and the psychologist, it was decided that it would be best for me to come home and spend some of my recovery time among my family and friends. And it also helps to be far away from the daily reminders of how useless I've become."

Marta wrinkled her brow.

Eduardo smiled. "At this point, the club has agreed for me to be away until Christmas, basically for another month. If I get much better before then, I'll go back sooner. But if we get close to the holidays, the feeling is that I might as well spend them here and return to the club after. So, you see, it's not all bad. You can help your friend buy that wheelchair after all."

Marta was excited by the prospect of working back at his house. She was amazed that he remembered the reason she told him during their interview two months earlier why she wanted the tutoring job. But buying the wheelchair sooner was no longer the impetus for her eagerness to work. She enjoyed Eduardo's company.

"Speaking of the wheelchair"—Marta did not attempt to

hide her pride—"I've almost saved all the money for it. And now I have to figure out where to purchase it and how to get it to Hugo."

"I can help you with that," Eduardo offered.

"Oh, that's too kind of you. But it isn't necessary." Marta was not prepared to accept any favors from Eduardo. He seemed to mean well, and she was already grudgingly indebted to him for his help with Pedro. She did not consider him a friend—he was still her employer.

His smile disappeared and he looked away. Guilt spread its prickly vines inside Marta's chest. But she was not about to let the unpleasant feeling change her mind. She was stronger than that. She pulled the hem of her dress over her knee and said, "It's good that you'll be around for a while longer. You'll be able to spend more time with Sebastián and Romina. They'll love it!" And more quietly she added, "And you might too."

Eduardo stood up. "I have to go. My head's starting to hurt. It's probably the bright light out here. But are you coming next week?"

"Yes. Two days a week?"

"You can come every day, for all I care. But whatever works for you as long as you're flexible." He put his jacket back on and lifted the collar up.

"Okay, let's plan on three days a week. And yes, I can be flexible," Marta replied.

He headed toward the front door and put on his baseball cap. Once outside, he turned toward her, his sunglasses already on his face. "*Chao*, Marta," he said. He pointed toward her. "I'll see *you* soon."

The promise in his words wilted the vines binding her lungs. Marta exhaled.

CHAPTER 14

Turquoise

After the injury, Eduardo spent a lot of time at home. He went to practices, but they were not regular, at least not every day. Sometimes he would be in his bedroom because he felt fatigued and nauseated, or had a headache. And sometimes he would go for a run but come back tired and irritable and went straight upstairs.

Marta worried about him and wished that she could do something to alleviate his discomfort. But the only thing she could do was to keep the children occupied and as quiet as possible so he could rest. Marta and the children began to venture farther afield on their walks and on longer trips that she had planned especially for them. They often took the city bus to explore the various parks, museums, and shops in Montevideo. They also visited Luisa in her office, and most thrilling of all was when they went to Sofía's bakery. By their second visit, Sebastián had picked his favorite cookie and did not care to try anything else, while Romina had to try every type of cookie and had already begun to eye the various cakes.

At the end of a particularly hot day, during which the children had been unusually active, Marta was exhausted. Isabella had just come to collect them and Marta was alone in the house. Eduardo had not yet returned from his practice, which went on longer than usual. He often hung out with his friends.

She was busy picking up the toys the children had left scattered around the living room, when Eduardo arrived home. His dark eyes scanned the room that was littered with toys, books, and shoes.

"Leave this for Señora Álvarez. You look tired," Eduardo said as he took Romina's teddy bear from Marta's hand.

Marta was tired but she had enough energy left to protest. "I can handle it. Señora Álvarez has a lot to do as it is. And I'm not so old and decrepit."

Eduardo's eyes grew large and concerned. "I did *not* mean that." He threw the teddy bear into the toy chest and leaned over to pick up a toy truck from the floor. "Let me help you then. I hope you'll have a drink with me once we're done."

Marta was startled by his sudden invitation. But a cold drink was a welcome idea. "I could do with a cold drink in this heat."

Together they collected the toys more quickly. Eduardo was twice as fast as she was. Once the last toy was in the chest, Marta took the shoes and headed upstairs to leave them in the children's rooms. She heard the fridge open and close, and then the clatter of glasses.

By the time she returned to the living room, Eduardo was sitting on the patio looking at the darkening sky. The pale moon was barely visible over the horizon. The crickets chirped, and the air was warm and filled with the tingling smell of freshly cut myrtle. Marta sat on the wicker chair next to him. He handed her a glass of white wine. She took a sip and felt the pleasant cool liquid flow down her throat.

"Thank you. This is perfect."

They sat in silence for a few minutes. The crickets chirped louder, and the moon's silvery path was clearly visible on the rippled surface of the ocean. As she looked out at the water, Marta took a deep breath.

"My mother once told me that if I swim in the moon's path, I would never drown," Marta said.

A faint smile spread across Eduardo's face.

"Now I know how silly it is," she continued, "but when I was a child it gave me hope. I knew that in any treacherous situation there would always be a safe path that I could take out."

"Have you been in many treacherous situations?" he asked, sounding amused.

"I've had my fair share, I think." Marta had already told Eduardo about some of her challenges growing up in Communist Bulgaria. And like the delightful memories of the fairy tales her grandfather used to tell her about the trials of a clever hedgehog, Marta's memories of her childhood now seemed happy too. The pain inflicted by some of her more recent experiences, however, was still sharp and not yet subjected to the soothing balm of time.

Marta took a sip of her wine and was about to change the subject but Eduardo asked, "Are the hard times over? You seem happy."

"I believe I am. Although happiness is such a difficult thing to define. It's such a fleeting feeling. There have been times when I've been content and I'd describe life as being easier. And there were times that were extremely difficult and I was miserable."

Eduardo was silent.

"But I do believe that even the most challenging times in life make us better in the end," Marta continued. "I'm so much wiser because of them."

"I wish I could be as positive as you are." Eduardo was staring at the ocean, dark thoughts seeming to furrow his brow.

"Are you unhappy?" Marta asked. "You have everything a person could possibly want, and yet you sound so melancholy. Perhaps my rambling has depressed you. I should get going. It's already pretty late." Marta stood up.

"No, stay." Eduardo took her by the elbow and pulled her down. His touch was gentle yet unyielding, a power to which Marta uncannily was willing to subject herself.

When he spoke again, his voice grew louder with each word, "Your words didn't upset me. I'm just fucking sick of feeling tired!" And then he mumbled, "Um, sorry."

"That's all right. I'm all grown up."

"Oh, good, I won't sweat it. So, where was I? Ah, yes. Basically, I've had a lot on my mind lately. And I can't make sense of it. I feel like I'm trying to score a goal, but I just can't get the ball into the net."

Marta recognized this more expressive side to him, which she had discovered early on in their acquaintance but just now realized how much she had come to enjoy it. "If it's of any use, I'm a good listener." Although she mainly talked for a living, in her classes, at conferences, at meetings, she had always been a better listener when it came to revealing anything personal. She was attentive and cared about what others told her, and they trusted her. When it came to trust, she could not say the same about herself, and only a few of her friends were privy to some of her most intimate stories.

Marta leaned back in her chair, took her glass in her hand, and fixed Eduardo with a steady gaze.

Eduardo looked at his hands. "When I play on a team, I'm usually a striker, you know, the player expected to score the most goals. Over the years, I've worked crazy hard and was lucky to score a decent number of goals. But I'm thirty-four, and I'm not at my peak anymore. I'm still able to play well, though, at least most of the time." He took a sip of his wine and wiped his lips with the back of his hand. "In the meantime, younger players are rising—which is great for the sport, don't get me wrong. But just how I replaced older players when I started, I see that the younger players are going to replace me."

He ran his fingers through his hair. "It hasn't been easy for me. Sometimes I think I'm overreacting, and that I should buckle up and keep playing my best and ignore all the other stuff. But then I feel low. And especially now with the injury—damn, I feel old—I'm seriously thinking of retiring from the sport. But, honestly, it scares me because it feels like I'm giving up." He exhaled heavily. "I guess I'm not ready yet."

All of a sudden, the decade that separated them in age seemed to shrink, bringing them ever closer together. Rooted in different causes, Eduardo's doubts and fears were very similar to Marta's. He was standing on the precipice of her own stage of life. But certain that Eduardo would not be pleased with this revelation, Marta remained still.

"I don't know what I'm going to do when I retire," he continued. "I've spent all my life playing football, and only since the injury did I start thinking that I need to figure out what to do next. I've never seriously thought about it before, and the unknown freaking terrifies me." His breathing was fast, and he fidgeted with the empty wine glass in his hands. "I don't want to play friendly matches, coach youth teams, and sit around for the rest of my life, you know? That sounds boring. I want to do something different. But I don't know that I can do anything other than play football." He placed the glass on the table. "I guess I have two big feet and one small brain."

Marta clutched her glass of wine, still half-full. She heard every word he said, but she was addled by the sudden awareness that they were more similar than she had ever thought possible. She chose to focus on his last words instead. She would advise him as an expert on the topic, which was always comfortable, and not from personal experience, which was often painful.

"Apparently," she began, "Mark Twain said that many years from now you'll be more disappointed by the things that you didn't do than by the ones you did do. And then something about letting go, taking risks, and venturing into the unknown." She looked at Eduardo. "What I'm about to say may sound like a lecture, but it wouldn't be far from the truth. It's close to what I often talk about in my classes. Are you ready for it?"

His eyes reflected the moonlight, and he nodded.

"You can't say I didn't warn you." She cleared her throat. "I'm a social scientist who studies human development. There are a few theories of human development, according to which we go through several stages from birth all the way until we reach full capacity at young adulthood. And they all stop there—it's a very unsatisfying prospect from the viewpoint of a middle-aged person!" Marta smiled.

Eduardo listened peacefully, his expression unchanged.

Marta took another sip of her wine and continued, "Only one theory, the one by Erik Erikson, continues with the stages well into old age. Each of Erikson's stages is a dichotomy of feelings, attitudes if you will, that dominate our experience at each period in our lives. I've always been impressed by the stark significance of the last stage. During this stage, we may experience either a sense of 'ego integrity,' or wholeness, or 'despair' depending on how our lives had progressed up to that point. In our sunset years, we're supposed to be looking back on our lives, and based on what we see, we may place ourselves on the integrity side, satisfied with what we had accomplished or experienced, because we remained true to ourselves. Or we may end up on the side of despair, regretting the things we were never able to achieve or discover."

Eduardo's face was solemn. "I think I'm confused. You can't be too surprised, you know—this is my first university lecture."

Marta laughed but shook her head.

"Anyway, how can we know that we won't regret a decision later in life?" Eduardo said.

"Well, if it's the right decision, we won't regret it, right?" she said. "But you're right. We can't really know until after the fact. And sometimes we may never know. When a person is faced with important decisions in life, he needs to strive toward the options that he believes would make him happy, even if they're not deemed by others to be the best choices the person could make."

Marta was getting into territory that was too abstract, and she had learned through her teaching that stories based on personal experience were more engaging and easier for her students to relate to them. She rarely relied on personal stories in her classes, however, but now seemed safe enough. After all, Eduardo had opened up to her, and it was natural for her to reciprocate him.

"About six years ago," Marta began, "I had to make the hardest decision in my life so far, and hopefully, ever. I had just received a letter informing me that I no longer had my job at the university. I had been given one year to pack my bags and find another job. But academic positions are rare and my prospects were slim. I applied for a few job openings and was extremely fortunate to get an offer at another university. The job was in the US, far away from Toronto, which would require a significant sacrifice—uprooting my whole family and relocating it to a new and foreign place."

"Hmm," Eduardo said. "It occurred to me that I know nothing about your family. I guess it's not surprising that you have one."

"I did, and still do, in a way. It all depends on how you define the word 'family.'" It was not an accident that Eduardo was ignorant of Marta's family. Unlike Bruce Mason and the other hopeless men she had met in the past, he had never asked. Otherwise, the remnants of her family were not a source of happiness for her, and she particularly bewailed her damaged relationship with Ilian. Marta closed her eyes, reminded of the desolation she sometimes felt as a result of her loneliness. She already regretted having broached the subject.

After a long pause, Eduardo prompted her. "So, what happened? Did you take the new job? You can't leave me hanging like this."

Marta squirmed in her seat. She was in the middle of her story, and there was no elegant way to change the topic. But the warm glow on Eduardo's face calmed her nerves, and she could not remember the last time another man had similarly affected her. She realized that she was at a point in her story that did not reveal her real dilemma, nor how she chose to deal with it, which was her original point. So, Marta continued.

"The job offer, as exciting as it was, demanded that I

make a very hard decision. I took my time to think about it and discussed it with several of my colleagues and friends. I talked about it with my husband, too, and he was supportive and adamant that I should take the new job. The day I finally decided to accept the job offer, I received an urgent call that my son, Ilian, who was twelve at the time, was hit by a car and was in the hospital.

"He had a broken arm and a few scrapes and bruises. But the doctors were unsure about the possibility of brain damage and indicated that Ilian would need an ongoing monitoring and possibly a prolonged rehabilitation. When I was finally able to think about the job offer again, I was forced to make the decision with a new knowledge. The critical question in my mind was: where would my son receive the best medical care? I consulted again, this time with medical doctors, and their advice was consistent. They thought that Ilian's healthcare would be better in Toronto. And all of a sudden, my choice was simple. I no longer needed to consult with anyone. I wasn't scared shitless of the uncertain future. I quickly made up my mind and I turned down the job offer, with no other employment prospects in sight. I was relieved, and I could breathe easier. But my husband could not."

Marta exhaled. She shivered and placed her empty wine glass on the patio table. She folded her legs in front of her and wrapped her arms around them. She looked at the ocean. The moon was high up in the sky, and its path across the water was slimmer. She was grateful for the cricket song. It reminded her of happier times during her childhood, and the images of people who loved her floated through her mind. She had not noticed that Eduardo had left her side, and she became aware of his presence again when he placed a blanket over her shoulders.

"Thanks." Marta wrapped the blanket tightly around herself. "We should call it a night. You must be bored to death by now."

"No, I'm not. That's a whole lot of 'despair.'" Eduardo said. "It can fill many of those great novels you seem to like."

Marta managed a weak smile in return.

"But seriously, you're a very strong person, Marta."

"Oh, I don't know about that," Marta said and exhaled heavily.

"But this isn't the end, is it? You still have a university job, so there must be more." Eduardo waited, but when Marta hesitated, he prodded her again, "Go on! I want to hear the rest, especially if it has a happy ending. Does it?"

Marta smiled faintly and resumed her story. "After I decided to stay in Toronto, I fought for the job I already had—fought hard and worked even harder. And in the end, I got the university to reverse its decision. The first few months of Ilian's recovery were rough, but he was able to make a full recovery and has been doing well ever since. Unfortunately, I can't say the same about my marriage. The strain on our already failing relationship was too much, and it didn't survive. And, sadly, with its demise, my relationship with Ilian became fraught . . ." Her voice wavered and she stopped.

They sat in silence for a while, surrounded by the ethereal glow of the moon. Marta turned toward Eduardo and added, "I don't know whether it's a happy ending. You tell me!"

Eduardo remained silent and continued to stare at the water. Marta felt drained, and she fought the urge to close her eyes and fall asleep right there on the patio chair. She was startled by Eduardo's somber voice. "It's late. I should take you home."

She looked at her phone. It was past midnight. But she refused his offer for a ride and moved to get up.

"I'm not sure how regular the buses are at this time of night. And it's too late. I'll drive you home," Eduardo insisted.

He offered his hand to Marta and walked her all the way to his car. She was not so much drunk as she was tired and dazed from the combination of the heat of the day and her strong emotions. Eduardo turned the engine on. The quiet rumbling of the car, the cool air of the night, and the loud cricket song lulled her to sleep.

Marta stirred drowsily at the sound of the engine turning off. Eduardo walked with her to her door in silence. While she shuffled for her keys, he said, "Marta, thank you for this evening. I learned a lot about that social scientist, and his theories and all."

"You're welcome. Any time." Marta found her keys. She stepped into the house and closed the door behind her. Her bed was not close enough.

CHAPTER 15

Yellow

Marta could not get her conversation with Eduardo out of her head. She was convinced that she must have been drunk to have been so recklessly uninhibited. In the bright daylight, when she was not lulled by the cricket song and mesmerized by the moonlight, she could not explain why she had revealed so much of her personal life to him. He had said that he admired her strength, but it was feeble to reveal to him that she was unable to hold her family together, and she felt exposed. But Eduardo had been similarly candid, even more so than her. Marta's feelings of discomfort subsided and were ultimately replaced by a calming sense of equilibrium. His equilibrium.

When Marta arrived at Eduardo's house a couple of days later, the children were not there.

"Sebastián and Romina are at a dentist appointment, but it's taking longer than expected," Eduardo explained.

Marta was not sure what to say next.

"It's not too hot yet," Eduardo added. "And I have a birthday card to mail to my mother. She still prefers the real thing, you see. What do you say to a brief walk to the mailbox?"

Marta had just hiked up the hill to his house but was unable to think of an excuse. Reluctant to admit it, she was glad to spend more time with him, and she agreed.

They walked side by side for a while. Feeling awkward by

the silence and still unable to figure out why he had invited her on the walk in the first place if he didn't want to talk, Marta asked, "How are you feeling?"

"Oh, it's not great. But I seem to be getting better, slowly but surely. So, it must be a good sign," he said flaccidly, which made it clear that he did not want to talk about his health anymore.

Marta remained silent.

They reached the mailbox, and after Eduardo placed his card into the slot, they turned back toward the house. He was preoccupied with his thoughts, seemingly untroubled by the silence, and Marta relaxed, unburdened by the need to talk. Instead, she focused on the carefully groomed yards of the neighboring houses. Eventually, they reached the house and saw Isabella's SUV in the driveway. The children's voices poured out from an open window.

Eduardo was gone for most of the day. In the afternoon, Marta thought that going to a movie theater might be an interesting experience for the children, and possibly more so for her. She had never been to a movie theater in Montevideo. Not knowing Spanish very well, it made no sense. But there was a recently released children's movie, and she thought the children would enjoy seeing it in a different context from their living room. They could catch the showing after Romina's nap, and Marta texted Eduardo to let him know that they would be coming back later than usual.

By the time Marta and the children returned home from the movie theater, it was well past six o'clock. The children ran into the house, their voices louder than usual, and they found Eduardo in the kitchen busily preparing dinner. He was happy to hear the children's excited reviews of the movie, and Marta patiently waited for her turn to say goodbye to them before she went home. While she waited, she noticed that the kitchen table was already set for four, and there were two wineglasses and an uncorked bottle of red wine. Marta assumed that it was going to be another special evening for Claudia. But come to think of it, she realized that since Eduardo had been back with his injury, she had not seen Claudia.

"Marta," Eduardo said, "one of these glasses is for you. Can you pour the wine? The food's almost ready."

The indirect but assertive invitation caught Marta by surprise. Before she could fully comprehend Eduardo's meaning, Romina was already at her side, pulling on her arm and pleading in her whiney voice, "Marta, please stay! Pleeease!"

"Yeah, Marta, stay with us," Sebastián joined Romina. "Papa's making my favorite food!"

"In this case, how can I refuse?" Marta replied.

Dinner was delicious and the conversation, however little, was erratic and lively. Eduardo had made polenta to complement the beef *tuco*, a flavorful tomato sauce with pieces of beef in it. Romina dropped her fork on the floor a couple of times and had to get out of her seat to pick it up. It was entertaining for her and Sebastián because they both burst into giggles every time she did it. With great concentration, Sebastián scooped an extra serving of polenta, but as he transported it from the serving bowl to his plate, he dropped a dollop of it on the table. He scooped it up with his fork, leaving a messy mark on the tablecloth, and another burst of giggles filled the kitchen. Marta observed their shenanigans and let Eduardo be in charge. He smiled occasionally and shook his head just enough to indicate that he was not oblivious of what went on, but continued eating his dinner uninterrupted.

Having eaten as much as she possibly could, Marta stared at the polenta remaining on her plate and mindlessly poked it with her fork. At a lull in the general noise at the table, she spoke, with a tinge of nostalgia. "Yellow's my favorite color—"

"Mine's purple!" Romina interrupted her.

"And mine's orange!" Sebastián jumped in his seat.

"And what's yours, Eduardo?" Marta asked. "Now that we have all revealed our secrets, we need to know yours too."

Eduardo leaned back in his chair and stretched his arm behind his head. "Oh, I don't know. I don't think I have a favorite color." He smiled and added, "How about light blue, the color of the uniforms of the Uruguayan national team?"

Marta laughed. "Not super original, but I guess it'll have to do—it comes with an explanation."

"And why do you like yellow?" Eduardo asked and winked at the children. Romina giggled.

"Maybe it's because it makes me think of delicate spring flowers, of warm sunshine, of fire and the energy it gives, lemons and their tartness, golden honey and its sweetness, and—"

"Corn," Sebastián said as he stood up from his chair and jumped up and down a couple of times.

"And fireflies," Romina shouted while dangling her feet vigorously.

Marta waited for the children to calm down and said, "And melancholy."

Everyone, including Eduardo, looked at her with a perplexed expression.

"Yes, melancholy! Which means 'sadness,'" she explained to the children. Romina was still confused and Sebastián sat back in his chair, dejected. "We have to experience melancholy in order to appreciate happiness!" Marta exclaimed. "Even Shakespeare described melancholy in *Twelfth Night* as yellow and juxtaposed it with smiling:

> *She pined in thought,*
> *And with a green and yellow melancholy,*
> *She sat like patience on a monument,*
> *Smiling at grief. Was not this love indeed?"*

Sebastián slid from his seat and headed toward the living room, and Romina followed him.

"Hey, hey, kids, stay in your seats!" Eduardo shouted after them. "We're not finished with dinner yet."

"But I'm bored," Sebastián complained. "And I wanna play."

"Me too," added Romina. But both children trudged back to the table and sat in their seats.

Noting their long faces, Marta sat straight in her chair and looked at Romina and Sebastián in turn. "Getting back to fireflies and corn, they are both great ideas! And I love them too! But are there fireflies in Uruguay? I can barely remember seeing fireflies once or twice in my life when I was a child back in Bulgaria."

"We see them at Granny and Grandpa's house," Romina said.

"Fireflies are getting more and more rare," Eduardo explained. "But a person can still find them on a summer night out in the countryside."

"I'd love to see fireflies again!" Marta said. "I've been enjoying the cricket concerts here. But I've not seen fireflies yet."

"You should come with us to Grandma and Grandpa's. I'll show you where the fireflies are," Sebastián said.

Eduardo smiled and stood up to clear the table. It was time for dessert: ice cream. Sebastián ate his ice cream as quickly as he possibly could while Romina swirled hers around until it had turned into liquid. When she was satisfied with its consistency, she picked up her bowl and started slurping from it loudly. Another burst of giggles accompanied every slurp, and Romina looked at Marta impishly. Marta resisted laughing at her, even though ice cream covered her upper lip and dripped down her chin. But since she did not show any signs of encouragement, Romina placed her bowl on the table and scooped the rest with her spoon.

Once they were finished with the ice cream, Sebastián said to Marta, "My favorite ice cream is in Italy."

"You must not get it often then? Italy is very far from here."

Sebastián ignored Marta's question and asked instead, "Have you been to Italy, Marta?"

"Yes, I have. And I remember liking the ice cream there too.

"I've been to six countries," Sebastián announced proudly. And he went ahead listing the countries. "Have you been to so many countries?"

"That's a lot of countries, Sebastián, more than one per each year of your life so far. I haven't counted the countries I've been to, but I'm pretty sure that there are more than six."

Marta relaxed back in her chair and the rowdy discussion of the different places the children had visited became a distant din. The scene was all too familiar to her: the messy table, the children's shrill voices, the father's resonant laugher. Marta was present in it, yet she looked on.

Romina rubbed her eyes and Marta stood up from the table, ready to go home. She hugged each child, and Eduardo sent them upstairs to brush their teeth. He walked Marta to the front door.

Before she left, she said, "I can't come to work tomorrow morning. Is that okay with you?"

Eduardo nodded.

"Remember the friend I told you about, the one who needs a wheelchair?" Marta said. "I've made enough money working for you and Isabella, and I would like to buy the wheelchair tomorrow."

"Have you thought about how to transport the wheelchair from the store to where your friend is?" Eduardo asked. "You don't have a car here, right? I'm happy to help."

Marta had not forgotten his earlier offer and how unsure she had been about accepting it. But she was not as opposed to the idea now as she was then. They had been talking, laughing, sparring—reluctant acquaintances emulsifying into unlikely friends.

"You're right," she said. "I haven't thought about it. But since you mentioned it, I could use a car." And they agreed to go together first thing in the morning.

Marta was about to open the door but turned toward Eduardo again. "You're a good father, Eduardo."

A faint smile flickered on Eduardo's lips.

Marta continued, "You're not afraid to show your love for your children, and you obviously enjoy their company and they know it. You're comfortable letting them be themselves but they know their limits. And, as you told me already, you genuinely want to do everything possible to be the best parent you can be. All of these are achievements not many of us can brag about, but especially for someone like you, who travels often and is so much in the public eye."

"I know who Elphaba is," Eduardo said, and his eyes flashed.

Amused, Marta exclaimed, "Oh, good for you! You looked her up."

"No, I read the book *Wicked*," he said with a shrug. "And I even liked it."

CHAPTER 16

Teal

T he next morning, when Marta opened the front door, Luisa barged right in and smacked a magazine on the middle of the dining room table.

"Congratulations! You're in the tabloids now."

"What?" Marta exclaimed and picked up the magazine.

On the front cover, there was a grainy photograph of her and Eduardo walking next to each other, looking down at the ground, and an insert of an unflattering photo of Claudia's scrunched face. The headline read in Spanish: "Who's Eduardo's mystery woman?" And the caption under Claudia's photograph read: "Claudia's raging: *How dare you take my man?*"

Marta looked at Luisa in disbelief. "What does this mean?"

"It means that you've become fodder for the gossip magazines, and you'll somehow have to deal with it," Luisa replied.

"How do I 'deal with it'?" Marta asked. "And what's there to deal with? Eduardo and I went for a walk in his neighborhood. And we weren't even talking, for crying out loud!" She sat on a dining chair and rested her head on her hand. "How could there be a story out of it?"

"Oh, they'll make a story out of anything as long as it would sell their papers and magazines," Luisa explained.

"What do I do?" Marta rubbed her forehead with a trembling hand.

But before Luisa could answer, the doorbell rang. Luisa rushed to open the door, and Marta heard her exclaim, "¡Dios mío!" Luisa was standing motionless with her hand over her mouth and her eyes wide open. With a curt *"Buenos días,"* Eduardo walked past her, removed the hood of his sweatshirt from his head and placed his sunglasses on the dining table.

"Luisa, it would be a good idea to close the door now," Marta reminded her.

Luisa shut the door and came into the dining room. Marta introduced them to each other, and Eduardo smiled and shook Luisa's hand. Not fully recovered from the shock, Luisa remained speechless. Noticing the magazine on the table, Eduardo looked at Marta.

"So, you know?"

Marta nodded. "Luisa just brought the magazine. And before she lost her capacity to speak, we were wondering what to do about it."

Luisa muttered "sorry" and sat on a chair across from Marta.

"How did you find out?" Marta asked, gesturing for Eduardo to sit.

"I got a phone call from Claudia this morning." Eduardo pressed his lips together, and a muscle on the side of his jaw twitched.

Marta winced at the thought of being at the center of a drama, and it wasn't even of her own making. A scorching wave of embarrassment washed over her. What if the ridiculous tabloid made Eduardo think that she was attracted to him?

Panicked, she said in between short breaths, "I hope Claudia isn't too upset. She does know that this story is entirely made up and there's nothing she needs to worry about?"

"No . . . I mean, don't worry about it," Eduardo grumbled, avoiding Marta's eyes. Marta was puzzled but let it go.

Eduardo ran his hand through his hair. "But how worried are you about the effect of this story on your life . . . your career, your family?"

Marta pursed her lips. "I don't know. I haven't thought about that yet. I've never had the honor of being in the tabloids before."

"Well, I've had plenty of it, and I can tell you, it's not a joke."

"Yeah, you've had it bad." Luisa finally found her voice. "I've always been impressed with how well you've been able to handle it."

Eduardo looked at her from under his eyebrows. "Thanks, but I've had help. That's what publicists and agents are for." He turned back to Marta and said, "There are a couple of ways to handle this. One's to leave it alone and hope the story will die out on its own soon. But it could also get a lot worse."

Marta sat up at the edge of her chair. "How could it possibly get any worse? There's no story here. We were just walking, damn it!" She was not able to control her indignation any longer. "Why are we even talking about it?"

"You'll have to trust me on this one, Marta," Eduardo said in a calm tone. "The second option is for me to address it directly in the media. It's what publicists call 'taking control of the message.' But that'll take time. I have to talk to a publicist, get the message right, you know."

Marta shook her head. "I honestly don't think this fiasco

would make much of a difference to me. The story is unlikely to be seen in Canada, right? It's far away from here."

"It could travel fast through social media," Luisa said.

"In that case, I can hope the news ups my coolness factor with my students," Marta scoffed. "But seriously, if it means that I can't take the bus or walk freely around town, that would be a problem."

"Okay, I'll call my agent right away and get going on a response." Eduardo was about to stand up, but Marta touched his elbow to get his attention. Agitated by how the tabloid story made her feel utterly exposed to the world, she could not shake off the guilt she also felt for having joined him on the walk in the first place. Her desire to be with him was the only reason for it, and she had found herself incapable of refusing his invitation, as trivial as it was. And now the seemingly innocuous event had inflated into a major problem that Marta wished would disappear without causing any more fuss for anyone else, especially Eduardo.

"Please, leave it," Marta said. "Let's hope it'll go away on its own. I don't want you to waste your time on something so stupid. By addressing it, you'll be validating a bogus story that's based on . . . nothing." She turned to Luisa. "I guess for the next little while I'll have to wear sunglasses and a hoodie to avoid being recognized."

Eduardo was deep in thought and did not react to her teasing remark.

Marta placed her hand on his shoulder and said, "Let's forget about this and go buy the chair for Hugo."

"Are you sure?"

"Yes, I'm sure. What more could come of it? We've already spent too much time on it as it is. You and I just need to make sure never to walk outside together. Simple." Marta was confident in her own ability to resist the temptation of another walk, and Eduardo was unlikely to suggest it again, considering the amount of hassle it had already caused him.

"Let's go," he said.

Luisa reached her hand out to Eduardo. Instead, he leaned over and gave her a loose hug. Luisa blushed, but she was beaming. Marta offered to take a photo of the two of them together.

As soon as Luisa was gone, Eduardo lifted his hood over his head and put his sunglasses on. Together they drove to the medical equipment store, but he waited in the car while Marta went inside and purchased the wheelchair.

Eduardo drove back to the Old Town and stopped as close as possible to the location where Hugo usually sat. It was still mid-morning, and the street was deserted except for a couple of pedestrians who were walking away from them. He took the wheelchair out of the trunk, unfolded it, and locked it into place. Marta pulled from her purse a red bow that she had purchased the day before and placed it on the backrest of the chair. She wanted Hugo to know that it was supposed to be a Christmas present, even though it was the first week of December. She took the handles and was ready to dart off, expecting Eduardo to follow her, but he did not move.

"Aren't you coming to give Hugo his present?" she asked.

"No, I think it'd be better if it just comes from you," he said and opened his car door.

Marta had to agree, and as she was about to turn and go, Eduardo added, "I'll see you later back at the house, okay?"

She waved and hurried down the street.

Hugo was sitting in his usual spot, but there was a young man, about the same age as Hugo, standing near and talking to him. Hugo looked surprised when he saw Marta walking toward him with the wheelchair.

"Marta, you didn't—" Hugo began.

"I don't want to hear any objections," she interrupted him. "We had a deal, remember?"

"What I was going to say is that you didn't take my money before you bought the chair."

"If you insist, you can give me the money now." Marta pushed the chair closer to him. "Merry Christmas!"

Hugo smiled. "Are you always early with your presents?" He turned toward his friend. "This is Marta, the Canadian woman I told you about."

"My name Carlos," Hugo's friend said in English.

Marta shook his hand and turned back toward Hugo. "Come on, Hugo, jump into that chair!"

She put the brake on and left the chair on the sidewalk. She stepped closer to Hugo, but he pulled away from her. Marta knew that he could not simply "jump" into the chair, and that she had to find a way to help him get in it. She was not certain how exactly it would work. But if his mother was able to help him move around, so could she.

Marta wondered whether Carlos's presence helped or hindered her plan. But before she could decide, Carlos said in Spanish, "I'll pull you up, mate. We've done it before."

Hugo hesitated again but nodded. Carlos came closer to him, and as he leaned over, Marta went back to the wheelchair. She took off the brake and turned around. Hugo was already on his feet, propped up by Carlos. She rolled the chair behind him, and Carlos lowered him into it. Hugo placed his feet on the braces, and Carlos showed him where the brake was.

Marta picked up Hugo's backpack from the ground and put his book and the metal can inside it. She attached the backpack to the back of the wheelchair.

Carlos took the chair by its handles and swirled it around so Hugo faced Marta.

"You're good to go, Hugo. Give it a spin!" Marta said.

Carlos let go of the handles and Hugo pushed the wheels forward. He rolled along the sidewalk for a while, clumsily turned around, and headed back toward them. Hugo grinned as he pushed the wheels faster and faster. Marta and Carlos stepped to the side to let him pass.

"Careful now!" Marta shouted after him. "There must be a speed limit for wheelchair driving."

Hugo stopped at the corner and turned around, less clumsily this time. As he approached them, he pulled next to them and put the brake on. He looked at Marta, his eyes watery but the smile still visible on his face. "Thank you, Marta . . ." He was panting and stopped to take a breath. "Thanks for letting me fly!"

Marta remembered the soaring seagull, the one she had noticed while sitting next to Hugo on the sidewalk. No longer able to restrain herself, she leaned over and gave him a hug. She was relieved that he accepted her gift without resistance, aware of how uncomfortable it had made him when she first suggested it. She compared Hugo's reaction to her own in response to Eduardo's assistance when he paid for Pedro's hospital expenses, and she felt reassured in having accepted Eduardo's generosity without becoming ridiculous. She was glad for his sake.

Pulling away from Hugo, Marta said, "This was just the takeoff!"

Carlos slapped Hugo on the back. "Looking good, mate.

I've got to go, but I'll see you soon." He said "*chao*" to Marta and left.

Marta bit her lip. "You don't have to rush into anything yet. It'll take a while for your arms to get stronger, and you'll have to 'fly' around a little bit at a time. But when you're ready, I can introduce you to my friend Sofía. She owns a bakery nearby, and with the Christmas season picking up, I know she needs help with local deliveries. I thought it might be a job you'd be interested in." Unwilling to make him feel pressured, she repeated again, "When you're ready."

Hugo unlocked the brake on his chair, and as he spun around, he shouted over his shoulder, "Show me the way to the bakery!"

Marta laughed and ran a few steps to catch up with him.

CHAPTER 17

Chartreuse

When Marta arrived at Eduardo's house later that afternoon, Romina and Sebastián were playing in the backyard by the fountain. Señora Álvarez told her that Eduardo had already gone to a business meeting before his afternoon practice, and that she would go home now that Marta was there. Marta nodded and ran to chase the children around the fountain.

Unaware of how much time had passed, they heard a car pull into the driveway and stop abruptly, judging by the piercing screech of brakes. The children thought it was Eduardo and ran to open the door for him. When Marta caught up with them in the vestibule, she found Claudia there instead. With long faces, the children said *"Hola"* and ran back into the yard to play. Marta was surprised to see her without Eduardo. She greeted her and explained in Spanish that Eduardo was at his practice, and she expected him to be back before dinnertime.

"Perfect," Claudia snapped in English. "I came to talk to you." And she marched straight into the living room.

Marta closed the door behind her with raised eyebrows. *So, Claudia speaks English after all.* Having barely talked to each other before, she guessed that Claudia's visit had been prompted by the tabloid story. And noting her cold demeanor, Marta grew increasingly more apprehensive. She followed her into the living room and gestured toward a chair as she sat on the couch. She looked at Claudia, expecting her to speak first.

Claudia remained standing. Her leg was fidgeting, and she twisted the belt of her dress around her finger. Having the opportunity to observe her more closely, Marta noted how her tailored dress hung loosely on her body rather than hug her nonexistent curves. But she could not help but admit that Claudia was stunning. Her lithe youth and vigorous energy were palpable. Marta found it difficult to be poised in front of so much natural beauty and youthful grace.

Claudia's icy voice, and her accented but good English, brought Marta out of her reverie. "I'm not going to beat about the bushes. Your presence in this house isn't welcome, and you must leave . . . forever!"

Marta was shocked by the audacity of Claudia's words. She anticipated Claudia to be upset, but she was not prepared for her to be so livid or her attack so directly pointed at her. Uncertain how to respond without escalating the conflict further, Marta said, "You speak English so well. I had no idea."

Claudia blinked, confused by Marta's words. She quickly collected herself and said, "Well, yeah. I count it among my achievements, considering that I didn't go to school past third grade." Then, as if she remembered her original purpose, she added, "Nice try, but you won't succeed at distracting me."

Marta was still focused on the words "didn't go past third grade." She had assumed that Claudia came from a privileged background. Her clothes, her confidence, and yes, her blue eyes all gave the impression of entitlement. And realizing how wrong she had been about Claudia, Marta was rattled by the thought of how terrible she was at judging people in general, not only men.

"You should be proud of your English. How did you learn it so well if you didn't go to school much?" Marta asked.

Claudia stopped fidgeting and sat on the chair. "At the modeling agency. I asked my friends there who speak English to teach me and insisted that we only speak English."

"But why didn't you finish school? Giving up on it so early limits your opportunities in the future."

Claudia twirled her belt again. "If you must know, I come from a very poor family, and I'm the oldest of six children. We lived on the outskirts of Buenos Aires, and my parents barely made ends meet. My father cleaned gutters and my mother sold fruits and vegetables on the market. There was never enough food for all of us. As soon as I turned ten, I dropped out of school and began working for a seamstress. I was helping the family a little bit." Claudia's face darkened, then she sighed. "Eventually, when I was thirteen, I was discovered on the streets of Buenos Aires by a modeling agency scout. And our lives changed. I support my whole family now and make sure that my younger brothers and sisters can go to school."

Marta's bewilderment grew as the story went along. The revelation of Claudia's difficult upbringing, and how important the schooling of her siblings was to her, warmed Marta's heart and she completely forgot Claudia's earlier hostility. The enormous responsibility Claudia had taken on also explained her apathy toward Eduardo's children. She had learned that children were a burden to be provided for. Marta was about to congratulate her on her strength and success when Claudia spoke again.

"Anyway, I've worked very hard at the successful career that I now have. And for my security, and that of my family, I also expect to marry someone who is rich and famous. And you, of all people, somehow managed to get in my way. So, you have to leave!"

It was Marta's turn to blink at Claudia's renewed resentment. Claudia was smart and ambitious, and her overpowering pragmatism was clearly rooted in her earlier life. But Marta was bothered on Eduardo's behalf, and instead of continuing to placate Claudia, she said, "I'm not sure what I've done to deserve such harsh words from you. But is my presence here not wanted by you or Eduardo? Because, since this is his home, only his wishes should matter."

Claudia sprang up from the chair. Her face and neck were covered with bright red patches that were visible beneath the thick layer of makeup. "Stay away from him, you frumpy, fat old woman!"

Marta swallowed hard. She had never been attacked like this before, and it took her a minute to regain her composure. Claudia's words were hurtful, although she knew that they were said more out of jealousy than reason. Claudia paced about the room, unable to look Marta in the eyes.

Marta took a deep breath and said, her voice unfaltering, "I can't stay away because I have a commitment to Eduardo and, especially, to his children." And she added with a sardonic smile, "And besides, you have nothing to worry about since I'm old, fat, and frumpy."

Claudia stopped pacing, and she was now twisting her hands. When she spoke, her voice was shrill. "Eduardo couldn't possibly be attracted to you. But I see how he looks at you. He can't stop talking about you. And now this tabloid story—it was the last drop. It probably means nothing to you since you're a nobody. But it's terrible for my career and . . . and . . . my reputation." She stopped, her breathing was fast and uneven.

Marta used all of her willpower to ignore the insults and remain civil. At the same time, she could not help but revel in the surprising news that she had been in Eduardo's thoughts when she was not around. But she pulled herself together. She knew, of course, that Eduardo could only talk about her in connection to his children.

"You can't be serious about the tabloid story," Marta said in an unsteady voice, revealing her increased agitation. "I would imagine in your line of business you must've learned to ignore baseless gossip. You know it's pure fiction. Yes, we went for a walk, but it was just that. And ultimately, Eduardo's the one in control of his own feelings, if that's ever possible."

A sense of dread kept troubling Marta, brought on by her increasing awareness that, as far as she was concerned, the tabloid story was not entirely misguided. But it was Eduardo's affections that mattered when it came to Claudia.

"Yes, but lately he's been pulling away from me," Claudia said and resumed her pacing. Her face was flushed, and strands of her hair had fallen in her eyes. "And I'm sure when you two are alone, you try to tempt and seduce him. You're desperate to have him!"

Claudia's accusations were absurd. Marta would never attempt to seduce Eduardo, and she wanted nothing more than for Claudia to leave. Her whole body was shaking, and she was grateful that she was sitting down. Her mouth was dry, but she was able to compose herself enough to say, "That's not true. Eduardo's my employer, and I've never made a move on him. And you're right. He's unlikely to find me attractive." Marta shut her eyes—she knew her last words to be true, but when she heard herself utter them, she felt a painful tightening in her throat.

Marta swallowed again and opened her eyes.

Claudia took a deep breath and looked to the side, as if she was thinking what to say next. She pursed her lips as she exhaled and headed toward the front door. Before she reached it, she turned around. "You should know that I'll do whatever's in my power to keep him!"

Marta flinched. She was perturbed by Claudia's callous assertion. She considered not engaging her any further, but she also knew that Claudia's plan had the potential to lead to more misery, not only for Claudia but for Eduardo too. And the thought of Eduardo's suffering made Marta even more indignant.

"Is this what you truly want, even if he no longer loves you?"

"But he's in love with *me*! We're a better match in age and style," Claudia shrieked.

Marta considered Claudia's words. Even though more than a decade separated each one of them from Eduardo, Claudia was the one younger than him.

"Youth and beauty are fleeting, and you wouldn't want his love to be solely based on them." Marta could no longer hide her indignation.

Claudia scoffed. "You think I don't know that? Once we have children, they'll keep us together." Her voice was sharp, but it wavered.

Marta stood up. "Children must *never* be used as an excuse for two people to stay together!" she exclaimed, and Claudia recoiled at her sudden outburst. "Especially when their relationship is irrevocably broken. It's well known that it's terrible for the children, and it never works for the couple."

Marta thought about Ilian and how hard she had tried to convey to him the same idea, but she had failed every time.

During one of the more heated fights with Chris, when Marta had thought that they were alone, she had noticed Ilian's pale face peeking through the open door. His eyes were wide with fear, and she felt as if her whole body pooled at her feet. She had rushed toward him to give him a hug, but Ilian had run upstairs to his room and slammed the door in her face.

Provoked and extremely upset by Claudia, Marta realized how hopeless she had been at handling this conflict too. She had no control over their conversation, and it was making her progressively more miserable. She returned to her seat, and once her breathing became steadier and her thinking less feverish, she decided that trying to end this encounter as cordially as possible was the only sensible thing to do.

Feeling composed enough, Marta said, "Claudia, would you please sit down for a moment? I want to tell you something I've learned about Eduardo."

Claudia narrowed her eyes, but she walked back into the living room and sat in one of the chairs.

Marta's hands were still shaking slightly, and she began. "Deep down, Eduardo is a kindhearted person. He is generous, and he cares about those who are less fortunate than him. And although he is very busy, he tries his best to find the time to do more than just play football—"

"And what does any of this have to do with me?" Claudia interrupted.

"I would encourage you to talk to Eduardo and connect on a deeper level with him. Find out what he likes and dislikes, what his passions and fears are. And try to figure out how yours match with his, what you have in common that is beyond beauty and vigor."

Claudia's tense face relaxed, but a confused expression

wrinkled her brow. She pulled herself up and declared, "Eduardo's only passionate about two things: football and me. And I'm a strong and independent woman. I'm not going to match myself to his interests and desires."

"That's not what I meant. By all means, be yourself, but also consider your partner's feelings. Listen to him and be there for him when he needs you. He is more vulnerable than you think. And . . . don't assume that he is only interested in beauty and sex."

"But sex and football are the two things most important to him. And it's not surprising because he's a top athlete in his prime."

Realizing that she failed yet again at mollifying Claudia, Marta shook her head and said with unhidden exasperation, "I do believe that you're very much mistaken. But even if you're right, then you might want to look for *love* elsewhere."

Claudia's expression soured. "I wouldn't need to look somewhere else if it wasn't for you!" she shouted.

"I gathered as much," Marta replied. "But you also need to understand that I'm not the right person to discuss this with. It's utterly useless, especially if your purpose is to cling to Eduardo's heart."

Marta had had enough of this conversation, and she desperately wanted it to end. She jumped from her seat and opened the front door.

"I don't have anything more to say to you that would be helpful to either one of us. And, I'm afraid, I have to ask you to leave because the children need to come inside. Goodbye, Claudia."

Claudia hesitated as if she wanted to say something more, but eventually gave up and stormed out of the house. Marta shut the door and exhaled in relief. She would make sure never to be alone with Claudia again.

Marta walked back into the living room and looked out the window facing the ocean. A boat ripped across the ocean's wrinkly surface like a scalpel cutting through withered skin, but instead of a red bloody mark, the boat left a white frothy trail behind it. Marta's heart was beating rapidly, and there was a loud buzzing in her ears. She closed her eyes and took a deep breath. When she opened her eyes, the boat was gone, and the ocean remained unscathed. Its immense power to self-heal seeped through her pores.

Clear thoughts flooded Marta's head, and she was startled by her need to defend Eduardo and her extreme agitation at Claudia's baseless provocations. Or were they? Was it possible that Eduardo had taken a special place in her heart and she was not aware of it until now? Marta was confused by her thoughts and needed more time to think about everything to do with Eduardo.

The children were having peanut butter sandwiches for a snack when Eduardo came home. He placed a sandwich on a plate and joined them at the kitchen table.

"How did the wheelchair delivery end?" he asked Marta.

"Very well. Hugo was so excited!" She told him how she had taken Hugo to Sofía's bakery and had introduced him to her as her new delivery guy. "And Hugo's already 'flying' around, making deliveries as we speak."

"That's great! And how was your afternoon, kids?"

"Claudia comed," Romina said through a bite of bread.

Marta had not intended to tell Eduardo about Claudia's

visit. She did not want to further insert herself into their affairs. And she was exhausted by the avalanche of emotions she had experienced in one day, many of them brand new or long forgotten, and she needed time to process them.

"Romina, don't talk with your mouth full," Marta reminded her.

Eduardo stopped eating and looked at Marta; his eyes narrowed and a shadow of concern clouded his face. "What did Claudia want?"

Marta fidgeted with a spoon. "She seemed more upset by the tabloid story than I expected. But she was mainly confused about your schedule and wanted to know where you were."

"I wonder why she didn't ask me instead." Eduardo relaxed and took a bite of his sandwich.

"That's exactly what I suggested she do," Marta said with a rueful smile.

CHAPTER 18

Green

Marta woke up early one morning and sat in bed with her laptop. She wrote a lengthy email to Gabrielle, which had been long overdue. Marta described everything about her life in Montevideo: the new places she had visited, how Gabrielle would be impressed with how much her Spanish had improved, and how much Marta still enjoyed working with Eduardo's children. She only referred to Eduardo as her injured employer.

Once she sent the email, Marta went into the kitchen. As she poured the boiling water into the coffee pot, she jerked and spilled some of the hot liquid on the counter. Sofía emerged from the basement carrying a large cardboard box filled with evergreen branches.

"Today's the day . . . we decorate . . . the Christmas tree," Sofía announced in Spanish, still breathless.

"There's a specific day for this here?" It was the first week of December.

"Yes, and I thought you might like to decorate one for your room. So, I brought you mine."

Marta was touched by Sofía's thoughtfulness, but something bothered her. "I would feel better if the tree was placed in the common part of the house. Or wherever you usually keep it," she said. She also did not want to tell Sofía that she preferred real trees. The memories and emotions associated with real Christmas trees were too numerous to describe with her limited skills in Spanish.

Marta's mother loved Christmas, possibly more so because it was considered a religious holiday in Communist Bulgaria and people had not been allowed to observe it. Celebrations of the New Year were supposed to replace Christmas, and instead of Santa Claus, Father Frost came to deliver presents to the children. However, Marta's mother had insisted on celebrating Christmas secretly, and she made sure to do all of the necessary preparations for it. She would spend hours lining up at the grocery store for bananas and oranges because those unassuming fruits were an expensive delicacy only available around New Year's Day. Only years later, Marta found out that bananas were plentiful in the stores in Canada, and they were usually the cheapest fruit she could buy. Fortunately, the traditional Bulgarian Christmas Eve dinner was vegetarian, and thus not difficult to source and prepare—beans and cabbage were cheap and plentiful.

The most arduous task of all was to find the fir tree, always real because the artificial ones were not available back then. The lots that sold the trees were scarce, and sometimes Marta's mother had to purchase the tree all the way across the city. Like most people at that time, she did not own a car, and she dragged the tree through the slushy streets and carried it on the cold trams. Once she arrived in their small apartment, she beamed with pride even though she was panting with exhaustion.

"Marta," she had called as soon as she entered the door, "the tree's here. Now Christmas can come!"

The tree was often miserable. It sported a *Charlie-Brown-Christmas* look, with only a few branches or no branches at all on one side. Once decorated, the tree was cheerful enough, but no matter how gangly it was, it had always smelled divine. And the fir scent reminded Marta of spiced cookies and aromatic beans, cheerful songs, dim candlelight, modest homemade presents, and . . . warm hugs.

As an adult, Marta had kept up the tradition as best as she could once she moved to North America, but without the deprivation and the challenges that her mother had to overcome. Ilian would holler early on Christmas morning, announcing that Santa had arrived, and she would scramble to get to him before he had opened all the presents. With time, his excitement dwindled, and in the past few years, they had a modest meal together, but the tree remained a constant. This was the first Christmas that Marta was not going to spend at home with her son or her mother, and she had toyed with the idea of skipping it entirely. But her mother would not approve of her giving up so easily, and Marta was going to make the best of Christmas while in Uruguay. Maybe it would be a fun adventure for Sebastián and Romina to decorate a real tree.

"Do you know if I could find fresh fir trees in Montevideo?" Marta asked.

"They are very hard to find," Sofía replied. "And even if you do, they would be outrageously expensive."

Marta was undeterred. As soon as she arrived at Eduardo's house, Romina opened the front door and ran out to greet her.

"Today we make the Christmas tree!" Romina shouted.

"I heard," Marta said.

Inside, she found Sebastián and Señora Álvarez surrounded by a couple of large cardboard boxes. While Señora Álvarez extracted the disassembled artificial tree from one box, Sebastián pulled out ornaments and garlands from the other.

Eduardo came rushing down the stairs. "I hope you celebrate Christmas. And if you don't, you might have to this year. The kids wouldn't have it any other way."

"I guess I'm lucky because I do celebrate Christmas. It's one of my favorite holidays."

"We're all lucky then," Eduardo said and turned to say goodbye to the children. He was on his way to his daily practice. Marta ran after him into the vestibule.

"Eduardo, you seem to be doing much better these days. How's your concussion?"

"I think it's better. I haven't been feeling any symptoms for a few days, even after an intensive practice."

"Are you leaving us soon then?" Marta tried to sound indifferent.

Eduardo's eyes brightened. "Not before Christmas. At this point, being so close to the holidays, it was decided that I should get back to my team first thing in the New Year."

"Oh, that's great! I'm sure the kids will be happy." Marta looked down at her feet and added, "There's something I'd like to ask of you."

"Anything. You name it." But when Marta lifted her face toward him, he lost his spark. "What is it?"

"I've always had a real tree for Christmas. There's something special about it, you know," Marta began, and a smile lit Eduardo's face. He crossed his arms and leaned casually on the wall. Encouraged, Marta recounted all the benefits of picking a real tree and decorating it, and how much fun it would be for the children. Finally, she got to the point. "Would it be all right with you if there's a real tree in the house this year?"

Eduardo, still smiling, shouted toward the living room in

Spanish while holding Marta's gaze. "Señora Álvarez, please put the tree back in storage."

"*Sí, Señor*," she replied from the other room.

Eduardo dropped his arms and pulled himself away from the wall. "You might want to consider buying it later. In this heat, real trees don't last long. But I don't envy you for convincing Romina and Sebastián that today you'll be doing something different than decorating the tree. I wouldn't want to miss this spectacle, but sadly, I have to go. I'm already late." He picked up his duffle bag and slung it over his shoulder.

"Thank you," Marta said. "And you're right. I hadn't thought of the heat."

Eduardo opened the front door and walked outside toward his car.

Marta shouted after him, "But I have an idea!"

Eduardo gave her a thumbs-up and jumped into his car.

Marta returned to the living room. The children were noisily sorting through the ornaments and had not noticed that Señora Álvarez had taken the box with the tree away.

"Sebastián, Romina! I would like us to do something special today."

Romina jumped up and down and Sebastián screamed, "Yeah!"

"Okay, in that case we need to start with finding a real Christmas tree. Let's go on an adventure!"

The children seemed unsure at first, but adventure must have sounded good to them because they went into the vestibule and put on their sandals without any prodding. In the meantime, Marta's mind raced. She had no idea where to go in search of a real tree, and how she would be able to bring it back to the house if they did find one. She picked up her phone and dialed Luisa.

Marta explained her predicament with as few words as possible.

Luisa laughed. "You're such a spoiled North American who has to have everything just as you're used to," she teased. But before Martha could protest, she added, "I'll give you all a ride."

An hour later, Luisa, Marta, and the children returned to the house, immediately followed by two men in a pickup truck. The children poured out of Luisa's car while the men carefully slid a fir tree out the back of the pickup truck. Once the men had carried it into the house in a large pot, Marta handed one of the men a couple of bills and they left.

She looked at the tree with unreserved pride. She had thought of the idea of a live tree but was not sure whether she would be able to find one. But the one she did find would last until Christmas, and afterward, she thought she could donate it to a charity, or to someone who could plant it somewhere. Marta inhaled deeply. It was the middle of summer outside, but she felt as if it was Christmastime in the winter. The evergreen aroma gently permeated throughout the warm house, and the children were untamable.

Romina had picked up one of the garlands and was dragging it toward the tree, and before Marta could notice, Sebastián had already placed a couple of ornaments on the lower branches. Marta gathered the children around her and tried to slow them down. She wanted them to savor every moment.

"Kids, before we decorate the tree, we need to have some music," she said.

Marta connected her phone to the speakers, and the first notes of "O Holy Night" filled the air. The children finally stopped moving, absorbed by the music. Marta's shoulders relaxed. Images of little Ilian, either wrapped up in a garland, or with cookie dough smudged on his face, or covered in shreds of wrapping paper drifted through her head. The lightness in her chest was replaced by a sense of heaviness. Grown-up Ilian had told her that he was going to spend Christmas with his father. Marta knew this meant that they would have a simple dinner together, the same as on any other night. His father never cared about Christmas, and he especially disliked the decorations and the fuss about presents. Marta realized how much she missed Ilian, and she made a mental note to call him later that evening. Hopefully, he would pick up the phone. But right now, she had to focus on decorating the tree, as Romina was trying again to place the garland on it.

Marta was perched on a step stool as she placed the last few ornaments on the taller branches of the tree where the children could not reach themselves. After she fastened the last ornament, she stepped down and turned on the electric lights. A brief "Aw!" came from Romina's lips. Her eyes were wide, and she clapped her hands together. Marta gathered the children around her on the couch and told them, just as her mother had told her, that if they squinted while looking at the tree lights, they would see stars. "Oh, yeah!" both children exclaimed while squinting at the tree.

The music was still playing in the background when Eduardo entered the living room. At first, a genuine surprise was visible on his face, and it was eventually replaced by a warm smile that spread to his eyes. Romina ran to greet him, and he picked her up in one arm while patting Sebastián's head with the other.

"Papá, the Christmas tree!" Romina said. "Isn't it pretty?"

"It's beautiful!"

"And it's magic. See the stars? Close your eyes! Like this," ordered Romina, while scrunching her whole face.

Eduardo squinted his eyes. "Yes, I can see them. Romina, you must be a fairy."

"No, Marta magicked it."

"Hmm, did she?" Eduardo said and looked at Marta. His eyes sparkled with the same intensity as Romina's did when she was delighted with a lollipop. Marta felt lighter, effervescent, in unison with everyone else.

Eduardo moved closer to the tree, still holding onto both children. "And it smells amazing." He lowered Romina to the ground and said to Marta. "So, you did find a real tree? And I can see that it'll last at least until Christmas."

"I did!" Marta announced like a child who had just been praised for figuring out how to tie her own shoes.

When Eduardo spoke again, his sober tone subdued Marta's exuberance. "How did you bring this tree all the way to the house? It must be heavy."

"The way all single women do—by paying men to do it."

Eduardo's face turned grimmer. He took his wallet out of his pocket and pulled out a stack of pesos. "The tree must've cost you a small fortune. Allow me to pay you for it."

Marta looked at his hands in a desperate attempt to hide the tears brimming her eyes—of course, she did not belong in their group. Eduardo had just made it clear. Abrupt resentment boiled inside her. Able to compose herself just enough, she mumbled, "It wasn't a big deal. This whole real-tree idea was mine, and no one else needs to pay for my spoiled North American ways."

Eduardo frowned in confusion.

"Never mind! That's how Luisa fondly refers to me." She was relieved to see that he put the money back in his wallet.

When he looked at her again, his face was illuminated by a familiar mischievous grin. "Well then, what other magical powers do you have, Marta?"

Not long ago, Eduardo's lighthearted teasing would have amused her, but now his words saddened her. Marta's feelings for him were too strong for frivolous banter. She managed to smile and whispered, "I can turn children into little monsters?" Speaking louder, she leaned down toward the children and said, "Next time I come, we'll make Christmas cookies!" The noise the children made reached fever pitch.

Marta sighed as soon as the front door shut behind her.

CHAPTER 19

Coral

The following morning, Marta stood still at the edge
of the water where the waves kept crawling up the
shore. As they withdrew, broken shells and smooth
pebbles tumbled in the foamy trail. Tiny holes emerged in
the sand just before a new wave blended them into obscurity.
With each retreating wave, Marta's feet sank deeper into the
sand. At first, she enjoyed the cool tickle of the water grazing
her ankles, but suddenly she felt as if she were being sucked
down into the familiar vortex of what her life had been.

She wondered what made the little holes. She lifted one
foot and dug into one of them with her big toe. But there
was nothing but sand. Marta was disappointed that she did
not discover a small creature buried in the sand, gasping for
air through the hole. Knowing that the holes had a purpose
would have been reassuring to her.

Marta gazed at the vast ocean gleaming in front of her. At
least the tabloid story had fizzled on its own, and she was
free to roam around and be amused by the mystery of her
fanciful air ducts. She finally extracted her feet from the wet
muck and pranced back across the hot and dry sand. She
stopped when she reached the patch of grass that separated
the shimmering haze of the beach from the noisy street. She
took a deep breath and dove into the bustling city.

Once at home, Marta poured herself a glass of lemonade
and was about to go to the backyard but was stopped by a

knock on the front door. She opened the door and exclaimed in surprise.

"Hugo!" Seeing him in his wheelchair still made Marta giddy with excitement that he was able to move around independently. She helped him push the wheelchair over the shallow doorstep and led him to the backyard. Once they settled around the patio table with two glasses of lemonade and a plate of cookies, Hugo glanced at her and blushed.

"What's up?" Marta asked.

Hugo fidgeted in his chair and took a sip of his lemonade. Finally, he said, "I've been thinking that I might want to publish my poems online." He looked at his clutched hands resting on top of his legs.

"Oh! That's cool!" Marta said, pleased that he had considered her earlier advice.

"But I don't know where the best place is to publish them."

"Let me get my laptop and we'll see what we can do."

Once she retrieved her laptop, she placed it on the small patio table in front of Hugo and opened its cover. While the computer booted up, Marta said, "I have to tell you, I don't know anything about publishing online. But I wonder whether Ilian would be willing to help us."

"Who?" Hugo asked.

"Ilian's my son. He is about your age and does almost everything on his computer, and he knows his way around the internet. He might know what websites to use to publish your poems. I'll ask him." Marta picked up her phone and typed a message. Hugo took a bite of a cookie while he waited.

Marta set her phone down on the table. "Hopefully Ilian will reply soon. He doesn't always, but it's worth a try." She also reached for a cookie and took a bite. "Ilian is taking a course in English lit, and they're studying plays—"

A beep sounded on her phone. She smiled while she read the message. "Wow! Ilian's on it. That was fast." She typed a quick reply to his text while she continued to talk. "He'll let me know when he's found a good website for your poetry." She set her phone down again and leaned back in her chair. "What made you want to publish your poems online all of a sudden? Would you let me read some of them?"

"Yeah. Actually, I brought you a Christmas present. I know that you, of all people, wouldn't mind early presents." Hugo pulled a notebook from his backpack and handed it to her. A red ribbon was sloppily wrapped around it.

Marta opened the notebook and examined the first page. The poem was handwritten in English and comprised of two verses. It was titled, "At Dawn." Hugo's poem was a metaphor for a person's life, a path stretched from dawn to dusk. It painted a picture of a difficult and treacherous road, but the ending was uplifting; despite the hardships, the narrator felt he had lived a good life. Marta saw herself walking along the path and felt the visceral anguish of the poem. The ending, however, gave her hope, and she was assured that as long as she continued to make the right choices, her path would end with her integrity intact.

But how could she be sure that she was making the right choices? It was the same question Eduardo had asked her during their evening conversation on his patio, and she thought she knew the answer then. But she was not so sure anymore. Her growing feelings for Eduardo were concerning and his behavior toward her was confusing. And she had been mistaken before. Marta had thought her former husband had been in love with her at a time when he no longer was, and she had ignored all the signs, even when they were painfully clear.

Marta lifted her head. "It's beautiful, Hugo, and it's poignant. And other than the melancholy tone, it has no trace of communist ideology."

Hugo laughed in his grunting way. "I don't know what made me want to publish them now. I thought it wouldn't hurt to try. And it would be cool even if only a handful of people read them. It'll be more than one!"

Marta nodded. "That's the spirit of a true artist. An artifact becomes a piece of art only when it touches the life of at least one person other than the artist."

"I know you think that. I remember when you told me about your parents, something about them falling in love over poetry?"

Marta was impressed that he remembered.

"I thought, I can't hope to ignite a spark of passion in anyone's heart unless I let others read my poems. And I'm still unsure if anyone will be interested in them, but at least I'll know I tried."

Marta was about to say something when her phone beeped. "Ilian found a website for you. Shall we try it?"

Hugo hesitated but Marta gently nudged him. "Are you in a hurry?"

He shook his head.

"Okay, let's do it then. Here's the computer ready to go."

They spent the next hour looking at the website, reviewing what others had posted already, creating an account for Hugo, and figuring out how to post and what it took to keep track of visitors to his site. "At Dawn" was the first poem they shared with the world.

Later that night, Marta read all of Hugo's poems. There were about a dozen of them, and less than half were written in Spanish. His poetry was concise and painted vivid images with a few resonant words. The topics of his poems were quite diverse. She had expected them to be dominated by the strong and unforgiving passions of a determined and rebellious youth. A couple of his poems were forceful in revealing his youthful idealism, but several dealt with tender and romantic feelings such as unrequited love, the ache for a gentle touch, and the sweet tenderness of first love. Not fully polished, his poems were raw, honest, intense, and touched upon universal themes, many of which were likely to be of interest to many of Hugo's peers. Marta turned the light off, and visions of the relentless breathing of the ocean surf lulled her to sleep.

The next day, Marta brought Hugo's notebook to Eduardo's house. She read one of the poems to the children, but they were not as taken with it as she was, probably due to the lack of rhyme. They spent the rest of the morning on the beach and came home for Romina's nap. In the meantime, one of the neighbors' children came to play with Sebastián, and when Romina woke up, she joined them in the front yard. Through the open front door, Marta could see that they were searching for bugs among the gravel rocks on the side of the driveway. She remained in the living room and opened Hugo's notebook.

Her quietude was shattered by Romina's piercing cry. Marta jumped up and ran into Sebastián at the front door, who shouted that Romina had fallen down. Marta found her sitting on the asphalt, and both her knees were scraped and bleeding. Small pebbles and dirt covered her wounds, and she was crying inconsolably. Sebastián's friend left, and Marta picked Romina up and carried her all the way to the bathroom on the second floor. She remembered seeing a box of Band-Aids in one of the drawers there.

Marta washed the wounds with soap and water and put a bandage on each knee. By that point, Romina was only hiccuping and her face was red and wet. Marta gave her a hug and wiped her face with a towel.

"Okay, you can get up now," Marta said.

Romina stood up, but winced and began crying again, refusing to go any further. "It hurts," she whimpered.

Marta knew from her own experience that once the initial shock was over and the surface wounds were cleaned and bandaged, the pain was not as noticeable. "Why don't you try again? Otherwise, you'll have to spend the rest of the afternoon in the bathroom by yourself."

Romina stood up and, complaining bitterly, she descended the stairs, pausing at each step and not proceeding to the next until both of her feet were on it.

Marta sat on the couch with the children but remembered to look at the time, and she jumped. It was past five o'clock. Eduardo was very late, and with Romina's minor accident, Marta had lost track of time. Today was Luisa's birthday, and Marta had made a reservation for dinner at a restaurant in the Old Town for seven o'clock. She still had to go home to change, and unless she left immediately, she would be late.

Fortunately, Eduardo came home just then.

"Thank goodness you're back!" Marta exclaimed. Before he had a chance to say anything, she quickly recounted Romina's accident. And after assuring him that all was well, she left. Only once she was seated on the bus, Marta realized that, in her haste, she had forgotten Hugo's notebook on Eduardo's couch.

CHAPTER 20

Indigo

For the next two days, Marta was busy helping Luisa prepare a house to be shown to prospective buyers. She had no idea that the homes people visited during an open house were first scraped of clutter and trimmed with just the right number of decorations: a vase of fresh flowers in an entryway, a fleece throw casually spread on one end of a couch. Marta learned that it was possible to achieve the look of careless order even if it was an oxymoron.

The next time she arrived at Eduardo's house, he opened the door holding Hugo's notebook. "I believe this belongs to you," he said as he handed it to her.

"Yes, thank you. I forgot it in my mad dash."

"I never had a chance to explain why I was so late the other day." Eduardo led Marta into the living room. "At the end of my practice, my neurologist came, and we had an unexpected meeting with her and the coaches about my health and next steps. I should've called you, but I kept thinking that the meeting would be over quickly, and by the time it was actually over, I rushed to get home as fast as I could."

"It's fine. You came home in the nick of time."

Eduardo narrowed his eyes. "Are you sure you're not angry because I was more than an hour late?"

Marta felt a pang of guilt for treating him so harshly the first time he was late to meet her. She shook her head and looked around the room in search of the children. "How are Romina's knees?"

"She's fine. She's already forgotten about them. She's drawing in her room, and Sebastián must be playing in his."

"The kids are awfully quiet. In my experience, it's never a good sign."

Eduardo laughed. "You might be right. But I'll take the peace and quiet while it lasts and deal with the horrible consequences later."

Marta fidgeted with the cover of Hugo's notebook. After observing her hands for a while, Eduardo said, "The notebook was left open on the couch . . . and because I wasn't sure what it was—I couldn't help myself and read a few of the poems in it." He paused again and asked cautiously, "Are they yours?"

"Oh, no. I can't write poetry to save my life. No, they are Hugo's. He gave me the notebook as an early Christmas present."

"I can't say I know anything about poetry, but I like them. Especially the first one. It seems to describe a sad path, but it ends on a positive note. And, as you know, I like happy endings."

His reaction to the poem was almost identical to Marta's, which compelled her to say, "Yes, it's a happy ending of a sort. I guess, one that we would all be satisfied with if we're lucky enough."

"It touches something inside you. I can't describe it." There was nothing forced in Eduardo's enthusiasm for the poem. "Has Hugo written many poems? Has he published any?"

"Not until a few days ago. He asked me to help him post

his first poem online. Like most artists who are just beginning, he's shy about his poems and doubtful that anyone would be interested in reading them. But now we wait and see." Marta smiled. "He thinks it would be a miracle if he gets a hundred views. But I think with enough time, maybe a few months, he might get there."

Eduardo rested his elbows on his knees and looked at his laced fingers. "You said he posted the poem on a website?"

Marta nodded.

"Do you think he would mind if I posted a link to his poem on my social media accounts? You know, I have a fair number of followers, and some of them might like it too. In any case, it never hurts to spread the word."

Marta was taken aback by the unexpected offer, but by now she had been given enough opportunities to recognize this gesture as true to Eduardo's generous nature.

"I don't know. But maybe . . . maybe you're right. You could help Hugo's online visibility. At least, it won't hurt . . ."

Marta was aware of her incoherence and stopped to think of what to say next. If she were to allow Eduardo to go ahead with his plan, it meant that he would become more closely connected with Hugo . . . and with her. But then, Eduardo had already been introduced to Luisa, and it would be natural for him to meet her other friends too.

"Actually, I don't think Hugo would mind, considering that he himself wanted to publish his poems online. He said he's ready to share them with others." Since the purchase of Hugo's wheelchair, Marta was officially no longer working for Eduardo, having refused to receive any money from him. At first, Eduardo had protested but eventually conceded, and as an alternative, he had proposed that she continue to visit with the children. Therefore, friendship between Marta and Eduardo was no longer a possibility. It had become a reality. "Yes, I believe he'll be fine with it."

"Okay. Let's do it." Eduardo stood up and sat next to Marta on the couch. She pulled out her cell phone and sent him the link.

Eduardo clicked on the link and squinted as he read the small font on his phone. Marta watched his eyes move as he read the lines. Once he finished reading, he typed quickly. "It's done," he said with a slight shrug.

"Thank you. It would be amazing if you manage to turn some of your soccer fans into poetry buffs. Now that would be what I'd call true sorcery."

Marta's hands were filled with shopping bags, and she kicked the front door shut. She had been at the market getting supplies for the Christmas gifts she was planning to make for her friends. She was about to head upstairs to drop off the bags in her room but was startled by a loud knock. She dropped the bags on the floor and opened the door. Hugo zoomed right passed her. Once he was in the middle of the room, he spun around to face her. He was flushed and breathless, and his eyes sparkled. Marta had never imagined that Hugo could get this animated.

"My poem," he announced, still panting. "It's getting hundreds of views. And somehow I'm making money too!" He paused to catch his breath. "It must be someone's cruel joke! Or it's one of those malicious bots I've heard about. I can't explain it."

Marta could not help but laugh at Hugo's reasons for his incredulity. "Calm down, Hugo. I think there's a far less sinister reason for your success. The bot's name is Eduardo Rodríguez." And she proceeded to tell him about Eduardo's role in promoting his poem on his own social media accounts. Then she noticed Hugo's creased brow. "I hope you're not upset with me. I thought it wouldn't hurt to spread the word about your poems. And since Eduardo offered himself, I thought, who'd better to do it than someone who already has a sizable presence online? It was all kindly meant . . . but I see now that I should've checked with you first."

Hugo shook his head. "No. It's very flattering to know that so many people have read my poem. I guess Eduardo's even cooler than I thought. Why else would he want to help someone like me? Someone among the thousands, maybe even millions, of strangers who think that they know him because they've seen him on TV." He looked sideways at Marta. "Or he must like you a lot."

Marta blushed. "I believe he genuinely liked your poem, Hugo. I had nothing to do with it, other than . . . inadvertently provide him with an opportunity to read it. And his daughter has two scabbed knees to prove it."

"Whatever you say. I plan to publish a new poem every week. I've already written dozens, and I feel inspired to write more. Because I'm able to move about a lot more, I meet more people, and they all give me new ideas."

Marta felt his exuberance and was reminded of her students. She had managed to avoid thinking about her work while on her leave, but now she felt the sudden urge to go back to her teaching.

Hugo interrupted her thoughts. "Do you think that's a good idea? Not to publish them all at once?"

"Yes, I think it's a great idea," Marta replied. "This way, you keep the people who are interested in your work coming to your site regularly. And you also provide them with something to look forward to every week. It's better given in small doses than all at once. You don't want to overwhelm them."

Hugo laughed. "I agree. My poems can be overwhelming."

"And also consider, once you publish everything you've written already, you may need more time before you write your next one. But by posting slowly and regularly, you give yourself more time to write the new ones so that you remain consistent. I don't know much about online publishing, but from a human behavior point of view, you don't want to have too long of an interval between stimuli or postings of new material. People would easily lose interest."

"They may lose interest even with regular stimuli, as you call it," Hugo said.

"Yes, but you can still try to do your best to avoid that. By the way, how do you access the internet when you don't have a computer?"

"I use the computers at my local library. And sometimes I borrow Carlos's laptop. Another reason to publish less often!" Hugo remained quiet for a while before he said, "Marta, I've decided to apply to university."

Marta took a sharp breath. "Hugo! That's wonderful news! Oh, I can't tell you how happy it makes me! You'd have such a great time in university, I know it." She gave him a hug. Hugo patiently waited for her to calm down. Finally, she sat back in her chair and asked, "And have you thought about what you might want to study?"

"Yeah. And you'd probably guess it easily. I'm thinking of political science. That or history, or some combination of the two."

"Oh, I'm sure that whatever you want to study, you'd find

interesting and you'll do great. I knew it from the moment I first met you. I had a feeling that there's a bright future ahead of you. All that reading was bound to amount to something."

Marta was satisfied with the small part she played in encouraging Hugo, and she could not stop smiling. More temperate thoughts finally broke through the excitement.

"Is university expensive in Uruguay?" she asked. "How can you and your mother afford it?"

"Public universities in Uruguay are free," Hugo explained. "I hope to get into Universidad de la República. It's the biggest and oldest university in Uruguay. If I do get in, I'd have to pay only for books, transportation, and stuff like that. I figure, if my poems are as popular as the first one I published, and I keep working for Sofía part-time, maybe I would be able to afford it."

"I'm so glad to hear it," Marta said. "You're lucky, Hugo. Uruguay is such a special place, no matter how disgruntled you may be."

"You're right. I do count my blessings almost every day." His eyes avoided Marta's face. "And I wonder whether there'll be a day when I could pay you back, even for a fraction of what you've done for me already."

Marta held onto the armrests of his wheelchair. Her face was close to his, devoid of her former joy. She waited until he finally looked up at her, and then she said with mock sternness, "Listen carefully, Hugo. I'll tell you a secret. I'm an extremely selfish being. Whatever I've done, I've done it for myself."

Hugo's face brightened, and she let go of the armrests and straightened up. "And you can't expect me to be proud of that. So, let's keep it a secret. But do let me know when you graduate, or get a job you love, or make enough money to get married and buy a house. To the ruthless capitalist that I've become, those would be enormous returns on my small investment, and I'd be foolish to ignore them."

Hugo grinned.

CHAPTER 21

Burgundy

Marta made several batches of four different types of Christmas cookies. She made half of them at home and half with Romina and Sebastián. She wanted to make a lot of cookies because it was her tradition to give boxes of them to family and friends. And although her family was not nearby, she had friends in Montevideo. That also included leaving a big batch at Eduardo's house for his whole family, who were coming to spend Christmas with him and the children.

Marta was about to leave Eduardo's house for the holidays, but Romina ran up to her and squeezed her tightly.

"Can you stay?" she asked.

Marta tucked a strand of Romina's hair behind her ear and told her that she could not. She had made plans with her friends already, and besides, the house would be too crowded.

Eduardo had been watching them, and when Marta finished, he said, "There's always space for one more."

Marta graciously declined again. She knew that there was no space for her wherever Claudia was.

During the last few days before Christmas, Marta also delighted in making Christmas presents for everyone, amazed that she had never found the time to do it before. She wanted to leave something with each one of her friends in Uruguay that would remind them of her long after she had gone home. She had noticed a seller in the market who was selling linens that she had weaved herself. Marta decided to buy plain white pillowcases and to paint them herself with special fabric paints. She was not good at crafts. But she thought that she could handle this simpler task and was excited by the creative aspect of the fabric-painting. From a different seller at the market, she bought the materials to make presents for Eduardo and his children.

Marta had a wonderful time decorating the pillowcases. She made each one unique, but with her limited artistic skills, she had to make them pretty simple. She decorated Sofía's with grapes, plums, peaches, and apples—she had always associated Sofía with food, her warm and cozy house, and grapevine-covered yard. Hugo's had an unrolled scroll with a quill hovering over it, as if an invisible hand was writing with it, leaving illegible scribbles—Marta did not want him to abandon his passion for poetry. Pedro's was scattered with shells of different shapes and colors, and at the center of it, there was a large, tightly shut oyster shell. As for Luisa, she did not have any specific ideas. After pausing to think, Marta splattered the whole pillowcase with drips of all the colors of paints she had, a la Jackson Pollock—Luisa, in her mind, was this happy, colorful, and indescribable mix of life.

Marta and Sofía were to host the Christmas Eve dinner at their house. Pedro was Sofía's only family member in town. Hugo was coming with his mother, and Luisa was bringing her new boyfriend, Guillermo, who was also in town for the holidays. During the day on Christmas Eve, Marta and Sofía were busy preparing the feast. Sofía did most of the cooking, but Marta made the dessert, which was a traditional Bulgarian pastry made with filo, squash, and spices.

At around nine o'clock in the evening, all the guests were finally assembled around the table in Sofía's dining room. Everyone was dressed simply but had added a piece of jewelry or put on a crisp button shirt to celebrate the festive occasion. Marta wore a sleeveless red linen dress, which hugged her torso closely, and the loose skirt reached just above her knees. She had put on a touch of lipstick, and she felt radiant.

After everyone had eaten the main course and had at least a couple of glasses of wine, the mood around the table was cheerful and loud. They shared old stories about their respective childhoods and, somehow, always ended with an embarrassing situation that made everyone explode in untamed and contagious laughter. In their merriment, they nearly missed a loud knock on the front door. Marta was closest to the door and went to open it.

She exclaimed at the sight of a pair of familiar dark eyes.

"I'm sorry for the interruption," Eduardo said as both Sebastián and Romina gave her a hug. "The children wanted to see you and give you their Christmas presents."

"But isn't all of your family at your house right now? Did you just leave them?" Marta also wondered about Claudia, but the only explanation she could conceive for Eduardo's visit was that Claudia must not be at his house. It was not unusual for people to spend some holidays, especially those most tightly connected to their childhood, with their own parents.

"Yes, we told them that we had to visit an old and evil enchantress, and that she would turn us all into frogs if we didn't visit her tonight," Eduardo replied.

"No, we didn't!" cried the children, giggling.

"Those aren't good manners for a host," Marta said. "Speaking of bad hosts, I'm keeping you all at the door. Please come in." She stepped aside to let Eduardo and the children into the house.

As soon as Eduardo noticed the people gathered around the table, he said, "Maybe we should come back some other time. We don't want to disturb the party."

Instead of replying, Marta took the children by their hands and led them into the room. A wave of boisterous voices engulfed them, and Romina held tighter onto Marta's hand and hid behind her skirt.

Luisa jumped up, pulling Guillermo with her. Eduardo gave her a hug and, flustered, Luisa clumsily introduced him to Guillermo. She assured him that, although Guillermo was from Argentina, he was a big fan. Guillermo smiled nervously and shook Eduardo's hand.

Next came Pedro. His voice boomed as he greeted Eduardo and grabbed his hand without being introduced.

Eduardo laughed and, able to guess who Pedro was, he asked, "How's the heart?"

Pedro froze. But his usual jovial disposition returned. "I feel great!" he exclaimed. "Especially now."

Pedro returned to the table, and Romina and Sebastián followed him. They still remembered the "funny man" who had fixed the night-light in their house.

"I believe Hugo's the last one of my friends you haven't met yet," Marta said to Eduardo.

As they approached him, Hugo rolled away from the table to face them and stopped. He shook Eduardo's hand shyly. Obviously more awestruck by Eduardo than he had let on earlier, he mumbled, "We've met before."

In response to Eduardo's questioning look, Hugo told him about his visit to his school a couple of years earlier and recounted their brief conversation at the time.

Eduardo's face brightened. "I do remember you! You were one of the few kids who didn't like football, and the only kid I can remember who wrote poetry. How are you?"

Hugo's face and ears turned bright red. He looked down at his lap. Finally, he muttered, "And thanks for helping spread the word about my poems. It's been unreal."

Eduardo shook his head. *"De nada."*

Hugo looked toward the table and pointed to his mother, *"Mi madre."* Eduardo waved at her, and Hugo's mother smiled and nodded in return.

Once the commotion caused by the arrival of Eduardo and his children subsided, Sofía said, "Come! Have a seat!"

Eduardo remained standing next to Marta. "Thank you, but we've only come for a brief visit." He was about to address the children, but Sebastián handed a small paper bag to Marta.

"Merry Christmas," he said.

Romina gave her a scroll of paper, which was fastened with a red bow.

Marta opened each present carefully. Romina's was a drawing of a woman, who had two long black lines for hair, two brown dots for eyes, and wore what looked like a yellow triangle for a dress.

"It's you!" Romina chimed.

"It's beautiful, Romina! Thank you." Marta showed it to the whole room and announced, "This is what I look like in the eyes of a three-year-old. It's wonderful!" She gave Romina a kiss.

Next, she opened the paper bag and pulled out a string. A tiny gray elephant—the long trunk was what mostly gave it away—made out of clay dangled from it.

"It's a Christmas ornament," Sebastián explained.

"I can tell," Marta said, and she went to the tree Sofía had decorated and put it on one of the front branches.

Now that the presents from the children were opened, both Romina and Sebastián were ready for new excitement and joined the others at the table. While everyone was talking to them, Eduardo handed Marta a small box. It was wrapped in shiny white paper and tied with a gold ribbon.

"Please open it when you are alone," he whispered.

Marta was intrigued by the mystery but sprang up the stairs and dropped the box off in her room. Soon, she returned to the dining room with three gift-wrapped boxes.

Sebastián immediately noticed and ran toward her. "Are these for us?"

"Yes," Marta replied, and she handed a box to each child. They ripped the wrapping paper as fast as they could and pulled out bracelets that were weaved with black leather straps and strings in each child's favorite color: Romina's was purple and Sebastián's was orange.

Marta helped them put the bracelets on their arms, and while Romina carefully examined hers, she found a small silver medallion weaved into it. She could see that a word was engraved on it and asked, "What it say?"

"Strength," read Marta. "This is called a 'charm' in English. It is supposed to bring you strength. For example, when Sebastián's too pushy and tries to change your mind, you can tell him that you know better than him."

Romina giggled, because any suggestion that she could be stronger than her older brother made her proud and silly.

"What say your, Sebastián?" Pedro called from the table.

"Kindness," Sebastián replied.

"Kindness is the greatest gift for someone who is already strong," Marta explained. Sebastián blushed, and she knew that eventually he would be able to understand her message.

"Wow, these are beautiful! May I see them closer, please?" Luisa asked, and the children ran to her to show her their bracelets.

Marta handed a similar package to Eduardo. *"¡Feliz Navidad!"*

He tore it open and pulled out another bracelet, this one weaved entirely with black leather straps. Eduardo tried to put it on but seemed to have difficulty with the clasp. Marta offered to help him, and while she fussed with the clasp, she could feel Eduardo's eyes on her face.

"Done," she said at last, and stepped back.

Eduardo looked at his silver medallion that read, "Integrity." He smiled and leaned toward her as if to give her a hug.

Marta recoiled instinctively but regretted it immediately. She had been growing progressively more envious every time Eduardo hugged Luisa. Flustered, she looked at the table. Relieved that no one had noticed, she walked toward the children, but not before she heard Eduardo's stifled grunt behind her.

"Sebastián and Romina, it's time to go," Eduardo said as he hurried toward the table and took each child by the hand. "We've stayed here too long already, and we'll be missed at home."

Neither child was eager to go, but Marta reminded them that there would be more presents waiting for them at home, which accelerated their departure. At the door, she gave each child a hug and wished them, *"Feliz Navidad."* Eduardo looked distant and somewhat impatient. He barely looked at her, muttered "Merry Christmas," and disappeared into the dark.

Marta returned to the room and found everyone oddly quiet and still. She took her seat at the table and surveyed the group, trying not to look as despondent as she felt. "What's up? Why are you so quiet all of a sudden?"

Pedro spoke first. "I no like him. He much pretty and moody."

Marta was taken aback until Luisa exclaimed, "Oh my God, I love his smile! He's so much lovelier in person, isn't he?"

"I'm right next to you," Guillermo exclaimed in mock indignation. "And I don't like playing second fiddle."

Luisa burst into loud laughter and gave him a playful kiss.

The volume in the room continued to rise, and the merry atmosphere returned.

But Sofía whispered, "I sense trouble around him."

This was too much for Marta. She excused herself from the table and ran upstairs. Once in her room, she collapsed onto the bed, aching on the inside, though her eyes remained dry. She wished that she had a switch to turn off her feelings toward Eduardo at will, or at least to temper them, but that was one area of herself over which she had no control.

After a while, she lifted herself up and noticed the small box that Eduardo had given her. Marta thought that it might be better to open the box later when she was less upset and her heart was beating more steadily. But her curiosity overtook her willpower. She undid the gold ribbon and carefully unwrapped the paper. The plain box sat on her palm, and Marta stared at it for a while with apprehension, knowing that whatever was inside would reveal something about Eduardo's feelings for her. Finally, she pulled the lid open. On a bed of soft navy velvet, there was a pair of simple, yet extremely delicate, pearl earrings.

CHAPTER 22

Red

Marta was still mesmerized by the earrings when she was startled by a knock on her door. She quickly tucked the jewelry box in the top drawer of her dresser and opened the door. Luisa walked into the room, concern written all over her face.

"I had no idea you've had feelings for him," Luisa said as she sat on the bed.

Marta dropped next to her and closed her eyes. "I'm sorry, Luisa. I haven't been completely open with you. Yes, I've had feelings for Eduardo for a while, but I can't speak them aloud. Especially because they're unrequited."

Luisa took her hand and said without any blame or resentment, "Judging by his behavior tonight, I doubt he's indifferent."

Marta wanted to believe that Luisa was right, but Eduardo's reserve when he left proved her wrong. "I like him, Luisa. I love him! He may not have read many books and hasn't learned much about real life, but I misjudged him. All his life, he's been required to stay focused on one thing, and that's football. But he has an extremely kind and generous heart. If you only knew . . ."

Marta did not go as far as to divulge that she found him irresistible too—an uncanny combination of athletic and bright, spirited and kind—someone she never thought existed. If they had only met at a different time, in different circumstances.

"He loves his children," she said. "He cares deeply about his family. He has a curious mind. And most impressive of all—he knows he has a lot to learn."

Luisa was silent. By now, Marta had become aware of the intensity of her feelings for Eduardo, but never having revealed them to anyone else before, she was alarmed by the depth of her despair. She did not see a future for the two of them. Their time together was limited, and soon they would be separated in almost opposite corners of the planet. And besides, there was Claudia.

A hot tear rolled down her cheek, and Marta swiped at it with the back of her hand. She was weary but forced herself to speak again. "But my feelings for him don't matter because he loves someone else. And please don't resent him on my behalf. He deserves to be appreciated for the person he is."

Luisa wrapped her arms around her and would not let go until Marta's sobs subsided. "Have you told him how you feel?" she asked.

"Of course not. He has a girlfriend, remember?" Marta pulled away from Luisa's arms and wiped her face.

"Claudia must think he at least likes you if she's so jealous of you."

"That may be true, but he's never told me as much himself." Marta was rocking back and forth.

"Has it ever occurred to you that Eduardo may be afraid to tell you because he thinks you'd never consider him an equal? He probably thinks he isn't smart enough for you."

Marta stopped rocking. *Not smart enough for you . . . not smart enough for you . . . not good enough for you . . .*

She had heard these words somewhere else before. Yassen's sad face appeared among her muddled memories.

Marta had met him during her first year at university in Bulgaria, and they had become good friends. He was kind, smart, and was studying to become an engineer. A couple of months after they met, Marta found out about a scholarship competition in the US. At the age of nineteen and never having traveled outside of Bulgaria, she was determined to apply.

Her mother encouraged her, even if it meant that they would be separated for a few years, at least. But when Marta wavered in the face of the magnitude of the decision she was about to make, her mother assured her that it was for the best.

"Men in general," she had said, "come and go. Husbands sometimes leave or die. And it's crucial, Marta, that you do everything in your power to become self-reliant. Only then will you be able to take care of others too."

Marta submitted her scholarship application, fearful of the unknown, but confident that she had made the right choice.

One fall afternoon, Marta and Yassen went for a walk in the park. The damp air soaked through her clothes and she shivered. The raw and musty smell of plant decay filled her nostrils, sure to remind her why fall was her least favorite season. Marta buttoned up her jacket while she chattered away about her hope of winning the scholarship competition.

"Even though it's unlikely I'll be chosen, it feels good to know that I applied," she said.

Yassen was quiet. In fact, he had been quiet the whole time. He looked troubled, and abruptly he blurted out, "I love you, Marta."

Stunned by his confession, Marta stopped walking and

looked at him straight on. He averted his eyes and she leaned to the side to try and catch his gaze. When his eyes finally met hers, Marta was struck by the mix of hope and trepidation she saw in them.

She was aware of the gravity of the situation, but she was unable to find the right words. She thought about how the main heroines in the books she read were effortlessly eloquent in such delicate moments. But now when it was her turn, words failed her miserably.

She cleared her throat. "I don't know what to say." Unable to withstand the hopefulness in his eyes any longer, she looked at her feet, and her voice trembled as she said, "I like you as a friend. Can we remain friends?"

Yassen sat on a nearby bench and Marta followed him. She could tell that she had not compared well with the sophisticated ladies in her novels, and in a frantic attempt to improve the situation, she asked, "Has no one refused you before?"

Yassen scoffed. "Not as ineptly as this."

Marta was distraught. She could feel his pain, yet she was incapable of soothing it. Instead, with every word she inflamed it further. She needed to make him feel better, but she knew deep down that she could not because she was not willing to utter the only words that would have satisfied him.

Instead, she said, "I'm so sorry, Yassen. I know how stupid I must seem, but you caught me by surprise. All I can do is to be honest with you."

"Jeez. Thanks for *that*."

Marta shivered, unsure whether it was from the cold or from the intensity of his anger. She kept twisting one of the buttons on her jacket. Desperate to get out from this excruciating situation, her final solution was to explain. "I want you to be my friend. Honestly, I do. But I don't want to commit to anyone right now—not just you—in case I have to leave the country soon. I know it's a long shot, but I don't want to make plans until I hear from the scholarship agency."

Yassen gave her a sideways look. "Face it, Marta, you're hoping for someone better to come along. I'm not good enough for you."

The button on Marta's jacket snapped and disappeared into the dry leaves that had accumulated beneath the bench. She considered arguing with him, but instead she stood up. "You can always call me. I hope you do."

Marta ultimately won the scholarship. She traveled to the US, where she met and eventually married her husband. Yassen never called, but his words still rang in her ears: *Not good enough for you . . . not good enough for you . . . not smart enough for you . . .*

Marta heard Luisa's distant voice, and it grew louder. "Marta. Marta! Are you all right?"

Marta blinked and said, "I'm fine." She brushed a wet strand of hair off her face.

"You should tell Eduardo how you feel."

Marta forced a smile. "I've told him he's a good father."

Luisa sneered. "Marta, that's hardly an admission of love."

"But I can't do anything more than that for obvious reasons. Besides, he hasn't been forthcoming, either."

"Perhaps it's because he isn't getting any encouragement from you."

Many families celebrated Christmas, or Family Day as it was officially called in Uruguay, with a picnic on the beach. Marta and her friends, having celebrated Christmas Eve together, had no plans for the day. It was hot, and Marta would have loved to go for a swim in the ocean. But when she considered that the beaches were probably crowded, she was no longer interested in the idea.

After lunch, Sofía brought the dishes from the patio table to the kitchen and went upstairs to take a nap. Marta remained outside. She enjoyed the birdsong and the scent of flowers drifting in Sofía's garden.

She was disturbed by the clicking sound of high-heeled shoes. Luisa leaned over her, gave her a peck on the cheek, and sat across from her. She pulled a book from her purse and placed it on the table. "I'm reading this book a friend recommended to me a while ago. It's very romantic, and it mostly takes place in Rome. But I've never been to Rome, and I can't understand its appeal as a romantic place. You always hear Paris described as the City of Love. Have you been to Rome?"

"Oh yeah, I've been to Rome and Paris. And I can totally understand why the author has chosen Rome. I fondly remember young men driving by and shouting out of their cars: 'Bella donna!'" Marta laughed. "I wonder whether Italian men would still be as enthusiastic about me. I honestly doubt it, but I would like to visit Rome again, just the same. Or better yet, I should visit Bangladesh. Apparently, men there would write poems in adoration of my eyes. I really like the sound of that. At least, this is what an old friend from Bangladesh told me a long time ago."

Luisa laughed. "My friend assured me this book has a happy ending. I wouldn't read it otherwise, especially during the holidays. I thought you might like it too. It's uplifting, you know. But I remembered our conversation not that long ago, and you didn't seem to favor happy endings."

"So, they get married in the end? How boring," Marta said. "But you're wrong, Luisa. I love fairy tales, especially the dark, twisted ones. Many have a happy ending, most often in the form of a wedding feast. But in real life, marriage isn't the sole ingredient of a happy ending. For example, in my case it came in my early twenties. I had just arrived in a brand-new and terrifyingly unfamiliar country, I didn't have a job yet, and I knew next to nothing about what I was getting into. If my fairy tale ended there, it would have been a mundane and uninspiring one. Though I did grow up in an Eastern European country during communism, and my life wasn't devoid of angst."

"You know, you've never told me much about your life back in Bulgaria."

"Haven't I?" Marta had not realized that all the stories about growing up in Bulgaria she had told to Hugo and Eduardo but not to Luisa. They were stories from her past, and as such, they had become lasting and real. But her dreams and hopes for the future were still solely her own, many destined to be evanescent, and Marta did not find it peculiar that she had only shared them with Luisa.

"Well, perhaps I didn't because it was boring," Marta continued. "My life—the one filled with purpose and adventures—truly began after I got married. I slew many dragons and solved countless riddles. I moved to yet another country, Canada, and had to face the still terrifying reality of functioning in a new culture while using a second language. And I had a child while also balancing a full-time professional career. And I was bruised and battered by the thorny obstacles and fiery challenges I encountered along the way. And all of that happened while I was married to that same man. But when I'd first married him, it wasn't the ending but the beginning of a long period in my life that was at times blissfully happy and at times extremely melancholy. Eventually, our marriage had to end, and that was *not* a happy ending, either."

"I'm thinking life isn't about happy endings but about promising beginnings," Luisa said after a long pause. "And I wonder what those would look like for you and me."

"Perhaps we just need to turn the page. And it seems to me that you and Guillermo have already done that."

"Yeah, I believe he may be the one, Marta. Life's been happier and steadier with him. And I finally feel at peace."

"I can't wait for the next chapter," Marta said and leaned back in her chair.

CHAPTER 23

Magenta

I t was the quiet week before New Year's Eve, and Marta had a chance to visit with all of her friends. Pedro had fully recovered from the heart surgery and had been gradually increasing his work hours until eventually he reached his usual schedule. Hugo had worked long hours leading up to Christmas making deliveries for Sofía's pastry shop. Sofía had become so accustomed to having him around that she continued his employment for as long as he wanted it. He was not making a lot of money, but enough to save for his modest needs during his university studies. He also met many new people, and Sofía's regular customers were always happy to see him. Hugo had not felt useful and appreciated for a long time, and those feelings energized him. He had less time to read but he smiled more.

Eduardo was getting ready to leave for Spain in a few days, and he was busier than usual. He had asked Marta whether she would like to spend time with the children that week. On Thursday, the day after Christmas, she visited with them. Eduardo's family had just left, and the house was in disarray. Señora Álvarez was giving instructions to two younger women in maid uniforms, who then efficiently stripped beds, vacuumed floors, and scrubbed bathrooms.

Marta meant to keep the children out of the way, but first she had to see their Christmas presents, which they were ecstatic to show her. There was Sebastián's new train track expansion, which included a drawbridge and a two-level tunnel, and Romina's wooden art easel, which was placed by the window in her room. They spent the rest of the morning reading books and blowing soap bubbles on the front lawn, where Marta had spread a blanket in the shade under the trees. After lunch, the two maids left and the house was peaceful again.

While Romina had a nap, Marta stood by the window and observed Sebastián who was playing with a soccer ball by the water fountain in the backyard. Eduardo caught her unawares, and Marta felt oddly self-conscious.

"Thank you for the earrings," she mumbled.

"*De nada.* I hope you like them." Eduardo looked at her, but Marta remained silent. She still burned from the emotions his gift had stirred in her, and liking it was too tepid to be among them.

"Sebastián reminds me of my childhood," Eduardo said as his gaze turned toward his son. "As I told you before, my whole family—we were all involved in football. My older brother is a former football player, and my sister married a football player. So, you see, we're all indebted to the sport." His smile had yet to reach his eyes. "I'm sure you don't approve of this fountain," he said, catching her off guard with the abrupt change in topic.

It was an odd way of asking, but he seemed to care about her opinion, and Marta did not want to disappoint him by being blunt about the truth. "It's not for me to approve or disapprove of your choices. This is your home, and you can decorate it however you like."

"It was a present from my family when I first bought this house. My parents and my brother and sister had contributed the money, and together they had hired a local artist to make it especially for me."

Marta examined the fountain. "It shows that your family loves you and is very proud of you." She still thought the fountain to be as tacky and excessive as she did the first time she saw it. But she also understood the importance of family, and that ultimately, the loving gesture was more meaningful than the actual gift. If she were in Eduardo's position, she also would have graciously accepted it and displayed it regardless of her feelings about it. "And you're wrong. I do approve of the fountain."

Eduardo's smile reached his eyes, dark patches of a summer night's sky sparkling with the brilliance of countless stars.

Marta recognized the burning sensations permeating her body, and she tried to quell them. "Tell me more about football. For example, I've never been able to figure out how offside works."

Eduardo eagerly explained that offside was an easy concept but was hard to see in action. Then he left her side and ran to the kitchen. When he returned, he sat on one of the chairs in the dining room and invited Marta to join him. He placed a piece of paper on the table and drew a picture to help him convey his thoughts more easily.

"I understand the theory of it," Marta said, examining the drawing, "but I still wonder how it all plays out in real time during a game when everything happens super-fast."

"It depends on the situation. But often, you do your best to avoid offside."

This time, Marta looked him directly in his eyes.

"But when you are close to the goal and the ball is coming

your way"—Eduardo hesitated—"you go for the ball, and
. . . hope for the best . . ." His words trailed off, and his face
was dangerously close to Marta's.

They were startled by Romina, who came into the room
and asked to watch a movie. Marta was relieved; his closeness
was disconcerting.

All four of them sat on the couch and watched *My Neighbor
Totoro*.

"I find this movie confusing," Eduardo confessed. "I've
watched the entire thing twice now and still don't know
what it was about."

"The story is ambiguous." Marta agreed. "But I think
it's intentional. It's about several ideas. First, it's about the
environment, and the forest spirit, Totoro, is possibly the
embodiment of it. And then there is the importance of family
and the support and love that parents and siblings give."
Marta looked at Romina. "I admit, I've always found the
story sad. The mother is sick throughout, and it isn't clear
whether she recovered. But in my experience, children love
it," she added and patted the top of Sebastián's head.

Ilian used to watch the movie while he was tested and
treated for his injuries at the hospital. And Marta believed
that it was the kindness, whimsy, and optimism of Totoro
that charmed the children.

She was about to leave for the day when Eduardo handed
her a glass jar wrapped in cellophane and tied with a slim
yellow ribbon.

"A bit of magic of my own. But it only works after dark,"
he whispered.

Marta was curious but slipped it into her purse.

Once home, she placed the jar on the dresser in her room
and went downstairs to help Sofía with dinner. By the time

dinner was over, Marta was drowsy and offered to wash the dishes in the morning. But Sofía sent her straight to bed. Marta turned off the light and pulled the light cotton cover over her shoulders.

She closed her eyes and listened to the dissonant cricket symphony—it was loud and sleep eluded her. She opened her eyes, which were immediately drawn to a few faint lights that were flickering above her dresser. She blinked a few times, but the yellowish-green specks kept shimmering. Remembering Eduardo's gift, Marta jumped out of bed, picked up the jar, and removed the cellophane. *Fireflies!*

She had not noticed them in the daylight, but they produced a bright glow in the darkness of the room. She went to her balcony where she carefully removed the lid and released the fireflies. They swirled and zigzagged in the air. Marta watched their mesmerizing fairy dance as smiling couples whirled and undulated with the rhythmic tempo of a graceful waltz. As their light dissipated in the dark, the elegant music was drowned out by the grating cricket sounds.

CHAPTER 24

Navy

Her journal was almost full, and Marta still had two whole months left of her leave. She decided to go in search of a new one while still in Montevideo and wondered whether Luisa might want to come. Marta planned to ask her at the end of the day after leaving Eduardo's house.

In the afternoon, Marta and the children were at the playground closest to the house. Sebastián ran around playing chase with another boy while Romina dug in the sandbox by herself. Marta sat on a bench talking to a mother. Her Spanish had improved significantly over the course of four months. After a while, the mother left with her child. Marta surveyed the playground and found Sebastián digging in the sandbox next to Romina.

A shadow blocked the sun from Marta's eyes and she looked up. Eduardo smiled and sat next to her on the bench.

"I came home early." He nodded toward the sandbox. "Sebastián and Romina are playing well together?"

"Yes, they are. But give it a minute."

Romina looked up from the sand, and seeing her father, she beamed and waved at him. Sebastián turned around and shouted, "*Hola*, Papá."

Eduardo waved before turning back to Marta. "What have you been up to today?"

"Well, in the morning, the children wanted to do art,"

Marta began. "We painted for a while—we had to try out Romina's new easel, you see—and I tried to help Sebastián understand about perspective. Romina was having fun making patterns with dots of various colors, which made me think of Impressionism. Of course, I couldn't explain that to her, but I told her that her painting is similar to that of some great artists. She was pleased with herself because she thought that she was being silly."

"That's Romina, all right!" Eduardo said.

"Then I decided that it was a good time to go to the art gallery and look at some of the art there," Marta continued. "Sebastián tried to find different ways of showing perspective in the paintings, and Romina was thrilled to see the 'dots' in the impressionist paintings. Once we returned to the house, Romina had a nap while Sebastián and I took turns reading a book—his reading is improving so fast. And when Romina was up, we came to the playground. How was your day?"

"Compared to yours, very boring."

"It couldn't have been that boring. You're back to doing what you love, playing football, right? And feeling your strength coming back must feel good. It's all about motivation, the true drive for everything we do." She stole a glance at Eduardo and then looked away.

"How do you know so much, Marta? And you are so . . ." he appeared to be searching for the right word, but finally settled on, "smart."

Eduardo's unaffected praise was kind and pleasing, but Marta also knew that men who found her smart were often intimidated by her, and she seemed to repel rather than attract them. She had no right to expect Eduardo to be attracted to her, but nonetheless, it troubled her. Compliments also made her self-conscious, and she often aimed to diminish them with diffident denials.

"You're too kind. In all honesty, I know very little. There's so much more to know. And smartness, like beauty, is all relative. It's possible that I seem to know a lot because I'm older now. I'm at an age when I've had a family, and my child's fully grown up. I also had to deal with the loss of people I loved." Marta swallowed. "There are some lessons that we can learn only from experience. There are no books or teachers that could give us the wisdom that we gain through living."

They remained silent for a while, watching the children play. Eventually, Marta perked up. "On the brighter side, we could also grow wiser because of the choices we make. Some of us decide that it's more important to always search for new things to learn or experience. You know me, I'm an awfully curious creature—"

"You don't say." Eduardo appeared to be amused by her curiosity, which was in complete contrast to her former husband, who was annoyed by it, and he often thought her nosey and called her a gossip.

Heartened, Marta continued, "It's all related to that 'integrity' thing I told you about: the choice to remain true to oneself over making choices that are most convenient or aimed to please others."

"Yeah, it's good in theory, but it's very hard to put into practice. Don't you think?"

"True." Lately, Marta had not been sure how to put the theory into practice either.

"If you consider me to be on top of my game—" Eduardo began.

"I most definitely do." Marta was too eager to reassure him.

Eduardo smiled and continued, "—and in order to stay there, I've had to be extremely focused and dedicated to mainly one thing. And I'm expected to spend all of my time and energy on it, usually at the expense of other things. It limited my experiences."

"On the flip side, having many different interests and passions has its downside too," Marta said. "In order to make the time to learn various new things, I had to consciously choose not to be at the top of my game. And here I am now in Uruguay learning Spanish and teaching English instead of plumping up my dossier for promotion."

Eduardo looked sheepish. "My point is that I may be good at football, but I've never been particularly good at school. I didn't read a lot, and now I hardly ever do." Then he continued more confidently, "Maybe it's because I wasn't encouraged as a child. My parents saw my physical talents and put all their resources, everything they knew, toward my training and preparation to be a professional footballer. I don't know, maybe if they'd steered me in a different direction, I would've excelled in that, too."

"Yes, I totally agree," Marta said. "And to add to that, our society has come to expect a certain . . . style from professional football players." She thought better than to mention his silver sports car and fashion model girlfriend. "And subconsciously, you've aimed to mold yourself to those expectations. But you speak four languages!"

"None of them very well."

Marta remained serious and shook her head. "You're extremely good at what you do, and that makes you intelligent and capable in the physical area and, to some degree, in the spatial and interpersonal areas."

"And what are those?"

"Correct me if I'm wrong, but it seems to me that the best football players are not only good at running fast and accurately passing the ball. They also must assess what's happening on the field and strategize about their next moves, often in less than a second. They also have to be aware of their teammates and be able to work well together with them, right? These are all superior skills, either mental or social, in addition to the obvious physical ones."

"It's true," Eduardo said. "Most people who don't play football assume that all we do is kick a ball. But there is much more to the sport than that. I'm currently the team captain of the Uruguayan national team. It's a big responsibility, and it does require the skills you mentioned. Especially when the team is in trouble, boosting the morale—especially of the younger, less experienced players—is key."

"Exactly! And similarly, most people assume that university professors only teach. And while that's one of our primary responsibilities, we also conduct research and train students on how to do their own, and we make sure our departments run smoothly."

"Wow, there's a similarity between our careers. Who knew?"

Not long ago, Marta would not have thought that she had anything in common with a soccer player, especially in terms of their careers. But Eduardo continuously taught her that if she were to look close enough, she would find similarities even in the most disparate things, and the two of them were a prime example. Luisa's reproach still ringing in her ears,

Marta decided that now was a good opportunity to tell Eduardo that she thought better of him than he may have assumed. And the topic of intelligence was the perfect turf.

"You see, people usually tend to think someone is intelligent because they focus mainly on two things. First, on the person's language, or how many rare words she knows. And second, on how good he is in math and logic. And these are the kinds of intelligence that are usually valued in academic settings, such as schools and universities."

"Yeah, that's obvious. So, what else is there?"

"Well, there is another really important way of looking at intelligence. A fellow by the name of Howard Gardner came up with the theory of multiple intelligences. According to him, there are as many as eight different types of intelligence, one of which happens to be being good at movement, balance, and coordination—talents typical of professional athletes and dancers. People tend to be better at some types of intelligence than others, but that doesn't make them less smart."

Eduardo leaned back and stretched his arm along the top of the bench behind her. "Wait a minute. Are you saying that I'm intelligent because I'm good at football?"

Marta smiled. "Yup, I guess you can summarize it that way."

Eduardo looked away.

Unable to read his emotions, Marta felt the need to explain further. "And, you know, one of the big advantages of being a professional football player is that you get to retire early while most of your life is still ahead of you. And you'll have all the time and all the money to do whatever you like, including improving yourself in areas you've never had the opportunity to try—"

"I can't say I haven't thought about that before," Eduardo interrupted her with a slight urgency in his voice. "I've always wanted to learn to play the guitar. Or make a kite."

"Great. I hope you do."

Eduardo was no longer smiling and was breathing quickly. He looked at her and said, "I had no idea you think of me in this way—that you could possibly see me as being more than a dumb jock."

Eduardo's plain and sincere words humbled Marta. But she forced herself to be cheerful, though her voice quivered. "Of course I do. I believe I've had enough opportunities to glean beneath what's readily obvious from your chiseled surface. And to be brutally honest, I was surprised at first."

Eduardo was about to say more, but Sebastián ran toward them and shouted, "Marta, I'm hungry. Can we go home?"

On the way home, Eduardo barely said a word and Marta felt awkwardly shy and mute. As soon as they entered the house, he sent the children to wash their hands. Marta was about to leave, but Eduardo called her name and she turned toward him. His demeanor was extremely serious, with none of his usual lightness about him.

"Marta, I know we don't have a plan with the children for tomorrow. But could you come for dinner? The kids will be gone to Isabella's by then, and I have something to talk to you about."

Marta was puzzled by the invitation, but sensing his urgency, and unable to suppress her own excitement, she said, "Of course. I'd love to."

On her way home, Marta sat in the back of a nearly empty bus. There were a few people sitting toward the front. Marta picked up her phone and was about to dial Luisa's number but hesitated, unsure whether what she wanted to tell her was newsworthy at all or simply wishful thinking. Unable to resist the urge any longer, she touched Luisa's name on her cell phone screen. When Luisa answered, Marta blurted, "Eduardo invited me to dinner at his house tomorrow night, but—"

"*Finally!*" Luisa's voice pierced her ear.

"But I'm not sure it's a date. I've had dinner at his house before, and it's possible that it might be one of those again. The children won't be there, though. Maybe he wants to discuss something that concerns them when they're not around."

"Marta, you can choose to be as rational and negative as you like, but I choose to be an optimist. I suspect that tomorrow is the night. He's figured out where his heart is, and he'll tell you in as many words as it takes to get it through your thick head."

Marta laughed. She hoped her friend was right.

CHAPTER 25

Maroon

T he sound of the birds' energetic song filled the room. As sleep lifted its gossamer veil from her eyes and her thoughts became increasingly more lucid, Marta smiled. Unable to suppress the giddy anticipation of her upcoming dinner with Eduardo, Marta leaped from her bed and opened the small armoire. She ran her hand over the olive-green silk dress she had chosen to wear that evening. And she pulled the jewelry box from the top dresser drawer and lifted its cover. Every time she looked at the pearl earrings, she felt a warmth envelope her as if she were wrapped in a hug. Marta left the open box on top of her dresser.

She expected this to be a leisurely day on her own. Humming, she bounced down the stairs and walked into the kitchen. While she waited for the kettle to boil, her cell phone rang. It was Eduardo, and he sounded desperate. He had to attend an unexpected meeting in the morning, and it was Señora Álvarez's day off. He was wondering—no, he was begging for Marta to come over and spend the morning with Sebastián and Romina. Their dinner plans were still on. Marta was conflicted about the change of plans, but she realized that most of the things she wanted to do that day she could do with the children, too, and she agreed. She inhaled a custard-filled pastry, emptied her coffee cup, and ran back up the stairs. Her favorite yellow cotton dress had to do, and she tied her hair in a loose ponytail.

Eduardo opened the front door while Marta was still walking up the driveway. He was dressed in a pair of jeans and a white linen shirt. He wore the bracelet she had given him for Christmas on his left wrist.

"Thank goodness you're here!" he said. "The kids are crazy this morning. I've got to go, but I'll be back before lunch."

Marta reached the door, and Romina jumped into her arms and squeezed her in a tight hug. Sebastián pretended to spray her with a water gun, which was fortunately empty.

"*Adiós*, Papá," they shouted in unison as they waved to Eduardo, who was already at his car. He waved back and left.

"What shall we do this morning?" Marta asked, and she shut the door behind her. Sebastián was still pretending to spray her with his water gun, and Romina still held tightly onto her neck. "Okay, it looks like I'll have to decide. How about we go to the farmers' market?"

Her suggestion was greeted with disappointment, but Marta reminded them that they could buy peaches and the children suddenly were eager to go. The visit to the market was the usual busy affair, and the children were happy.

When they got back to the house, Eduardo was not back yet. Marta made tomato sandwiches for lunch. Sebastián ate quickly, and Marta had to feed Romina by the end because she was nearly falling asleep at the table.

"Marta, aren't you hungry?" Sebastián asked. He was awfully observant for a young child. Marta replied that it was too hot, and that she was not hungry and would only have a glass of the juice.

Half of Romina's sandwich was still on her plate, but Marta picked her up and carried her to her room. By the time she took her sandals off, Romina was asleep. Sebastián was not as tired, but he had lower energy than usual. Marta suggested that they read a book, and he picked one from the bookshelf and sat next to her on the couch.

"Read this one," he said.

"Please," Marta reminded him.

"Please, Marta, read this one."

Marta smiled and gave him a peck on the forehead. By the time she finished the book, Sebastián was asleep with his head resting on her arm. She gently laid him on the couch and covered him with a blanket.

The house was quiet. Marta longed to go for a swim. The day was hot and she felt sticky. The thought of the cool ocean water made her feel even more impatient. It was a few minutes after one, and Marta sent a text to Eduardo asking when he would be back. There was no reply. She took a book from her bag and sat on one of the patio armchairs. She did not realize how much time had passed when Sebastián walked onto the patio and rubbed his eyes.

"I'm awake now," he announced and snuggled in her lap.

Marta placed her chin on top of his head and hugged him snugly. His head smelled like the sweaty head of a child, which reminded her of Ilian. Not too long after, another figure appeared at the patio door. Romina stood there holding her teddy bear, her hair messy and tangled from her nap. Marta smiled and reached out to her. Romina came over and sat on her lap as well. Marta could hold both children like this for a long time.

All three of them were startled by a sharp buzzing noise: a text message. Eduardo was late and he wouldn't be home until later in the afternoon. It was followed by a curt apology. Marta was frustrated with his lack of acknowledgment that he was asking for a lot more than their original plan. And he had put her in an impossible position since she could not leave the children by themselves. Marta threw her phone on the patio table and exhaled.

"Kids, what do you say we go to the beach?"

The beach was always an easy option for Marta. She did not have to do a lot to entertain the children while they were there. They played in the sand, splashed in the water, and hunted for interesting shells.

When five thirty rolled around, there were no messages from Eduardo. Marta was tired and wanted to salvage whatever she had left of the day for herself. She gathered the children's toys, hats, and shoes, and they started the usual hike up the hill to the house.

Eduardo still was not home at six. Marta was extremely upset. Eduardo's behavior reminded her of a supercilious teenager and not the mature, thoughtful man she had come to admire. She no longer felt desired but jilted. She also did not know when Isabella was supposed to collect the children. But while the children were with her, she did her best to be cheerful. To her relief, the doorbell rang. Isabella had not expected to find Marta and had no idea where Eduardo was.

After Isabella and the children left, Marta tidied up the books and toys that were scattered on the floor of the living room. She was about to leave when she heard the front door open and shut louder than usual. She hurried to the vestibule. Eduardo was there, but he was not a pretty sight to behold. His white shirt was untucked and wrinkled, his hair was disheveled, and he reeked of alcohol. Marta had never seen him inebriated before. As a professional athlete, and especially after the concussion, he hardly drank any alcohol.

As soon as he saw her, he muttered "Sorry," and brushed

past her into the kitchen. He took a glass from the cabinet, filled it with water, and drank loudly while some of the water poured down his shirt.

Marta followed him into the living room. This was clearly not a good time to make her point about being upset with his tardiness and lack of responsibility.

Eduardo was agitated, and he was pacing from one end of the living room to the other. Determined to go home, she picked up her purse and grocery bag, and was about to turn toward the front door when Eduardo finally spoke, his voice low and raspy. "Please, don't go."

"But I must. You seem upset, and rest is what's best for you right now." She was unable to ignore his wild state. "And to be honest, I find you frightening."

He scoffed. "You have nothing to be afraid of."

Marta felt provoked and could no longer resist the urge to reproach him. "I may not have a reason to be afraid, but I have plenty of reasons to be furious. Did you ever consider that I have my own life, and I have plans, and they all went to nothing today because of you?"

"Claudia's pregnant."

At first, Marta was startled by the unexpected revelation, which was delivered in a calm but firm tone. But then she remembered her conversation with Claudia, and his news was not that surprising. And considering how distressed Eduardo was, she wondered whether there was more.

Eduardo leaned on the windowpane and stared out of the patio window toward the ocean. "She got pregnant even though she kept assuring me that she's on the pill." He looked like a wounded animal. His face was dark and his eyes flashed with rage. "How can I trust anyone, Marta? What should I do?"

Marta stood still and her mind went blank. For once, words failed her. All she could think was, *Selfish, unfeeling Claudia!* His pain was palpable and thoughts whirled in her head, but she did not know what would be the most suitable, reassuring thing to say at this moment. Marta's anger at his earlier neglect subsided and was replaced by sympathy.

"I'm angry," Eduardo continued. "No, I'm furious because I've been used, manipulated, and most of all, stuck in a situation I didn't choose for myself." Marta trembled in response to distress. Eduardo turned toward the window, and they both stood in silence for what felt like an eternity.

"The pill is not one hundred percent foolproof," she managed to say. "It's possible for a woman to get pregnant while on the pill."

"I know," Eduardo said. "They teach you this in elementary school." He ran his fingers through his messy hair and said more calmly, "I'm very aware that you want to find the good in every situation, but trust me, there's nothing good in this one." His breathing was shallow and fast.

After a long pause, Eduardo muttered, "I have no choice but to marry her now."

The silence between them was impenetrable.

"There's always a choice, but often not an easy one," Marta said.

Eduardo's eyes narrowed. "Claudia doesn't want an abortion."

Marta rushed to clarify, "That's her choice." She looked down at her hands to avoid his stare and whispered, "I thought . . . you loved her?"

Eduardo took his eyes off her and paced the room again. "I thought so too, but lately we've been drifting apart, and the pregnancy . . ." he trailed off. He stopped pacing. "Since my injury, we've bickered a lot as if we couldn't seem to agree on anything. And for the past few weeks, we haven't been together at all." He peered through the window. "The day after the tabloid story came out, Claudia told me you had refused to leave my house, and she demanded that I get rid of you or else—"

"I'm sorry. Looking back, that walk was a big mistake." Marta's face was burning.

"No, no. There's nothing for *you* to apologize for," he said gruffly. "Anyway, Claudia's threat had the opposite effect than the one she had expected. I told her that I wanted to take a break for a while, that I needed some time to think over our relationship. She was angry and upset but seemed to accept it. Until this morning, when she summoned me to tell me the news in person." Eduardo resumed his pacing, which was slower and more meticulous.

Saddened and filled with sympathy, Marta contemplated telling him about her conversation with Claudia, revealing that Claudia had been even more conniving than he may have realized. This might have relieved him from the obligation he felt keenly to do the honorable thing and marry her. But Marta thought of the unborn child, and when she finally spoke, her demeanor was firm.

"Whatever you decide about the nature of your relationship with Claudia, you should never lose track of the most important issue at hand. The child should have two loving and devoted parents."

Eduardo stopped pacing and sat on the couch. "Come. Sit over here," he said and gestured to the space next to him. When Marta hesitated, he added, "Please."

She sat next to him, making sure that their bodies did not

touch. They sat in silence until he spoke again. "What would *you* have me do in this situation?"

Marta shut her eyes. She was certain that she was not the best person to advise him, and Eduardo would not have asked her if he had been aware of her feelings for him. She opened her eyes. "I don't know, and . . . it doesn't matter what I think." Her voice shook, but she forced herself to continue. "No one really knows what you should do, but . . . you have a good heart. Let it be your guide."

Eduardo was staring at his clasped hands, and she thought this may be a good time to leave. She was desperate to go before she said something she might regret later.

Marta stood up and picked up her purse and grocery bag yet again. Once at the door, she turned to Eduardo. "You have some big decisions to make, and I'm afraid I'm of no use to you. Promise me that you won't drink more tonight."

Eduardo nodded and clutched his face in his hands.

Once home, Marta closed the box with the pearl earrings and placed it back in her dresser. She stared at the specks of dust that had been disturbed by the puff of air emitted by the closing drawer. Illuminated by the dimming rays of the setting sun, the dust specks spun in circles, perpetually perhaps.

CHAPTER 26

Scarlet

Marta woke up with a throbbing headache. Her thoughts were racing, and she kept tossing in her bed. After a while, she could no longer stand it and got up. She stepped into the shower, eager to feel the prickling cleanse of hot water. But no matter how high she turned the tap, and even at its maximum, the water still did not feel hot enough for her numb body. The steam was thick, and she let the water run down her back. Eventually, she turned the shower off, threw on a bathrobe, and sauntered into the kitchen.

Marta went through her usual actions involved in making her morning coffee, but on this particular morning, she approached the task with unusual deliberation. Her movements were gentle and fluid, as if she was practicing Tai Chi in the park. She never stopped moving until she sat at the kitchen table with a cup of coffee in her hand.

She took a sip, and the coffee tasted more bitter than usual. She put a bit of sugar in it, but now it was too sweet. Marta leaned back in her chair and closed her eyes. She could not stop thinking about Eduardo's revelation, and how it had shattered the dream castles she had built over the past two days. Although the dust created by the rubble clouded her thoughts, Marta realized that he had not made his final decision yet. She opened her eyes and sat up straight. Perhaps, if she revealed her true feelings to him, she would give him all the information he needed to make a sound decision. After all, that was what a true scientist would want. Marta slouched back in her chair. Eduardo was not a scientist, and what if he chose to be with Claudia anyway? Marta flinched and rubbed her upper arms, suddenly feeling cold.

She was startled by a loud knock on the front door. Certain that it was Luisa who had come to hear everything about the night before, Marta remained seated. The knocking resumed, louder and more determined, and Marta stood up and opened the door.

Luisa was beaming. But after regarding Marta, her face dimmed.

"What happened? You look awful."

Marta stepped aside to let her in.

"Are you all right?" Luisa persisted.

Marta nodded, and Luisa walked with her to the dining table. Luisa noticed the half-full coffee pot, and she poured some coffee for herself.

"I have to go home. I can't stay here anymore," Marta said.

"I gather it wasn't a romantic dinner after all."

"No, quite the opposite." Marta did not want to talk about her conversation with Eduardo, but she could not see how she could avoid it, not after her broadcast of the news when she called Luisa from the bus. Marta regretted her sudden folly, and now she had to deal with the dreaded consequences.

"But what happened? Was he rude to you? He didn't hit you?"

"No! He was drunk but he wasn't violent. He was extremely upset."

Marta recounted her entire encounter with Eduardo. As she spoke, she came back to the same realization that she needed to leave Uruguay before her six-month leave was up. By the time she finished talking, she had made up her mind.

"He obviously no longer loves her," Luisa concluded after hearing the whole story. "But you didn't know that, and now it's too late."

Marta gasped. "I have to go back home *now*!"

"You have to say goodbye to the children, at least."

"I know, and I'm not looking forward to it. But children are resilient, more so than we usually give them credit for. But I'll comfort them, and myself, with the thought that I'll see them again. And not that much time will have to pass for them to forget me. Or I'll become a dim memory, one that as adults they would introduce with, 'I vaguely remember my English tutor from Canada . . .'" Marta placed her face in her hands.

Eventually, Luisa left and Marta opened her laptop. She had to book her flights to Toronto. She would fly back in a couple of days, which gave her enough time to pack and take leave of her friends. She was not expected at Eduardo's house, but she would go anyway on the following day. But first she wanted to see the children. Marta picked up her phone and dialed Isabella's number. Fortunately, they were free in the afternoon. She told Isabella that she would be coming to say goodbye in case Isabella wanted to prepare the children.

Marta had a plan, and she felt better. There was a purpose to her movements, and they were brisk and efficient. Just before she reached for the doorbell at Isabella's house, Marta took a deep breath and smiled, and only then did she press the button. Romina and Sebastián greeted her at the door.

"Is it true you're leaving tomorrow?" Sebastián asked.

Marta kneeled down, her face at level with Romina's. She placed her hands on each child's shoulder and said, "Yes, it's true. Something unexpected has happened, and I have to go home to Canada sooner than I had planned." Marta stood up and reached inside her purse. "But I brought you some presents to remind you of where I'll be when I'm not here with you."

She gave Sebastián a plastic figurine of a hockey player dressed in the uniform of the Toronto Maple Leafs. "Your papá is a football player, and football is the most popular sport in Uruguay. But in Canada, hockey is most popular. Have you seen a hockey game?"

Sebastián shook his head, and Marta explained how it was similar to football, but instead of playing on grass, the players skated on ice and pushed a rubber disk with a stick. Marta pointed to the figurine and said, "One day, when you come to visit me, we'll go to a hockey game!"

Next, Marta pulled out a picture book from her bag and handed it to Romina. "This is one of my favorite children's books. It's called *Princess Prunella and the Purple Peanut*."

"Can you read it?" Romina asked.

Marta nodded, and Romina led her into the living room, and they sat on the couch. Sebastián placed himself on Marta's free side. When Marta finished reading the book, Romina exclaimed, "Puh, puh, puh. All the words are with puh!"

"Yes, it's fun, isn't it? And when you come to visit me, we'll also prance in pretty petticoats and pounce on peppermints!" Marta gave each child a long hug.

She was about to leave, but before the front door closed behind her, Romina cried, "*Marta!*" and ran toward her. Marta lifted her up and Romina gave her a kiss. When Romina ran inside the house, Isabella finally closed the door. Marta's smile disappeared.

The next morning, Marta noticed that Eduardo had tried to call her several times late the night before when her phone was usually silenced. She sent him a brief text to let him know that she wanted to see him that morning. His response was immediate: he would be home and he would expect her.

After completing item one on her list, Marta made herself a cup of coffee and concentrated on what she would say to Eduardo in person. But in her thoughts, it was difficult to get past "I'm leaving for Canada tomorrow." It all depended on how he would react and what he would say. She decided to leave it to the moment. Hopefully, it would not be too embarrassing for her.

She dressed in a navy lace dress and slipped on her favorite scarlet flats. They always filled her with a dose of spunk, and Marta was particularly in need of it now.

Eduardo opened the door. His face was tense, but he forced a smile and invited her in. He was more formal than usual, which did nothing to relieve Marta's unease.

They sat across from each other in the living room, which reminded Marta of their first meeting. How much their relationship had changed in those short four months! He had now fixed her with a steady gaze and was not letting go of her face.

Eduardo began: "Marta, I'm—"

He was interrupted by loud footsteps coming down the stairs. Eduardo closed his eyes, and Marta turned toward the staircase. Claudia appeared, and she was dressed up even more than usual. She looked impeccable.

As soon as she noticed Marta, she beamed, and without

greeting her, she said, "Marta, did Eddy tell you? We're engaged!"

She stopped to look for the effect of her words, but Marta remained composed. The news was acrid, yet stale, but she absorbed it, securely tucked in her shell.

Claudia continued on her victory march. "Isn't it wonderful? He asked me to marry him last night."

Marta looked at Eduardo, who had covered his eyes with one hand and was rubbing his temples. She turned back toward Claudia and said, "Congratulations, Claudia. Have you chosen the date yet?"

Claudia looked at Eduardo coyly, but he was fixated on his hands. "No, not yet. Eddy's not sure of his plans for the next few months, but we'll be working on it. *¿Está bien, mi amor?*" Eduardo moved his head in a barely perceptible nod. Claudia hesitated as if unsure of what else to say, and she leaned over and gave Eduardo a quick kiss. "I'm going shopping. *¡Chao!*"

Smoky silence filled the house. Marta sat still while Eduardo fidgeted with her bracelet on his wrist. "Do the children know?" she finally asked.

"No, not yet." He looked directly at her. "Marta, I'm very sorry. Claudia was supposed to be gone by now. And I tried to tell you about the engagement, but it all happened so fast."

Marta remembered the missed calls. "That's all right. I'm not at all surprised. You made the right decision."

"Do you really think so? Do you think that I'll be truly happy with her?"

Marta felt the burning traces of Eduardo's eyes on her face. "I'm leaving for Canada tomorrow."

"What? So soon? But why?" Eduardo was feverish.

"It's for the best. Besides, the children don't need tutoring in English."

"But, Marta, do consider! You can't leave so soon. At the very least, you have to tell the kids."

"I've already said goodbye to them." Eduardo looked at her incredulously, and Marta explained, "I visited Isabella yesterday. I'll miss them a lot."

Eduardo was restless. He kept running his hand through his hair. He seemed to struggle to say something. Sensing that her emotions were about to overtake her resolve, Marta stood up and headed toward the door. Eduardo leaped from his chair, and with a few long strides, he reached her, grabbed her by the hand, and gently forced her to turn around. Marta could feel his breath in her hair and could sense his closeness draining her self-control. She pushed his chest with her hand to keep him at a distance, and she shivered as if a jolt of electricity ran through her body. Through the thin fabric of his shirt, she could feel the hard muscles of his chest and the violent beating of his heart. She was about to remove her hand, but he encircled it with one of his and lifted it up to his lips. He placed a soft, lingering kiss on top of it and cradled it with both hands.

Marta closed her eyes. A myriad of feelings flooded her senses, the most powerful among them was the now familiar warmth that enveloped her aching heart. But this time, it did not ease her pain. She opened her eyes and looked at Eduardo, pleading. He released his grip on her hand and she withdrew it.

"When will I see you again?" Eduardo asked.

The word "never" would be apt, but it was too melodramatic. Instead, Marta forced herself to say, "If you bring the children to Toronto, I could take them to play in the snow."

She opened the front door and turned around one last time. "*Hasta siempre, Eduardo.*" Her voice quivered, and a tear rolled down her cheek.

Eduardo stood tall and strong, the pain still raw in his eyes but mellowed by affection and regret. Marta quietly closed the door behind her.

CHAPTER 27

Black

P edro heaved Marta's suitcases onto the carousel, where they jostled toward the black rubber flappers and tumbled into the void. He pulled Marta aside to give her a hearty hug. When he withdrew, his eyes were filled with tears, and he said in a voice raspier than usual, "Marta, here you change everyone life, no your life." He wiped a tear on his sleeve and continued, "I say, you need unclamp."

"What do you mean? I'm vastly better because of meeting all of you," Marta said.

"Yeah, but you go home—hands empty." Pedro was right, as was often the case.

"You know what, Pedro, maybe there isn't a pearl inside this oyster."

"You no fool me!" Pedro winked.

Marta gave Sofía a hug and thanked her for cosseting her and providing her with delights Marta believed to be reserved only for Peter Pan.

"My guest room is yours whenever you want it," Sofía said in Spanish. "Just come back!"

Marta leaned over Hugo's wheelchair. "Keep everything in perspective. Don't let anyone dictate your principles. And I want you to tell me everything about your studies, the courses you love, the professors you hate. The works!"

"I will," Hugo said and his voice choked.

Last was Luisa. Marta hugged her, and their bodies shook intensely; their tears came too fast. Marta did not want to let go of Luisa. She was a rare friend, and Marta would miss her infinite energy and carefree nature, which perfectly balanced her own introverted and thoughtful disposition. Finally, Marta picked up her carry-on bag, turned one last time to wave to her friends, and disappeared behind the security barrier.

Marta's tears kept running, and she hoped that her neighbor on the plane did not notice. She leaned back in her seat and closed her eyes. Eduardo's face loomed large in front of her, the pained expression clearly visible and the unmistakable feeling in his eyes, which she could no longer deny. Marta opened her eyes and touched the top of her hand, the one Eduardo had clutched in his. She imagined she could feel his burning lips on it, and it still felt warm where he had kissed it.

But her tears were not merely flowing for the loss of Eduardo. Marta had come to realize that yet another circle in her life was closing, and it was at the exact same place where it had started—she was not going home in better spirits. Uruguay had been a bright place, providing her with ample opportunities to feel truly independent and to be of help to others. Nevertheless, Marta felt desolate from a sense of loss, and she ached to know its source.

Marta grasped the satiny bronze doorknob and exhaled. She was home at last. It was the same house in which she had nurtured her family and eventually lost it. Marta used to think that the houses on her street were pretty and unique, but upon her return from Ciudad Vieja, they looked tepid.

There were hardly ever any people walking on the sidewalks, and the closest coffee shops were a few blocks away.

It was cold and dark inside the house, and the musty smell was a sharp reminder that the house had not been occupied for months. It was the coldest part of winter in Toronto and Marta shivered, her body not yet adjusted to the abrupt change of seasons. She dropped her bags inside the door and headed to the thermostat. Once the hot air started blowing from the vents, she went into the kitchen to get a glass of water. She had a peculiar feeling—the house was familiar, yet removed, as if her own house no longer recognized her.

She climbed the stairs to her bedroom, threw her coat on the floor, and lay in bed with her clothes still on. She pulled the bed spread over her body and fell asleep. It was New Year's Eve, but Marta did not notice the bright reflections of the fireworks in her neighbor's windows, nor hear the muted thunder in the distance.

She woke up and squinted. The sunlight reflected off the snow outside, and it was bright in the room. Marta grumbled and dragged herself out of bed. She pulled the curtains shut and went straight back to bed. She kept drifting to sleep but she was uneasy, and her body kept jerking itself awake. At some point, she got up to go to the bathroom and noticed that it was three o'clock in the afternoon, but she had no idea what day it was.

Marta spent two full days in bed. She only drank water. There was no food in the house, and she was not inclined to do anything about it. On the third day, she woke up with a dull headache. Her starved brain eventually managed to signal to her that it was the lack of food that was making her ill. She was not hungry, but she had enough sense to force herself to go to the grocery store. She bought yogurt, bread, and a few bananas and apples.

Back at home, she walked past the bathroom and froze. There was a bag lady in her bathroom staring right at her. The woman's hair was matted, her clothes were wrinkled, she had dark patches under her eyes, and her skin was pasty. Marta was about to ask her how she got inside her house, and as she moved closer to the woman, she gasped. Marta touched her own reflection in the cold glass. She was a sorry sight but felt empty inside, and there were no tears in her eyes.

Marta took her clothes off and went into the shower. The hot water revived her. It was cold outside of the bathroom, and she ran to her closet and dressed quickly. Once she had a few spoonfuls of yogurt and a banana, she felt her strength come back and her headache subside. She went back to bed.

The next morning, after her breakfast, Marta felt a sudden jolt of energy after days of doing nothing. She took her coat and left the house. As soon as she stepped on the sidewalk, the cold air painfully prickled her face and her bare hands. Marta returned to the house and put on a hat and a pair of mittens, and wrapped a thick scarf around her face. She walked for two hours without any purpose or a sense of time.

As the days went by, Marta kept more or less to the same routine. She would get up, eat a small amount of food, and go out for a long walk: sometimes along the lake, sometimes in High Park, and sometimes along the streets in her neighborhood. She did not care where she was. All she wanted to feel was the breeze on her face. She often spent a long time facing the lake where the wind was the strongest.

She imagined that it blew through her head and carried away all the memories of Eduardo like dry leaves picked up by a gale.

Marta noticed that her clothes were getting too loose, but she ignored them. She did not often look at herself in the mirror, but when she felt that her face was rough and hot, she glanced at herself. Her cheeks and forehead were severely chapped and were bleeding in places. Marta wondered why she had not noticed the pain earlier.

At first, it was quiet in the house, but on the fourth day Marta's phone beeped. She ignored it. Over the next few days, her phone kept beeping or ringing with increasing regularity. She silenced it. When Marta eventually looked at it again, she noticed dozens of texts and missed calls from Luisa. No one in town knew that she was back yet.

Early one morning, the doorbell to Marta's house rang urgently. It was followed by loud bangs on the door. Marta tried to ignore it and hoped the person would go away. The doorbell rang again, ceaselessly; whoever it was, he or she was persistent. Marta walked down the stairs while fumbling with the belt of her bathrobe. She finally opened the door, and her friend, Gabrielle, took a sharp breath and placed her hand over her mouth. Without a word, Marta left the door open and headed toward the back of the house. She heard Gabrielle close the front door and exclaim, "Ugh!"

Gabrielle followed Marta into the kitchen. Dirty dishes were piled everywhere and the garbage needed emptying badly. Marta was drinking water by the sink. Once she placed the glass on the counter, Gabrielle took her by the shoulders and examined her carefully. She placed her hand on Marta's forehead, shook her head, and pursed her lips. She took Marta in her arms and held her for a long time. When she pulled away from her, Gabrielle noticed that Marta's expression had not changed.

"Marta, what's going on? Are you ill?" Gabrielle's voice was shrill, and her face concerned.

Marta opened her mouth and tried to say something, but her throat was dry, and only quiet, unintelligible sounds came out of her mouth. She had not spoken to anyone in two weeks. Gabrielle shook her head, grabbed Marta by the hand, and led her all the way upstairs to the bathroom. She left Marta by the door and turned on the faucet to fill the bathtub. She took Marta's clothes off and Marta did not protest. Once she was in the bath, Gabrielle left her alone. Marta could hear the water running and the loud clatter of dishes coming from the kitchen. Every few minutes, Gabrielle would come to check on Marta and disappear again.

Once Marta was done, Gabrielle helped her back into her bathrobe and walked her to her bedroom. She pulled a nightgown from the dresser and tucked Marta in bed.

"I'll make you supper and some tea," Gabrielle said. But before she came back with the tea, Marta was asleep.

Marta woke up to the smell of warm food. She found a tray, with a bowl full of spaghetti and a small plate of salad, sitting on top of her bedside table. She realized that Gabrielle must have gone shopping for food and had cooked a simple dinner for her. Marta picked up the salad plate and ate a couple of bites. Shortly after, Gabrielle entered her bedroom. Marta managed to smile.

"Thank you," she whispered.

Gabrielle's eyes filled with tears. "Finally! Oh, Marta, you have no idea how worried we all are about you. I'm not going to ask you what happened, not until you're stronger. Until then, I'll take care of you."

"No," Marta whispered again. "Your husband needs you."

"Nonsense, he can take care of himself. Besides, I'm only going to spend a couple of nights here, and once you're on your feet, I'll come during the day to check on you. Okay?"

Marta nodded.

"Do you have a facial cream? Your face looks terrible. Have you been going outside a lot, or is this some exotic disease you brought from the Southern Hemisphere? Which reminds me, it would be a good idea to take you to your doctor."

"No," Marta said weakly. "I'm fine. It's from the cold."

"Okay, you're off the hook. But if you don't get better in a couple of days, I'm taking you to the doctor."

"The cream is in my bathroom."

Gabrielle stayed with Marta for two full days. The food and the facial cream made the biggest difference. Marta had more strength, and the color returned to her skin that was not otherwise burned from the cold. The cold burns were getting better too. She almost looked like herself. Before Gabrielle had to go home for the night, she and Marta sat at the kitchen table and held onto steaming cups of tea.

Gabrielle asked cautiously, "Do you want to tell me what happened?"

Marta shook her head. "Nothing happened, Gabrielle. In some respects, one might say that's the problem."

"Well, something did happen to bring you to such severe depression. You were on the brink, you know."

"Thank you for all your help. I'm feeling better, and I promise you that from now on I'll take care of myself."

"You'd better. Your son still needs you. And please call your friend Luisa in Uruguay. She's extremely worried about you."

"How do you know her?"

"She found me through the departmental website. Smart woman!"

"That's Luisa, all right," Marta said and smiled wistfully. "I'll call her, I promise."

As the days went by, Marta improved steadily. She kept to the same routine: her days comprised mainly of her long walks, but she now read books and listened to music. She also kept her house in order and made food for herself, albeit in small amounts because she never felt hungry.

She finally called Luisa. She was ready to apologize for not responding to her calls and texts, and she dreaded to have to explain the reasons for it. But fortunately, Luisa had the good sense not to interrogate her about it.

"Marta, I'm so glad you called!" she said instead. "You must be doing better, or at least that's what Gabrielle tells me. She's been very good about keeping me in the loop because I didn't want to trouble you until you're ready."

"I'm sorry, Luisa," Marta muttered.

"No, no, don't mention it. All that matters now is that you're feeling better. And you called me!"

"How are you? How's everyone?" Marta perked up.

"We're well. We miss you terribly, and everyone's sending their love." Luisa hesitated. "The day after you left, Eduardo came by Sofía's house. He was on his way to the airport, finally leaving for Europe. I'm not sure why he came, to be honest. Seemed to me that he wanted to make sure that you were truly gone . . . Oh, and I almost forgot. He wanted me to tell you that he and the kids had planted the Christmas tree in the backyard."

Marta closed her eyes. She was not ready to talk about Eduardo. She opened her eyes again and said, "Luisa, I'm very sorry, but I can't do this. Please, let's agree that we'll never talk about him. Can you understand?"

"Yes, I can."

Luisa was a great friend.

A few days later, as soon as Marta opened the front door, Gabrielle declared, "Stop wallowing in misery and self-pity! It's time to raise your head high, put on a new pair of stylish but comfortable shoes, and walk into the sunshine." It was mid-February, and it was still cold and snowy outside.

Marta smiled. "Gabrielle, I've been walking practically nonstop."

"Keep walking more. Maybe it's time to start running. I don't know. You need to get back to living. And it's high time that you tell me what happened in Uruguay that made you so miserable."

"I came home empty-handed." Marta sighed.

"What did you expect to bring? Diamonds?"

"Integrity."

"What do you mean? Have you completely lost your mind?"

"I'm fine, really. I just don't want to talk about it."

Gabrielle went into the kitchen and, after a few minutes, returned to the living room with two cups of tea. She placed them on the coffee table and sat next to Marta. A deep crease etched into her forehead.

"You know that no man deserves this much sacrifice," Gabrielle said. Her face lit up. "You don't want to turn into Miss Havisham now, do you? Although, I have to say, you got pretty close there, sans the wedding dress."

Marta remained serious. "Perhaps. Although it wasn't

my intention to make a sacrifice at the altar of men." Her tone was acerbic, and she shifted in her seat. "In the past few weeks, I've spent a lot of time thinking. And sadly, I can't seem to put my finger on it. In Uruguay I was happy, I had friends, I felt useful, and I was even loved. Yet, I feel destitute, even more miserable than before I left."

Marta was still frustrated with her inability to understand the source of her despair. She had undergone various crises in her life: the career she had almost lost, her son's major injury, the divorce from her husband, but never before had she felt so shattered, unable to pick up the pieces and move on. Her eyes were shifting, unable to focus on one place.

"Since my mother passed away almost a year ago, her loss has been excruciatingly difficult for me to process. The pain tends to vacillate between the numb and the unbearable, yet it always lingers. But the worst part of it was when I received the phone call in the middle of the night. Devasted, I writhed in agony"—Marta swallowed and looked straight at Gabrielle's still eyes—"but there was no one to fold me in the warmth of a loving hug." She shut her eyes and lowered her face to her quivering chest.

Gabrielle wrapped her arms around Marta and rested her chin on top of her head. "For what it's worth, you're not alone," she whispered.

CHAPTER 28

Silver

D aily walking had become a habit for Marta, one that she craved. She thought about a lot of things: her son, her future plans for her research, her friends back in Uruguay, and . . . Eduardo.

Marta wondered if there was something she could have done to achieve a different outcome. Was her current misery entirely her fault as Pedro seemed to believe, or was it—at least in part—due to the circumstances? If she were more open about her feelings and more receptive to those of others, would she have been in a happier place now? Marta was frustrated with her inability to find answers, and it exhausted her. But should a new opportunity present itself with a different man, she was determined to be less guarded.

A change of scenery always helped, and a visit with Ilian was long overdue, even if he did not care. One Friday, Marta drove to Montreal and spent the whole weekend with him. Upon first seeing her, he paused.

"You've lost weight," he said.

"I've been exercising a lot," Marta replied. Ilian seemed to have grown even taller, although he was still the scrawny child Marta would always love. The unruly clump of hair that usually covered one of his eyes was still there, and he kept sweeping it aside with his hand. He had the fine elvish qualities of his father, but his hair was dark and his eyes were the same amber color as Marta's. Except that they kept drifting away from her face. Marta quickly changed the subject.

She was interested in how his semester was going, and she was given the usual indifferent response that it was fine. Unwilling to give up easily this time, she kept asking him specific questions. Ilian told her that he was doing well in his courses but was unsure what to major in, and that he had friends, although Marta knew virtually nothing about them.

He did not ask, but she made a point of telling him about her trip, and Ilian listened patiently and showed mild interest in how Hugo's poems fared online. When she told him that they were a great success, especially because of the intervention of a soccer star, Ilian's only reaction was a calm, "Cool!" He was not into sports himself, and soccer was out of his scope.

At the end of Marta's visit, Ilian concluded, "Forget the UNESCO sites. If you got to be around kids, I know you were happy."

He still knew her so well.

The first thing Marta did upon her return from Montreal was to look up Hugo's website. While discussing her trip with Ilian, she realized that she had not checked on Hugo's poems since she left Uruguay. There were more than half a dozen on his website, and the activity on the site had remained steady. Judging by the comments, Hugo had some regular readers. Most of the poems were written in English, but Hugo had begun to publish some of the ones in Spanish too.

Marta recognized many of the poems from the notebook he gave her as a Christmas present. But reading them again, she realized that, while still powerful and poignant, many of the ones that were written in English would benefit from some editorial help. Marta was hopeless at poetry and would not be useful to Hugo. Instead, she wondered whether she knew someone who might be able to help, and she thought of Julia Evans. Marta sat up in her chair and typed a brief email to her colleague in the English department at her university. Julia replied quickly and offered for them to meet at her office. She also suggested that a graduate student might be interested to do the work for a minimal fee.

The next morning, Marta walked down a hallway in the English department, looking closely at the numbers on each door. The door to number 106 was open. Marta knocked as she walked into the office. She was already a few steps into the room before she realized that it must be the wrong one. Instead of Julia, a man was sitting at the desk. He had just removed his reading glasses and looked up at her with curious anticipation. His blue eyes were unusually bright for his advanced middle-age, but he still had a full head of hair, which was a fluffy mess of tight, silvery-gray curls.

"Can I help you?" he asked.

"I'm sorry, I think I've got the wrong office." Marta spun toward the door, but realizing that he might be able to help, she turned back toward him. "Actually, I'm looking for Julia Evans. Do you know which one is her office?" She checked her phone and continued, "I had this office number written down, but judging by your appearance—obviously, it's the wrong one." Marta stopped herself and closed her eyes. She realized that she had made an embarrassingly thoughtless comment and wished she had already left.

He smiled and said, "Is there something wrong with my appearance?"

Marta shook her head. "Never mind, it was a stupid thing to say."

She took a step toward the door but heard his voice coming louder from behind her. "Wait a minute!" Marta stopped and turned to face him again. He stood up from his desk and was walking toward her. He was of short and slim stature and, obviously, not in the habit of vigorous exercise— the usual intellectual style of men with whom Marta was awfully familiar.

"Julia's office is two doors down the hall. But she just left. She received a call from the school that her daughter is sick and she went to pick her up and take her home. I don't believe she'll be coming back today."

"Oh," Marta said. "In that case, I'd better leave you alone. Sorry to disturb you."

She was about to go but the man stopped her again. "Please, it was rude of me not to introduce myself. My name's Roger Corbier." He stretched his hand toward her. Marta hesitated, questioning the need to trouble herself with more polite ceremony since she was unlikely to see him again, but she shook his hand. "Assuming you are looking for Julia in her capacity as an English professor, perhaps I might be useful too."

Marta was not prepared to receive help from a virtual stranger, but she also realized that she had nothing to lose by telling him the true purpose of her meeting with Julia. "As a matter of fact, you might be able to help."

Roger pointed Marta to a chair, and he returned to his seat behind the desk in the middle of the room. The office was large. Two walls were lined with bookshelves, and a large window looked out toward an internal courtyard. The desk was covered with piles of books, stacks of paper, and a computer on which Roger had been typing when Marta first entered his office.

"What can I do for you, Marta?" Roger's smile was friendly, and Marta felt as she imagined his students must feel during their meetings with him.

She told him about her young friend Hugo and his poems, and got straight to the point. "I'm looking for someone to help Hugo polish his poems because, while they're good, the language in some places could be improved. And Julia thought that a graduate student might be interested in the work."

Roger clasped his hands together and placed his index fingers on his lips. Eventually, he put his hands down and said, "An interesting proposition. In the span of a couple of minutes, you mentioned a few words I hadn't heard ever spoken in this office, or hadn't heard recently."

Marta wondered what he meant.

"I don't remember Uruguay ever being mentioned in my presence before, and I haven't heard someone speak about poetry in this office for a long time. The fact that I don't teach poetry explains the latter, of course."

"I guess you can't help me then," Marta said.

"No, I didn't say that. I said that no one has mentioned poetry in front of me for a long time. And because I don't teach a course on it, it doesn't mean that I don't read poetry or know nothing about it."

He appeared defensive, and Marta felt the need to give him a chance to explain himself further. "Okay, so what do you propose we do?"

"I have to admit, I'm intrigued by your friend. It's inspiring to see young people engage in poetry. And you said he has a following online? That's a significant achievement, both for someone so young and for poetry. I can't deny that I find the proposition appealing, and I would like to help him, or I guess, I should say, help *you* out."

Marta was about to protest, but he continued undisturbed, "And I like poetry and have read a lot of it. I don't teach a course on it because I grew despondent of having fewer than five students in my class—"

"But they must have been incredibly keen," Marta interjected. "I would have considered teaching them a worthy pursuit."

Roger leaned forward in his chair. "Are you a fellow university professor too?"

Marta described what she did and in which department she worked. When she finished, he leaned back in his chair and said, "Ah, a psychologist. It explains why you feel helpless with poetry but you want to help a poet."

Marta did not find his remark funny. "I may not write or formally critique fiction and poetry, but I'm able to appreciate when it's written well and makes me think about who people are, how they act, and whether life is worth living."

Roger cleared his throat. "Anyway, it doesn't really matter. It's good to know that there are people like you in the world. I can still be inspired."

"I'm not sure how I can inspire you. You know nothing about me."

"You may be surprised, but I already deduced more than you think."

Feeling provoked, Marta insisted, "Please, indulge me!"

Roger laughed. "Perhaps another time. For now, you'll just have to trust my hypothesis. The empirical evidence in support of it would have to be provided later."

Marta was amused by his mocking of the scientific

method, which was noticeable coming from a non-scientist. His dry sense of humor was familiar, invigorating. She felt a sudden affinity to Roger, so she had to leave. "I should get going. I don't want to waste your time any longer."

He stood up and came closer to her. "I believe I went too far with my teasing." He leaned back on his desk and held onto its edge with both hands. "I'm not at all creative myself, you see. I'm much more analytical, or in other words, boring." He smiled, and his eyes grew even brighter.

"How could you be an English scholar if you're analytical? I've always assumed that English profs were just as creative as the writers they study."

"You're mistaken. That's true for some of us, but alas, not me. I analyze the books; I don't write them. And it takes a rational mind, not necessarily a creative one, to do that."

Marta sat back in her chair. She was intrigued. He said something that piqued her curiosity, and she wanted to know more. They talked for a while, and with each passing minute, Marta found Roger easier to talk to. He was funny, and he had the same inclination to quote famous works of fiction—a tendency which Marta appreciated and found intellectually stimulating. She looked at the time; they had been talking for nearly an hour.

"I should go," she said.

"Perhaps we can discuss Hugo's poems over dinner sometime?" Roger offered.

The abrupt invitation reminded Marta of her dinner with Bruce Mason, her colleague from the physiotherapy department, and she shook her head. But before she could soften her refusal with a polite excuse, she was struck by a second thought, or more precisely, the image of a clamped oyster. Instead of retreating in her familiar and cozy shell, it was time to try a new approach. Ultimately, its outcome could not be more painful than what she had recently endured, and it was possible that it could even turn out better.

"I'd be glad to," Marta said.

On Friday night, Roger took Marta to a family-owned French restaurant, which offered only a set menu. They had a meal of succulent beef in a tarragon-infused cream sauce, accompanied by a couple of glasses of lush red Burgundy. By the time the dessert arrived, crème brûlée, Marta and Roger were both relaxed and talkative. Marta did not want the evening to end. Roger was just as interested in her life as she was in his. He was from an old Francophone family in Ontario, had lived in Toronto all his life, and was a widower. He had no children and generally lived a secluded life surrounded by books. Marta felt sorry for him at first, but then she realized that he was content; loneliness did not frighten him as much as it did her.

After dinner, they walked for a while on the cold streets of Toronto. Roger was not troubled by the stanch or traffic noise. He was easy and confident, and like Marta, he belonged in the city. Their conversation revolved around the books Roger had read, and when he talked about his favorite ones, Marta grew eager to read them. And she was fascinated by his perspective on the ones she had read already. He had analyzed them at a deeper level than her, and he had interesting ideas about the characters' motivation or the meaning behind their words. Marta was tantalized.

Eventually, they ended up in front of her door. As it had been her standard practice, after the first date, Marta would have thanked him and said good night. But tonight, she invited Roger to come inside for a drink. She surprised herself with her willingness to spend the night with him on their first date. Not that she had any rules about it. But she never thought herself capable of doing it. When she woke up in the morning, Roger was still in the house. By the pleasant smell in the air, she could tell that he was making coffee in the kitchen. Marta smiled. Pedro, for one, would be proud of her.

Marta and Roger continued to see each other regularly. He also proved to be perfect at the editorial feedback for Hugo. He found it "diverting," as he put it, and he didn't mind doing it on an ongoing basis, as Hugo continued to put out one poem a week.

During one of her daily walks, Marta realized that she had not thought of Eduardo in a few days. As soon as she arrived home, she opened her laptop and wrote an email to Luisa in which she told her all about Roger. She concluded:

"I have found someone who cares about me, and I'm happy. I'm not alone, and I have finally managed to leave Eduardo behind. He is a beautiful memory, one that makes me smile the same way all other good memories do."

Marta, however, was not smiling.

CHAPTER 29

White

Marta returned to work, and the days went by at a swift pace, the way time passed when a person was contented and occupied with the monotony of a predictable daily schedule. By her birthday in late March, Marta and Roger had been together for over a month.

Hugo called that morning and directed Marta to a new poem he had posted on his website as her birthday present. As soon as she hung up, Marta went straight to her computer. The poem was strangely titled "ME" in capital letters. It was longer than usual, a narrative poem that told a love story between a man and a woman from the man's point of view. The two protagonists were uncommonly different, and at first, they resisted each other. Only when the woman revealed her true feelings did their love triumph.

Marta was amazed by how romantic the story was, especially coming from Hugo. And she could not shake the uncanny feeling that it was familiar. She read it again, wondering why this particular poem had been her birthday present. Was the "ME" in the title supposed to stand for Marta and Eduardo?

She brushed the uneasy thought aside. It was ridiculous to assume that Hugo would write a poem about her and Eduardo, especially when he knew that Eduardo was engaged to someone else. Marta chose to accept the more sensible interpretation, namely that the poem represented people's longings and insecurities that came along with love. And she was fully convinced that this also explained the title "ME" and decided that the caps were irrelevant.

Marta was still distracted with the poem when her phone rang again. Luisa started the video call by wishing her a happy birthday in her loud and joyful tone and proceeded to ask her whether she had any special plans with Roger. Marta had barely finished answering her question when Luisa interrupted: "Guillermo and I are engaged!"

"Wow, congratulations! I'm so happy for you," Marta said and suggested the idea of going to the wedding if she were to be invited.

"Of course you'll be invited. But we haven't picked the date yet." When Luisa spoke again, her somber voice sounded as if she were a different person. "A couple of days ago, Eduardo came to visit me in my office with his kids. They had also remembered that it's your birthday soon."

Marta did not say anything. "The children miss you, Marta. And Eduardo's in town—"

"Please, Luisa, don't," Marta begged.

Luisa sighed. "I thought you'd be pleased to know that I told him you have a partner. And he said that he hopes you're happy, and that you deserve nothing less." Marta remained silent, and Luisa continued more brightly, "The children left presents for you, and I'll mail them to you tomorrow."

"Oh, they did? Show me!"

Luisa put each present in front of the camera as she introduced them to Marta: a heart-shaped stone from Sebastián that he had found on the beach, and he had written with a marker the word "love," on one side and "amor" on the other. "He said it's a 'charm' for you since you were the only one who didn't get one for Christmas."

That observant child. Nothing escapes him, Marta thought. She said, "A bilingual stone. How great!"

Next, Luisa showed her a picture from Romina: a childish drawing of what looked like a big gray cloud with zigzag lines on its belly and a small girl standing next to it. Romina had printed her own name with big sloppy letters with an arrow pointing to the girl.

Marta recognized the picture and exclaimed, "I'm Romina's Totoro!"

Later that evening, she was alone at home and sleep was eluding her. Roger had gone home for the night because he had to catch an early flight the next morning for a conference. Marta yawned as she made herself a cup of herbal tea and placed it on the desk in her office. Unable to fall asleep, she decided to do some work instead. While waiting for her computer to load, she noticed her journal tucked in the corner of her desk. She had not opened it since returning from Uruguay. She picked it up and turned to the last page. The final entry ended with an effervescent description of her anticipation of her dinner with Eduardo at his house. Marta smiled pensively at the irony—just as well, the events that had since unfolded were not worthy of reminiscence. Abruptly, she pulled herself up and feverishly typed on her computer. After all this time, Marta finally googled Eduardo.

She had been successfully avoiding any news of him. Not being on social media at all, she was largely in control of the news that reached her. At the top of the first page with the search results, there were several news articles and a few video clips. Marta clicked on one of the articles and read it partially. It was too full of statistics to hold her interest. She clicked on one of the videos instead, which contained a studio interview with Eduardo. He was dressed more formally than his team uniform, and his hair was dry and wavy, not flat and dripping with sweat the way it usually looked in his post-match interviews.

As soon as Eduardo appeared on the screen, Marta became aware of her heartbeat. She had not heard his voice or seen his face since the day she said farewell to him. He looked the same, except for the slight sadness in his eyes and his more subdued, thoughtful demeanor.

The interview was generally boring, mostly focused on Eduardo's style of play and his thoughts on his recent matches. Marta was about to close the videoclip but stopped when she heard the host's next question.

"I noticed the word 'integrity' is engraved on the bracelet you've been wearing ever since you've returned from your medical leave. What does integrity mean to you?"

Edwardo's face was mellowed by a wistful smile. "I'm fortunate to know a person who taught me about the importance of staying true to myself, as well as many other things, such as forest spirits, witches, and the nature of intelligence."

"I guess this person wasn't a teacher." The host forced a laugh and Marta grumbled at his thoughtless joke. Eduardo shook his head, but before he could respond, the host moved onto his next question, which was about Eduardo's impending marriage . . .

Marta slapped the laptop shut, took her jacket from the hook in the hallway, and left the house in search of a strong breeze.

Marta and Roger had settled into a mundane but sensible existence. They continued to live separately in their respective homes. Roger seemed perfectly happy with their relationship. But to Marta, it seemed solid but too cerebral, almost platonic. Their lovemaking, albeit irregular, was predictable, comfortable . . . reliable. Sometimes Marta wondered whether Roger would notice if she disappeared, or whether he would miss her if she left him. But she enjoyed their conversations, and she liked his dry sense of humor—as long as he made her laugh, she was happy. He tolerated her emotional and romantic tendencies, and every once in a while, she thought that he might even like her for them.

A couple of weeks after her birthday, in early April, Marta had just finished a meeting with a student in her office, and she looked at the clock. It was half-past four. Today was Roger's birthday. She left her office and headed home to change before she was supposed to meet him at a restaurant downtown. Afterward, they had planned to go to the Alliance Française to see a movie. Marta was unenthusiastic because French films were often good, but sometimes the artsy ones were brutally devastating, and she did not feel up to that type of experience on someone's birthday. But it was Roger's choice.

For Marta's birthday they had gone to the ballet, which was perfectly fine. Marta, as a former dancer herself, loved all forms of dance, and *Coppelia* was one of her favorite ballets. But a friend of hers had wanted to organize a small party for her, which she would have preferred. Roger was not willing to go. "Too much midlife banter could bring anyone to a crisis," he had said. And the ballet it was.

Marta had recently realized how she had been subconsciously acceding to Roger's preferences while he was less willing to follow her lead. She had planned to talk to him about it, but not on his birthday.

Marta turned the corner of her street and noticed some-one sitting on the front steps of her house. She inhaled sharply and stopped—it was Eduardo. As soon as he saw her, he stood up, and his beautiful smile warmed his face. The bracelet she had given him for Christmas was still wrapped around his wrist. She moved closer to him and said with an unsteady voice, "Hi."

"*Hola*, Marta." Eduardo was shyer and less certain of what to say next. As he examined her more closely, his expression darkened. "You look thinner. Are you okay?"

Marta had forgotten that she had lost weight since she came back from Uruguay. At one point, her loose-fitting clothes had reminded her of Claudia, which propelled her to put greater effort into her cooking. She had already gained some of the weight back, but apparently the change was still noticeable.

"I'm fine, thanks," she said.

Eduardo remained silent, and still addled by his sudden appearance, Marta asked an obtuse question. "How did you know where I live?"

"Luisa gave me your address. Actually, I had to pry it out of her. She's a good and loyal friend."

Mystified why he had come, and unannounced, Marta decided to be direct. "So, why are you here?"

Eduardo hesitated. "The children miss you."

"I miss them too," Marta said wistfully. But she pulled herself together—she was not inclined to prevaricate and was unwilling to return to the painful past. "But why are *you* here?" she asked again. "Is your wife with you?"

"My wife?" Eduardo sounded genuinely surprised. "Do you mean Claudia?"

"Yes, who else?" Marta snapped.

"It's all over between us." Eduardo's voice was quiet but more confident. "And I've come to tell you that I've made a decision I know I won't regret."

Marta noticed the significance of his words, but she asked instead, "And the baby?"

Eduardo paused and creased his brow. "Right. You don't know, of course. Apparently, Luisa tried to tell you, but you wouldn't let her." His face brightened. "Which turned out to be a good thing because it helped me to convince her to give me your address. She agreed that it'd be better if I tell you in person."

Marta was concerned, unsure of what news to expect.

Eduardo sighed. "A couple of weeks ago, Claudia had a miscarriage. And shortly after, she broke our engagement." He looked at Marta, but she remained still. "I do believe that she felt truly guilty for what she had done to us both."

By now, Marta suspected the real purpose of Eduardo's visit, and instead of being elated, she felt apprehensive. "I'm sorry to hear about the miscarriage. And I'm glad to know that things seem to have settled between the two of you." Still unwilling to risk reading too much into his words, Marta said, "I'm grateful for your thoughtfulness, but you needn't have come all this way to tell me the news."

"I read Hugo's poem, 'ME,'" Eduardo said.

Startled, Marta pulled back.

"Even after reading it a few times, it kept pulling me in. I was surprised by how familiar it seemed, and something about it made me hopeful." Eduardo had also recognized himself in the poem, which was prescient.

Marta grew increasingly more agitated and shuffled her feet. "It's a silly poem. Hugo was undoubtedly playing with the idea of fairy tales. We shouldn't read too much into it."

Eduardo took a couple of steps closer to her. "No, you're wrong. Fairy tale or not, it occurred to me that if Hugo imagined it, you and I could make it a reality."

Marta was now flustered, and she fidgeted with her fingers. Her emotions were coming on too fast, and her thoughts were unable to keep up. She needed time to understand what was going on and how to react most appropriately.

"What makes you think the poem is about us?" she asked.

A warm smile spread across Eduardo's face. "Because I want it to be."

Marta felt lightheaded, and she could no longer tame her feelings. "I want it too," she breathed.

She closed her eyes to compose herself. She felt Eduardo's arms wrap around her shoulders, and he gently kissed the top of her head. Instead of being soothed by his embrace, Marta was seized by cold prickly panic. The sudden prospect of a relationship with Eduardo terrified her. He was unfamiliar, distant, aloof, someone yet to be discovered. She needed time to learn to trust him again, to accept him as a friend, before he could become a lover . . . a partner. And how would their relationship unfold? Marta was not about to give up her career, to relinquish control over aspects of her life she had pursued tenaciously. And . . . *Roger!*

Marta drew back. Her face burned. "I'm with someone else now who happens to be a good man, and he loves me." Her gaze turned toward Eduardo. "I can't break his heart. I won't do it."

Eduardo remained visibly calm, but his breathing was quick and shallow. "But do *you* love him?"

Marta looked away to hide the tears brimming in her eyes. Eduardo's presence, his words, his affection, were exactly what she had desired but months ago, not now, not after she had finally relinquished him and expunged him from her heart. Her legs felt weak, and she lowered herself onto one of the wooden steps and wrapped her arms around her knees. She heard Eduardo move closer and felt the wooden board under her buckle slightly from his weight.

Marta wiped her tears with her sleeve and stared at the ground. "Eduardo, you and I . . . we're not as alike as we might think. We live continents apart, no matter where you are. You have your career and I have mine. We have our children."

Marta looked at him. She wished that he would say something, that he would argue. But his grave stare was focused on his hand, which was fidgeting with his bracelet.

"We can dance and dream together, but do you really think that we can live in the same place and think alike?"

Eduardo remained solemn and silent. Marta took a deep breath, and when she spoke again, her voice shook. "You know, I've often wondered whether what we have is love. After all, it has always been implied but never spoken."

When Eduardo looked at her, his eyes were huge. Marta recognized the wounded disbelief in them and turned away. She thought that she had said enough, but her lofty doubts flooded her consciousness again, and she had to release them. "Or is it an infatuation, the irresistible allure of a relationship that neither one of us has experienced before? But, like a dry leaf tossed into a fire, it will burst with a bright flame and quickly wither into ash . . ." She finished in a barely audible whisper, "And we'd be better off to have never been burned by the fire." Marta coiled into a tight knot.

When Eduardo spoke, his voice sounded colder than she expected. "I get it. I'm still not good enough for you."

Marta's terrified face shot up toward him. "No! That's not—"

"You're right," he interrupted her and stood up. "We can never be together as long as I feel inadequate around you."

Marta shut her eyes tightly. She had done it again.

Eduardo exhaled, and her pulse quickened when she thought she could feel his breath. Instead, she heard his steady footsteps disappear in the cool breeze. When Marta eventually looked up, the yard was empty and a black squirrel bolted across the lawn. Once she dragged herself inside the house, she closed the door behind her, leaned her back against it, and exhaled.

It was time to get ready for her evening with Roger.

CHAPTER 30

Gold

Marta lifted her tired eyes from the computer screen. She had spent most of the day working on a research paper, and she had not noticed it had grown dark. She stretched and stood up from her chair to let the blood flow back into her legs. She looked out the window. It was still dusk after a long day in June, and the black silhouettes of the trees in her backyard were discernible against the ink-blue sky. The moon had not risen yet, and there was a single star glittering over the treetops.

Marta was about to turn and get back to her desk, but instead she rubbed her eyes and leaned closer to the window. A glowing speck fluttered just outside the glass. Marta blinked again, but the neon light kept flickering, a lonely firefly. She exclaimed out loud in disbelief. She felt the exuberance of the little light permeate her body. An image glided in front of her eyes: a petite woman in a yellow dress, dancing in the arms of a tall man in a white linen shirt.

Marta shook her head, and the glow of her vision was replaced by a grim shadow—the recognition that she was dreaming of Eduardo, *again*. She had not been able to get him out of her thoughts ever since she last saw him in front of her house two months earlier, but she had managed to suppress them. Tonight, however, she would finally embrace the dream. She dreaded what she was about to do, but she had come to realize that no matter how strong the pain would be, she had to try. She could no longer tolerate the unknown.

On the following afternoon, as soon as Marta finished her meetings at work, she rushed to her car. A recent conversation with Roger kept worrying her thoughts. She had been desperate to do something spontaneous, frivolous, and she had asked Roger to go dancing. He had smiled and replied in his usual calm manner that he did not dance at home, and there was absolutely no chance that he could be persuaded to do it in public. And Marta should know better that he was not the type. She knew, but she was not about to give up. It had been a long weekend, and she wanted to go somewhere in the countryside. A cottage by a lake or a cabin in the woods.

"Our conversations are always stimulating, my love, and does it matter whether we have them here or in the countryside?" Roger could be annoyingly rational.

It had mattered to Marta. She had not yet gathered the cour-age to talk to Roger about their relationship and how his sometimes rigid and egocentric behavior, even if unintentional, made her feel belittled and unequal. But it did not matter now because she could no longer delude herself that choosing to remain with Roger was the right decision. And she was on her way to tell him.

When Marta burst into his living room, she was panting and her face was burning. She found Roger sitting on one of his armchairs reading a book. He took off his reading glasses and looked at her with mild amusement. Instead of greeting him with the usual kiss, she walked stolidly toward the window. It had started to rain outside, a light misty drizzle. The sky was still pale blue, and the colors were more vibrant than before. Marta opened the window and the fresh, crisp air grazed across her flushed face. She closed her eyes and inhaled deeply.

Eventually, she turned to face Roger. "Roger, I loathe what I'm about to tell you because I know it'll hurt you. And believe me, hurting you is the last thing I want to do. Even though I tried very hard to avoid it, I can't keep living this way." She stopped to swallow, but her mouth was dry. She forced herself to go on before she lost her nerve. "I've been faithful to you, but I'm in love with someone else."

She was feeling as awful as she had anticipated, and she needed to brace herself for Roger's disappointed, possibly angry response.

Roger had been listening to her intently, and instead of expressing anger or even hurt, his face remained tranquil. Marta was perplexed, but she also felt hopeful. When Roger finally spoke, his voice was hoarse, "Of course, you're free to go."

Marta took a sharp breath. These had been the exact same words she had uttered when her former husband had told her that he wanted a divorce. Realizing that Roger was also trying to spare her more grief by hiding his own, she felt suffocating guilt.

"I'm so sorry. I truly am. But continuing as we were would be unfair to you, and lately it's been driving me crazy."

"You don't need to apologize for the inevitable, Marta. I can't pretend that I'm not disappointed, but I also can't pretend that I'm surprised."

Marta was confused. She had told Roger about her trip in Uruguay and her friends there, but she had not told him about her feelings for Eduardo. "What do you mean?" she exclaimed.

Roger rubbed his forehead and looked at the carpet. He sat motionless for a while.

Marta waited patiently. The usual buzzing of her thoughts was gone, and she could hear the soft, arrhythmic drumming of the raindrops on the leaves outside.

Finally, Roger lifted his head and said, "I've been observing you lately. You're like a caged bird who longs to be set free, and I hate myself for being the person who trapped you."

Marta already regretted thinking of him as egocentric. "Roger, you haven't—"

"I know that it's hard for you to find a partner who's fully compatible with you because people like you are rare. And you're forced to choose, usually between the more dull, cerebral types like me, or the more free-spirited but often fickle romantics like the characters in the books I read." He examined the carpet again. "I'm a person who appeals to your intellectual side, which has been good—great, even—for me, at least. But I know that you want and deserve more."

Marta turned back toward the window. She did not want Roger to see the raw emotion probably visible on her face.

"You may not find your perfect match," he continued. "But I hope that the person who is fortunate to have captured your heart is also someone who is able to dance with you, and is willing to learn and keep up with your curiosity."

Marta was breathing fast. No one had spoken to her so graciously before. She was startled by how raspy her own voice was when she said, "How do you know all of this about me?"

She heard Roger move behind her, and she felt his hand rest on her shoulder. "Because I love you."

Marta felt her stomach shrivel and turn into a hard walnut. Roger was sincere and kind, but he was not making it any easier for her. She reached toward her shoulder and took a hold of his hand.

"And this is also the reason why I must let you go." Roger sighed.

Marta turned to face him, and she realized that the odd feeling in her stomach was that of being nauseated. Distraught by her increasing sense of guilt, she looked at his eyes. They were calm and clear, and there was no sign of uneasiness or regret.

He smiled and shrugged. "The empirical evidence no longer supports the hypothesis."

Marta stared at Roger's eyes for a long time. Gradually, her shoulders relaxed and she felt an immense relief. As he had said himself, the revelation was not new to him. He had been preparing for this moment for a long time. She also knew that Roger had not been joking when he declared that he had analyzed their relationship and had already accepted the logical conclusion to let her go. And he was right—they would be better friends than lovers.

"Thank you," Marta finally said. "You're an exceptional person, and I'll always love you for that."

He turned toward his chair, a faint smile visible on his lips. "Come and visit anytime you feel the need for a shot of witty repartee."

"I'll visit as often as I can." Marta leaned over him, wrapped her arms around his chest, and kissed the top of his head. "Goodbye, Roger."

Roger grabbed hold of her forearms and squeezed. His hands were warm and soft, but quivered. He let go of her, picked up his book, and placed his glasses back on his face.

Once outside, Marta was delighted by the sight of a perfect rainbow shimmering in the sky. The sudden realization that she and Eduardo could finally be together doused her like a hot shower. She had had to repress her feelings for so long and had endeavored hard to forget him. Now the very real possibility of Eduardo being back in her life was surreal.

Marta jumped into her car and drove as fast as she could while navigating through the busy Friday afternoon traffic. The rain had stopped, and the sun's reflection off the wet asphalt was at times blinding. She was forming a plan in her head. First, she would text Eduardo. No! It would be more romantic if she were to surprise him, and judging by his past actions, he would prefer it too.

By the time Marta arrived at her house, it was shortly after five o'clock. She ran straight to her office and turned on the computer. There was a flight to Barcelona leaving in less than three hours. She had never paid so much for an airplane ticket, but it did not matter. She headed to her bedroom to pack. She realized that she had no time left at all, and she either had to leave right away or miss the flight. She texted for a cab and decided that the black pants and delicate pink lace-trimmed top she was already wearing would do for the trip. She put on a cotton cardigan as an extra layer for the plane. Next, she went to her bathroom and threw her toothbrush and a comb in her purse. She peered in the mirror—she did not look frightening—and dug her passport from her documents folder in her closet. On her way out of the bedroom, she stopped and reached for her jewelry box. Marta pulled the pearl earrings out and put them on—for the very first time. Finally, she turned off the lights and locked the door behind her. At that moment, the taxi pulled up to the curb. It was lucky!

She was breathless by the time she reached the airline agent. He told her that he could issue her a boarding pass if she had no luggage to check in, and she had to speed past security and run to the gate before it closed. But she still had a chance to make her flight. Lucky again!

Only once she was seated on the plane did she relax. The space was cramped but she did not feel confined. She felt weightless. When the plane was in the air, she reclined in her seat and closed her eyes.

Marta got out of the taxi and skimmed the busy plaza. Small groups of tourists were scattered around it, and dozens of pigeons flew in the empty spaces between them. Marta wondered how she would find Eduardo when she saw him. He was pacing fast toward her with a brilliant grin on his face. Marta moved a few steps, but her legs felt weak and she stopped. She was trembling, and all she could see was his radiant face growing nearer. A couple of steps before he reached her, Eduardo stopped.

"So, you made a decision?" he asked, only smiling.

Marta nodded, rendered silent by the flood of her emotions.

"And you chose me?" Eduardo evidently enjoyed the agonizing delay of the moment they had both anticipated for so long.

Marta could manage a barely discernible nod.

Eduardo moved closer and tucked a strand of her hair behind her pearl earring. "You're so beautiful!" He took her face in his hands. "I wasn't sure what to expect, but I was prepared to wait for you for as long as it took. Months, years even. But I didn't think you'd come to me so soon."

Marta closed her eyes. She could bear the anticipation no longer. Eduardo lowered his head and kissed her with the gentleness of a spring breeze.

He broke the kiss and lifted his head. His eyes, black patches of summer night's sky, glittered right in front of her, and she felt her love for him overpower her again. He brushed his thumb over the small wrinkles around her eyes.

"Marta, I was never able to say this to you before, but God is my witness, I wanted to many times. So, let me say it now." His voice trembled.

"¡Te amo, mi alma! ¡Te amo!"

Marta was startled by a vigorous shaking. She rubbed her bleary eyes and wiggled her stiff body. She peered through the oval window. The plane had just landed.

During the taxi ride, Marta vaguely noted the spires of La Sagrada Família peaking over the rooftops of the buildings zooming past her, but she was too preoccupied with a feverish anticipation to notice any other sights. The taxi slowed down on a broad street. Elegant four-story gray buildings were lined on one side of the street, and a large park with old trees and lush bushes lay on the other. The taxi left Marta on the park side across from an ornate building with stone-framed balconies. The gold number on the black door matched Eduardo's address on her phone.

For a couple of minutes, Marta stood motionless on the sidewalk and stared at the building in front of her. She never wanted the pleasant fluttering in the pit of her stomach to cease. When she finally took a deep breath and stepped onto the street, a silver sports car pulled up to the front of the building and stopped. Marta beamed when she saw Eduardo exit from the driver side. She raised her arm in the air and was about to call his name, but no sound escaped her lips. The head of a young woman with long blonde hair emerged from the car, and as soon as Eduardo reached her, he smiled and kissed her, and they dashed inside the building.

Marta's arm limply hit her hip, and she stepped back onto the sidewalk. *Too late.*

Another one of her life circles closed, and the tight coil that she had assembled over the years cinched around her chest even tighter. Marta ambled toward the closest bench in the park and slumped onto it. She stared blankly. Her eyes were dry, but her vision was misty. She shivered although it was June in Spain. Snowflakes landed gracefully on the thin threadbare shawl over her shoulders. The remains of several burnt matches were littered around her feet. A bright glow coming from a large window lit her face. Inside the window, standing by a warm fireplace, a couple was laughing while holding tightly onto each other.

Marta exhaled. She was living in a fairy tale, but not the one little girls usually desired.

She became aware of a persistent movement. As she forced her eyes to focus, she saw a seagull pecking at a shell on the ground in front of her until it lost interest and flew away. The shell was gleaming, and Marta leaned over and picked it up. It was an empty oyster shell: on one side, coarse and grotesque, and on the other, glossy and oddly soothing. Marta ran her thumb over the smooth side, and it felt warm and soft, almost velvety. She was mesmerized by its iridescent sheen. She left it on her lap and reached toward her ears. She took the pearl earrings off and placed them on top of the shell where they disappeared, camouflaged in its shimmering creamy colors.

Marta stood up, still holding the shell in her hand, and rambled along a path in the park. She turned toward the first exit. At the stone gate, she noticed a woman sitting on the ground. She was dirty and disheveled and was clutching a bundle of rags. The woman stared at Marta, a hostile, defiant look. But Marta was not frightened. She knew that the bundle in the woman's arms was her baby, whom she was protecting instinctively.

Marta smiled and leaned down over a small plate. She placed the pearl earrings in it and paused to admire their soft glow amid the dull patina of the coins that were already there.

CHAPTER 31

Copper

E arly one morning, Marta boarded a train. As soon as she had returned from Barcelona, she felt an urgent, almost visceral need to visit with Ilian. And as if to inflame her desire further, he had surprised her with his wish for her to spend his twentieth birthday with him in Montreal. It was all it took for Marta to hop on the first available train, even though Ilian's birthday was not for another week.

She leaned her head on the dirty window and watched the blur of trees go by. As the train approached its final destination, Marta sensed the commotion around her but remained motionless until she could recognize every object that went by. She stood up and headed for the doors. She was resolved to tell Ilian the truth about the divorce.

Ilian had said that he would meet her at the station, but Marta knew that he often had more pressing priorities than her. When the wave of people withdrew from the platform, she pulled her phone out and was about to call a taxi when she heard his voice.

"Maman!" He was breathless. "I'm sorry . . . I'm late. I'm taking a summer course . . . and the class went over time, and . . . I couldn't leave."

Marta lifted herself onto her toes, and Ilian leaned down to give her a hug.

"That's all right," she said as she pulled back from him. "I'm glad you're here."

"I'm starving. Shall we go straight to lunch?"

Marta was too agitated to feel hungry but agreed.

"Come, I know just the place," Ilian said and picked up her small suitcase.

They approached a restaurant, and Marta noted the sign on the door, Chez Henri. She was puzzled but remained silent. Once seated at a linen-clad round table, Ilian quickly made his choice, a beef sandwich. He tossed his menu to the side, but Marta was still laboring over hers. Finally, she asked, "Why the French restaurant? You hate French food."

"But *you* like it."

Marta was not sure whether he was teasing her, or whether he was indeed trying to please her. She placed a napkin on her lap and muttered, "It's very kind of you."

Ilian creased his brow, and Marta recognized the ominous silence that was pushing them further apart. Now was the time for her to speak before the jagged breach between them became irreversible. She cleared her throat and said, "Ilian, I have something important to tell you. It's about the reason for the breakup of our marriage. I know I'm not perfect, and you blame me —" Marta pulled back, startled by Ilian's abrupt movement.

"I know the truth," Ilian said. He stretched back in his chair, his hand resting on top of the table. "Dad told me last time I saw him. But why didn't you tell me sooner?"

Marta exhaled in relief. "Because when you were younger, I didn't think that you could understand."

"What do you mean? I'm in the generation that totally understands 'gay.'"

Marta squeezed his hand, which was unusually cold and clammy. "And I thought it best if the news came from your father, once he figured himself out. It's his truth to tell."

Ilian was breathing fast. His eyes were full of tears but remained fixed on her face. He swallowed and said, "If you'd only told me sooner." His hand twitched in hers as if he wanted to pull it away, but he remained still.

Marta placed her other hand on top of his and held even tighter. "Let's not regret the past. It's numbingly vapid. But now, the future"—Marta beamed—"I can't tell you how exhilarated it makes me feel."

Ilian smiled through his tears and squeezed Marta in a tight hug. "I love you, Maman," he whispered, words she had not heard uttered from his lips in a very long time.

Marta had always liked French food, but now she loved it.

As always, September ushered in a new academic year. As soon as Marta walked into her first class, she was surrounded by the hum of many voices that hovered all around her but never touched her.

She sat on top of the table at the front of the room and dangled her feet until the buzzing around her lost some of its energy. Marta smiled. She cleared her throat and said in a crisp voice, "The topic of today's class is the language of love."

The classroom became still.

"Who wants to tell me what you would consider to be the most persuasive expression of love, whether in books or movies, and especially in your own experience?" The silence was replaced by a low but animated rumble. "And then, I'll tell you mine." As the wave of lively chatter drenched her, Marta laughed.

She reveled in the new energy she felt when teaching

her classes. She was inspired by her students, and they appreciated her candor. She did not notice the time passing, and it was Christmas before she knew it.

On Christmas morning, Marta took a sip of her warm eggnog and inhaled the faint fir scent drifting in the air. The Vienna Boys' Choir Christmas album was playing softly in the background, as it had become the tradition Ilian had always insisted on ever since he was little. They had just opened their presents. The soft cashmere scarf Ilian had given her was wrapped around her neck even though a small fire was crackling in the fireplace. The new cell phone Marta had given Ilian was lying on the couch next to his leg.

"Stay in touch!" she had reminded him.

Ilian was curiously examining the oyster shell Marta had also given him, and he was still turning it over in his fingers. He was puzzled at first, and she had just finished telling him how she had come to cherish it with the help of her friends in Uruguay.

During the rest of the day, in the short breaks while the food was cooking, Marta connected with everyone in Montevideo, and had a long video call with Luisa. Her wedding was set for mid-February, and she wanted to tell Marta about all the delights, and mostly the challenges, of planning a wedding. Marta listened patiently and assured her that she would be there. She had a week off work at that time, and she was thrilled to have a reason to spend it in Uruguay.

As the train began to roll, Ilian smiled and waved from his window. It was the day before New Year's Eve, and he was going back to Montreal to celebrate the arrival of the New Year with his friends.

Earlier, Ilian had been scrolling on his new cell phone while Marta was driving him to the station and she heard him say, "Hey, that guy you worked for down in Uruguay. The soccer player. Was his name Eduardo Rodríguez?"

The car swerved slightly, and Marta exerted herself to remain focused on the road. Hearing Eduardo's name uttered by Ilian, of all people, discombobulated her.

She could feel Ilian's gaze on the side of her face, and she finally managed a hurried, "Yes . . . yes, it was. Why?"

"My friends who are soccer fans are all abuzz on social media that he's announced his retirement at the end of the season. Apparently, it's one of the big news stories in the world of soccer right now. Did you know?"

The celebrity news was hollow: the name, familiar; the person, unknown. Marta managed to shake her head in response to his question and was relieved when she pulled into the parking lot at the train station and stopped. She turned toward Ilian and smiled. "Time to go."

On her way home, Marta finally allowed herself to concentrate on the fact that it was also the day when she had said farewell to Eduardo in Montevideo a year earlier. She trudged up the frozen steps of her house. As she was about to unlock the door, she noticed a large envelope resting on the doorstep. She kneeled down to pick it up. She examined it and caught her breath. The initials "ER" were written on the top left corner. She unlocked the door and went inside.

Marta felt tense. She could not tell whether she was happy that Eduardo had written to her, or whether she was unsettled by the anticipation of the news contained inside the envelope. She went into the living room and left the unopened envelope on the coffee table. She rubbed the stiff muscles on the side of her neck as she walked into the kitchen and made herself a cup of tea.

With the steaming cup in hand, Marta went back into the living room and sat on the couch. She took a sip and scrunched her face; the tea was still too hot. She placed the cup on the coffee table and exhaled. She recognized regret as the familiar emotion that gnawed on the inside of her chest—for what had been, for what could have been. She looked at the envelope sitting on the table in front of her, and a sudden burst of curiosity for what it could be replaced the regret.

Marta seized the envelope and tore it open. She pulled out a sizable stack of papers. She was disappointed not to find at least a personal note to tell her what this package was about. She skimmed the top page and noted the letterhead of the Universidad de la República in Montevideo. At first, Marta thought that it had something to do with her work, but examining it more closely, she saw that the letter was addressed to Eduardo. It was a copy of his admission letter from the university. Marta kept reading and her eyes slowed their rhythmic movement when they reached a section of the letter highlighted with a yellow marker. It appeared to be a response to a question Eduardo had previously asked, confirming that he could take some of his classes as an exchange student in Toronto.

Marta rushed to examine the next page. It was the beginning of a long legal document, fortunately written in English, that described a charitable foundation in Uruguay named "Integrity," which was devoted to supporting the education of poor and disadvantaged children, teens, and young adults. The contract was for the opening of a nonprofit charity branch in Toronto, and Marta was named its future director. Her heart was racing as her eyes skimmed through the rest of the document. As far as she could tell from the convoluted legal language, everything had already been planned and arranged, and only the space for her signature, next to the one Eduardo had already signed, had been left blank.

She turned the last page of the contract and discovered a small envelope with "Marta" scribbled across it that had fallen on her lap. With shaking hands, she snatched the card from inside. The card, like the envelope, was made of pale-yellow cotton paper that felt soft and smooth to the touch. The following words were written in uneven, but legible, handwriting:

[Love] is an ever-fixed mark
That looks on tempests and is never shaken;
It is the star to every wand'ring bark,
Whose worth's unknown, although his height be taken.

Marta looked up from the papers on her lap. She had recognized the Shakespeare's sonnet from which these lines had come, and she felt their meaning keenly. She also knew that the entire package was meant to answer the questions she had asked during their last meeting in front of her house; to soothe doubts she no longer harbored, to ease concerns that no longer troubled her. Her eyes drifted to the shimmering shape on the wall, the reflection of the winter sun off the surface of her tea. "Light bunnies," her mother had called them, and the illusion still beguiled Marta.

She shivered as if awakened from a dream. She picked up her teacup, but the tea was cold. She exchanged the cup for her cell phone and entered "Eduardo" into the recipient field of a text. With steady hands, she typed a few short lines and touched Send.

Marta heard a muffled bleep.

ACKNOWLEDGMENTS

Unlike my academic pursuits, which are typically a collaborative effort, researching and writing this book was an adventure I undertook on my own. But the novel only came to life after it received the support from various people.

I am grateful to my publisher, BQB Publishing, and its president, Terri Leidich, for believing in me and my book. And everyone at BQB, including Rebecca Lown, Robin Krauss, Allison Itterly, Glenn Leidich, Julie Bromley, and John Daly, who gave the book style, color, and shape. This also includes my editor, Andrea Vande Vorde, who helped me polish my writing, which I had done in my third language, and forced me to rework that vexing first chapter one more time.

Before reaching my publisher, I was fortunate to work with the excellent developmental editor, Ronit Wagman, and the beautiful and inspiring creative writing teacher, Sands Hall.

Life would be meaningless without family and friends. Among them was Felix, who patiently described the effects of multiple concussions and how to manage them, and kindly educated me on the game of soccer, the ins and outs of professional soccer, and some of the major players in it. And Naiden, who let me into the Wonderland that is his mind.

ABOUT THE AUTHOR

Born and raised in Sofia, the capital of Bulgaria, Stefka Marinova-Todd has spent her adult life in North America. A university professor of bilingualism at the University of British Columbia in Vancouver, Canada, she has a Bachelor of Arts in Developmental Psychology from York University in Toronto, and a master's and a doctoral degree in Second Language Acquisition from Harvard University Graduate School of Education. *Love and Impediments* is her debut novel.